Jeremy's Home
&
There's Always Hope

by

Susan Payne

Sweetwater

Jeremy's Home & There's Always Hope

The Wild Rose Press, Inc.
PO Box 708
Adams Basin, NY 14410-0708
Visit us at www.thewildrosepress.com

Publishing History
First Line Rose Edition, 2012
Print ISBN 978-1-5092-3174-4
Digital ISBN 978-1-5092-3175-1

Sweetwater, Book 3
Published in the United States of America

WESTERN UNION TELEGRAPH COMPANY
TELEGRAM

TO: JOSEPH MACGREGOR
DATE: JUNE 10 TH. 1874
        MACGREGOR RANCH
        SWEETWATER, KANSAS

COMING HOME FRIDAY ON AFTERNOON
TRAIN. STOP. WILL BE BRINGING IMPORTANT
GUEST. STOP. I THINK SHE IS THE ONE. STOP.
PLEASE BE HAPPY FOR ME. STOP. HAVE
TRANSPORTATION AVAILABLE. STOP.

                FROM: JEREMY MACGREGOR

Dedication

To my husband of fifty-four years whose sense of romance never fails to take my breath away.

Jeremy's Home

CHAPTER 1

Matthew stood on the platform outside the brick train station of Sweetwater, Kansas. A frequent traveler on this train, he was here to meet it and take a couple of visitors out to the Harrison Ranch about an hour north of town. Matthew's sister, Callie, had married Seth Harrison and now brought graduates from St. Michaels Foundling Home in New York to Sweetwater so they could begin a new life in the young western state.

The conductor, a friend of Matthew after so many trips, put the steps down and smiled at him. "You waiting on two young ladies, Matthew?"

When Matthew nodded, the friendly older man with white hair and mustache continued, "I thought maybe that was the case. They're real sweet girls. I'm glad Callie is taking them under her wing. Give my best to your sister, won't you?"

He turned to help the first of two young women. Both wore dresses that, though well-mended, had faded from too many washings and their feet were covered in heavy shoes favored by men who worked in the fields. Cloth poke bonnets hid their hair and faces as they looked down rather than either the conductor or Matthew. Each had a half-empty carpetbag clutched in a white fisted hand.

Taking off his hat, Matthew took a deep breath saying briskly, "Ladies, I'm so glad you came to Sweetwater. My sister, Callie, is anxious to renew your acquaintance and if you're ready, I'd be happy to take you out to the ranch." He knew better than to try to touch either of the girls, noting that one of them held on to the other's skirt and kept half behind her at all times.

Instead, he put out his arms as if herding sheep toward a pen and stepped forward urging them in front of him as he walked toward the buckboard at the end of the platform. The two young women shuffled ahead of him, keeping out of his reach.

Once settled on the bench seat, the women seemed to relax. Matthew went to untie the team's leads when a lady's stridently raised voice intruded on his thoughts as she instructed the ticket seller and porter which trunks and bags were to be taken off the train for her.

At the same time, he heard a man call out, "Matthew, how did you know I was coming on this train? I was wondering how to get home with all this luggage." A tall, lean man with auburn hair cut short on the sides and left long brushed back on top walked toward him with his hand outstretched as a welcome. He, too, was wearing an expensive city suit with gold pocket watch and cuff studs. His top hat was a dark grey and he sported a cane for no other reason than it had a gold top piece.

Smiling in recognition, Matthew replied, "I'm actually here as a favor for Callie. She has some visitors arriving for a few months but I think I have room for one more."

"Well, it's more than one more, I'm afraid." He walked over to the exquisitely garbed lady still ordering the box-men and now another porter around.

"Don't let that case get scratched. It's very expensive and could not be replaced without going all the way to San Francisco." Pointing at a different man, ordered, "And don't put that one on the bottom. It is irreplaceable out here in the wilds. I don't know how I could do without these things so make sure there's nothing left behind, won't you?" The woman sounded as if she had a lot of practice ordering men around to her satisfaction.

Jeremy Macgregor tried to interrupt the tirade and finally, taking her upper arms in his hands, turned the lady to him and received a blistering glare for his trouble. But he stood his ground saying, "Clarissa, I want you to meet a neighbor and good friend, Matthew St. Michaels. Matthew, this is Miss Clarissa Smyth."

The lady was exquisitely dressed with a very trim waist that flared at the hips due to several underskirts. The dress' bustle was made of at least three layers of cloth, each being of a different fabric and trim. There was a matching jacket with more than four trims and two styles of gold buttons at the tight neck and wrists. Her shoes were of the finest leather and buttoned up the side with black shiny buttons. Her hat rode high on her blond curls piled on the top of her head with wide ribbons hanging down the back. Matthew recognized the quality of the hat and gloves since he often sold such articles through his distribution business.

She turned to where Jeremy was trying to point her. She saw the tall, handsome man with dark curly hair, wearing a black suit with vest, white starched shirt and black string tie and a wide-brimmed Stetson in his hand. Much better than she thought this ragtag town could come up with - besides Jeremy, of course.

The lady's face changed immediately into a charming smile followed by a soft well-cultivated voice, saying, "How do you do, Mr. St. Michaels? It is so nice to meet a friend of Jeremy's. Please do excuse me. I must make sure that these men know what to do and how to treat my luggage properly." Then turned back to the growing pile of luggage standing on the platform.

Jeremy said, "Can you stop off at the ranch and tell my brothers I'll be waiting at the hotel's restaurant for someone to pick us up? They evidently didn't get my wire."

Matthew peered at the luggage, saying, "I can take the luggage and you could rent a buggy and horse at the livery in town. Mason always has some available to rent these days."

"That sounds like a better idea. Clarissa and I can be home before dark and she'll be able to see the ranch as we drive up. I'll get her some refreshment at the hotel first and follow you in a little while."

Then Jeremy turned to the now sweating ticket seller, saying, "I'll help load this into the wagon there and you men can get back to what you were doing." He handed the men a gratuity and began to carry the cases to the end of the platform and Matthew's buckboard. Grabbing a large trunk, Matthew carried it effortlessly.

Finally, on their way to the Harrison ranch, Matthew tried to get the two girls to loosen up and asked simple questions he already knew the answers to. "So, you're Faith?" At the girl's nod, Matthew said, "Then you must be, Charity?" The second girl, sitting the furthest from Matthew shrank back from his view.

Faith said, "I heard that other man call you St. Michaels. Are you from the orphanage, too, then? You say you're Callie's brother, her real brother?"

"I was at St. Michaels until I was fourteen and then I thought I knew it all and left. I spent many years on the street learning things I probably should never have learned. Then Callie came west and we found each other. I just felt like I had found family again. So, yes, I'm her real brother in every way that counts."

"I, we, knew Callie when she was still there. She was a little older and ended up working mostly in the kitchens but I remember her. She was always good to us and always had time to teach us things, like cooking and knitting and embroidery. We missed her after she had to leave and then we had to leave not much later. I'm glad she has made a good life for herself. That she seems to have found a good man. She wrote he lets her bring us there, some of the orphans, I mean, until we can find a decent position or maybe a husband." She spoke to him easily as Charity held onto Faith's arm on her other side as if one of them was going to run away.

"Mother Mary Margaret keeps Callie informed of any graduate in the west who might be in need of a job and family. I know Callie was hoping one of you would want to work as a cook for the ranch hands. Right now, she has two other St. Michaels' girls, um, young ladies, but one is training under the midwife here in town. Callie likes the idea of two people in charge of the cooking. Callie comes down to the cookhouse daily and has trained the two Mary's into great chefs in only a few months. Harrison ranch is getting quiet a name for itself as the ranch to get hired on for the cattle round-ups. No one has better food.

"And my wife, Abby, is looking for someone to help her with our two daughters, one less than a month old. She runs the dress shop in town and would like to get back to working with her customers." Matthew noticed Charity clutched Faith's skirt tighter so said, "But I don't know for sure. It might be one of the two Marys. Probably Mary Margaret since she loves to take care of Callie's son, Warren."

After a little over half an hour on the road, Matthew pulled the wagon through an archway announcing the Macgregor ranch. He pulled the wagon to a stop in front of the wide front porch on the massive two-story stone and log structure. Two ladies came out smiling and wiping their hands on their aprons, both obviously expecting - soon.

The shorter of the two women called out, "Well, Matthew, have you brought us some new friends?"

"Certainly, Emily and Mavis Macgregor, this is Faith and Charity St. Michaels. They'll be staying with Callie for the next few months. That way Mary Elizabeth can go and start her training with Rebecca in town." The four ladies nodded to one another, the two on the buckboard shyly acknowledging the married women.

"Would you like to come in and have some tea or something?" offered Emily.

Matthew answered, "I appreciate the offer, but we will have to get going after I drop off this luggage. The big news is that Jeremy and his female friend are following me in half an hour or so. I take it there may be an announcement as soon as the family meets her."

Tying the reins to the brake, he jumped down, going to the rear of the wagon where he removed the boards so he could reach in and pull the trunks and cases toward him. Taking each one carefully knowing he would hear about any scratches, he set them on the porch.

"I'd take them upstairs for you but I have a feeling I've been the bearer of news that has caught you both off-guard. The men due back soon?" he asked.

"Yes, they're planning to be back before evening. We better get a room ready for a guest and see to dinner," said Mavis, already trying to organize the work needed to be done.

Matthew climbed back onto the wagon seat and tipped his hat saying, "I'll come by and see Jeremy later this week, I suppose. Nice to see you both."

The wagon continued back to the main road as Matthew explained, "The Macgregor family has been in Sweetwater as long as the Harrisons have been here. They were both some of the first white folks here after the territory was opened. It's a small community and very friendly. I feel like I've been friends with these families forever but it's actually been a little over a year. I think you're both going to like living here."

Faith nodded but neither young woman agreed nor disagreed. Matthew stopped trying to get the women to talk and a little over another half-hour, the team was steered into the gate with the words, Harrison Ranch, over them. Here, too, was a large two-story house only in clapboard with wrap around porches surrounded by a small yard of grass and flowers. There were several other buildings as well as a large barn and stable with corrals. A bunkhouse with several men sitting on its porch waved to Matthew as he pulled up to the building that had once been the original homestead but now was the ranch hands' dining room and cookhouse.

There was a small reception awaiting the wagon's appearance in the smaller building. Anticipating their arrival was Mary Margaret, another graduate from St. Michaels, Jamie, the young boy who helped in the kitchen sometimes, Sully, the ranch foreman and, of course, Callie. She was a diminutive, maternal woman even though she wasn't much older than the girls in the wagon with him. She had taken it upon herself to help others raised in the St. Michaels Foundling Home and now on their own in the western states and territories.

Greeting the two young women as they got down from the buckboard, she hugged them and welcomed them to the ranch. Callie soon had everyone sitting at one of the long tables in the dining room for the ranch hands while Mary Margaret set out sandwiches and little frosted cake squares. Both of the new-comers accepted tea with sugar and some of the food, eating as if it may have been a while.

They knew Mary Margaret from the orphanage so felt freer to be open with the young woman. They were all soon discussing the ranch and the various other orphans already located nearby. It wasn't long before Callie joined them after she cleared away their luncheon. Mary Margaret explained she would continue to be lead cook until the new arrivals found if they liked the work or if they wanted to apply for something in town. St. Michaels was well known to have highly educated 'graduates' and the young women were trained in several areas, teaching and sewing being the two most popular.

Faith and Charity were shown to their bedroom at the back of the cookhouse. They would be sharing a bed as they had in the orphanage, which Charity preferred. She didn't want to be separated from Faith and was afraid when she realized how close they were to the men's quarters. Both of the new women were tired from the events of the past few days and then travelling. Neither hesitated to get ready for bed and soon were sound asleep, not hearing the noise of twenty men having supper right outside their room.

CHAPTER 2

At the Macgregor ranch, Jeremy was pulling into the long, curved drive in front of his family home. It was a large two-story house with a wide front porch, now holding his happy welcoming family, each male larger than the next. Mac, with his red hair had shaved his once bright red, bushy beard and was dressed in suit trousers, starched shirt and string tie. Mac always looked as if there should be a big blue ox next to him. Jamie, his hair color toned down to an auburn, was equally tall but less broad with it and he was wearing a suit similar to the one Jeremy wore.

The ladies, Emily with light brown hair pulled into a no non-sense bun and Mavis with darker curls pinned on top of her head, wore pleasant looking dresses with fashionable bustles that put the humps in the front to shame.

Jeremy thanked his lucky star for having Matthew meeting the same train he and Clarissa were on so his family had gotten some forewarning he was arriving with a guest. He didn't trust what his oldest brother might have said if Jeremy had arrived out of the blue.

The second to oldest brother, Jamie, was the first to come off the porch and hug his younger brother to him with a warm pat on the back. He turned to Clarissa as she was being helped down from the rented buggy and very gallantly brought her gloved hand to his lips saying, "And who is this charming young lady you have brought along with you, Jeremy?"

"Everyone, this is Clarissa Smyth, ah, my friend

from Topeka. I brought her home to meet all of you," Jeremy told the waiting group as Clarissa held her lips firmly in a tight, polite smile.

"Please bring her in and we can introduce ourselves as you get settled. We've put Miss Smyth in Mac's old room. We're in your parent's room now, so we have plenty of space," Emily explained. She hoped he understood that he could share if he wished. They were all adults, after all.

"I'm sure I'll be quite comfortable. I once had to travel in Mexico - a filthy, dirty country, so I'm sure this will be a refreshing experience." Then floated past the group as if she was a queen surveying her subjects.

Mavis went a bright red, opening her mouth to tell Miss Smyth her manners needed to be refreshed when Emily pulled on her sleeve. Mavis clamped her lips closed and said nothing to disrupt the warm homecoming they all expected.

The men carried the few remaining parcels in from the buggy and called a ranch hand to take the rented rig to be put away for the evening. It would be returned to town in the morning.

The men entered the house talking and laughing. It had been several months since they had seen one another and had a lot of catching up to do. Emily showed Clarissa to her room.

That fine lady looked it over then smiled saying, "How quaint." She looked at her trunks and cases, still packed and setting in the room. "I suppose the quilt is a family heirloom of sorts?"

"It is now. Mavis and I finished that very recently," answered Emily sweetly.

"I suppose there's not much else to do is there? I

didn't see an opera house or theater in town. Jeremy wasn't very forthcoming as to the amenities of his hometown. I will simply have to try to find things to keep myself entertained. This is fine. I'll be down for dinner when I've had time to refresh myself." She dismissed Emily as she turned around to face the mirror and with long practice, removed her hat without disturbing her hairstyle.

The happy family talked animatedly while sitting in the parlor of the home, a large stone fireplace taking up one wall, an upright piano and wing back chairs another. There were also leather sofas and miscellaneous tables holding lamps of colored glass and painted shades scattered around the room. Talk stopped completely as Clarissa finally made her entrance.

She had changed into a gown that showed a little more of her than normally was seen in Sweetwater, even at Miss Lily's house of ill-repute. The bustle out did the one on her day dress which had been considerable while the plethora of feathers in her hair as she approached the group had several of them dropping their jaw open.

Jeremy rose to meet her at the base of the stairs, saying gallantly, "You look lovely, my dear. No one would guess you have been traveling for days."

"As you know, I was lucky enough to procure a Pullman for my travels most of the trip. However, the last few hours to Sweetwater was in a regular coach car and there was a crying child most of the trip. Why people insist on taking their children with them I do not understand. I mean, isn't that one of the main reasons to travel? To get away from the little beasts?" She trilled a laugh expecting them to agree.

Mavis placed her hand protectively over her

stomach and Emily interrupted before anyone could say anything to counter what Clarissa had said. "I believe we can remove to the dining table. Gentlemen, if you would, please?"

Jeremy took Clarissa's arm and escorted her the few feet to the long table already set with candelabra and a centerpiece of flowers. Emily and Mavis disappeared into the kitchen and after a moment brought out some beautifully cooked beef bourguignon, buttered asparagus and creamed new potatoes. Jamie had been pouring the wine and offered his wife a kiss when he got to her seat then helped push her chair in for her before seating himself.

Clarissa's eyebrows rose at the sign of such public affection but didn't comment. Instead, she accepted the piece of beef that Jeremy, sitting next to her placed on her plate along with some asparagus but deigned to accept any of the potatoes. The rest of the diners ate hardy portions of all, including the freshly baked rolls.

Mac, normally not very sociable, was answering Jeremy's question as to how many foals were going to be born. Mac began to explain the problems with the stallion having a very nasty infection of the sheath and being unable to perform his duties to the mares.

Emily asked, "What about the bean harvest, dear"

Mac glanced up from his plate to his wife watching him expectantly and he cleared his throat before replying, "Ah, yes, I plan on planting a field of beans, probably lots of beans." Then smiled and took another bite of potatoes.

"I think you probably will, dear." Emily smiled benevolently at her handsome red-haired husband.

Jamie rose to help Mavis and Emily clear the table

of the serving dishes and used plates. Then Mavis brought in a fruit trifle while Emily brought in the dessert dishes. Everyone accepted a portion except Clarissa, who turned it down as being too fattening.

"After all, I know now you are married you aren't as concerned about your figures but I don't have that luxury to let myself go." She smiled coyly at Jeremy who jumped in with the compliment Clarissa had been angling for.

"I adore every lovely curve, my dear." He raised her hand to his mouth, imitating his older brother of earlier in the day.

Finally, Emily stood as did Mavis and Jamie, all of them taking whatever plates and tableware was left in front of them. Once inside the kitchen, Emily and Mavis both pushed Jamie back out to visit with his brothers and to keep Mac from saying anything that might offend Clarissa.

The two women took as long as possible before having to reenter the parlor to partake of the family gathering. They arrived to find only Jamie sitting in one of the wingback chairs and he stood to help his wife get comfortable then sat cozily next to her on the sofa. Mac went to the office almost immediately after dinner and Jeremy has just gone upstairs to say goodnight to Clarissa.

Mavis asked bluntly, "Do you think we'll see Jeremy again tonight or do you think they share a room?"

However, before anyone could make a conjecture, Jeremy returned and flopped down tiredly into the other wingback chair. "We don't share a room, yet. It's my hope we soon will and you can all wish me happy," he said confidently.

"Sorry, I was simply wondering if we should have put you into a room together," said Mavis.

"No, the room is fine. Clarissa even said so. But what's this about beans? Since when are we farmers other than for feed? What field did we put into beans?" he asked the group.

Jamie laughed, saying, "That's Emily's way of letting Mac know he is beginning to speak of...let's say less than appropriate dinner conversation, especially if we have company. There's more leeway if it's only Mavis and me there. We talk too much business for the ladies sometimes. Mavis has a very sensitive stomach right now and Emily is trying to keep Mac from revealing too much information about certain farm functions."

"I see. Well, that's always been Mac's way. It must make a lot of talk of beans at dinner time." He laughed just thinking of his oldest brother's habit of talking of all sorts of ranch life. Heck, Jeremy learned about sex listening to his two older brothers discuss cattle and horse breeding. The rest he learned at Miss Lily's.

At the Harrison ranch early the next morning, the three young women, Faith, Charity and Mary Margaret worked together as if they had been doing so for years. Callie had set up the kitchen similar to the one at St. Michaels so all three were used to the procedures. Mary Margaret handled the main stovetop cooking while Faith, her red-gold hair pulled back in a bun, was in charge of mixing and baking the biscuits. Charity, a blond braid wound at the back of her neck in a figure eight, was put to work packing the mid-day meals the men took with them to their work posts.

At six, there was a clang of a bell on the porch and

a tall, slim man came in smiling and bobbing his head, saying good morning to all three ladies then receiving a plate heaped with eggs, bacon, and biscuits with gravy. More biscuits and honey were already on the table. Faith poured coffee, refilling as necessary. The men all said their good mornings, ate their platefuls, grabbed their packed meals and told the young women 'thank you' when they left, wishing them a good day.

When the last of the twenty men filed out, Faith, Charity and Mary Margaret sat down as Faith asked in awe, "Is it always like that? It was like feeding locusts!"

"Well, Callie had them trained before we, Mary Elizabeth and me, got here but they are really quite sweet. When we first arrived, it took us a little while to learn this stove and we didn't get things all cooked at the same time. No one complained, not one."

She continued, "A couple of the men offered to help but then Jamie, he's sixteen now, joined us. Callie was big with child and Seth didn't want her standing at a stove or doing anything down here in the cookhouse. She spent most of her time in the big house but she always made time to teach us new recipes. She's really good at coming up with new soups and ways to cook beef." She chuckled. "We serve a lot of beef here."

"So, I take it this is how all the meals are?" asked Faith looking at the menu board hanging above the back shelves.

Mary Margaret nodded, then said, "Supper always consists of a soup, an entrée and four or five sides plus dessert. We dish up the meat as they pass by this counter and then they help themselves to the rest. Bread and preserves or honey, and things like pickles are on the tables. We set up the weekly menu in advance, using some of the left-overs for the soups.

"Sunday, we have a big dinner right after church and Sunday evening is a simpler meal, usually a one dish casserole or stew and left-over desserts from the weekly suppers. If there isn't enough, we make a pudding or stewed apples or something simple. We get time off during the day as well as Sunday afternoons after dinner. Jamie usually takes care of Sunday supper," Mary Margaret continued explaining what to expect to the new comers.

"That seems more than fair. I was working in a laundry and we had fourteen-hour days, six days a week without breaks and had to haul the water for near to a quarter mile. We were also in charge of cutting our own wood to heat the washing kettles," said Charity as she crossed herself. "This sounds like a peaceful blessing."

"There is always a week plan and a day plan hanging on the wall. It even tells what has to be done for the next day's meals, like when to make soup stock and things like that," explained Mary Margaret.

"This is starting to sound complicated, Mary Margaret. I'm not sure we're up to this just yet." Faith worried knowing Charity was still fragile and not ready for too strenuous a job.

"I'm not going anywhere and Jamie was doing the job by himself before he started to help train the horses. He's always on call if we need him. I enjoy cooking for the men but I like taking care of babies, too, and little Warren is such a cutie. He's just beginning to investigate his world. I love them when they start to develop their own personalities."

Faith was hoping to get Charity settled in her new home before any more changes occurred. There may only be a few weeks and it may take that long before Charity felt comfortable on the ranch, even surrounded by so many other people from the orphanage. Faith needed to disappear before anyone guessed her secret. She hated to accept anything more from Callie, but she may have to. It would be the best for all of the St. Michaels' graduates.

"It will be up to Callie but if you don't like it here, she'll help you get set up somewhere you want to be. She has brought in a couple of the boys, I mean men, from St. Michaels, too. Right now, they're out with the herds and will be back in a day or so. Real nice young men, even if I say so myself." Mary Margaret took pride in other orphans from the same foundling home in New York doing well. As if their reputation somehow enhanced her own. They were all their brothers' keeper.

"I think we can learn the recipes. I remember Callie teaching me how to make the first batch of oatmeal I ever made at St. Michaels. It was like glue but she fixed it and the rest of the children never knew I made such a hash of it," confided Charity quietly finally becoming comfortable with only the female St. Michaels' group there. "Callie showed me the secret and I never burned anything or made a pot of glue again."

"Well, that's enough of a rest. What's next on the day's plan, Mary Margaret, besides clean up?" asked Faith standing and patting down the starched white apron she had been given to wear over her skirt and shirtwaist. She didn't want too much time to think about her having to leave just as she finally found a home, she could be content in.

The three went to consult the day's plan and Mary Margaret showed them where the printed recipes were located for that evening's supper of coq au vin and dumplings.

It was several days later when Faith asked to talk to Callie in private. Charity looked toward Faith but Faith gave a little shake of her head. Charity stayed sitting at the table, peeling apples for that night's dessert.

Callie and Faith walked up to the side porch of the house and Callie offered Faith some tea and cookies.

"No, I can't eat anything, Callie. I have something to tell you and if you think it best that I leave, I'll understand. I wanted to get Charity settled first. You've been trying to do something good here and I don't want people to think anything else about St. Michaels' graduates," she said quietly.

"Well, why don't you tell me about the problem first and I'll decide," said Callie wondering what this poor young woman could have done to make her feel as if she had let St. Michaels down.

"Just after I mailed you the last letter, I was, I was…I may be with child." Then the tears she had been hoping to keep at bay rolled down Faith's cheeks and dropped onto the starched apron.

"Oh, Faith, what happened? Please tell me. It isn't the end of the world no matter how you may feel about it," Callie told her laying a comforting hand on the younger girl's arm.

As if seeing it all unfold in front of her, Faith closed her eyes so she wouldn't have to see the censure in Callie's gaze.

"Charity and I shared a shed off the main building next to a saloon. We were already sleeping when something woke me up. I heard a noise outside our room and then the door was kicked in." She sucked in a shuddering breath then continued knowing she had to tell the whole thing. "A man, he knew where we slept because he had been hanging around the saloon and would say things to us as we came home some nights. We always came home from work after dark and the men were sometimes out on the boardwalk, just making noise. We never answered them or anything." Taking another trembling breath, she continued. "They frightened Charity and so we tried to outwait them but this one man was there a lot of the time."

Callie patted Faith's hand and urged her to keep telling what happened because it got easier and became less of a burden each time the story was shared. Callie forced the tears in her eyes not to roll down her cheeks in empathy.

"He grabbed me, maybe because I was closest to the door but I fought him as much as I could. He ripped my nightgown and then he, he kept pushing into me, and Charity tried to hit him with a shoe but he threw her against the wall. I screamed at her to stay back. I was afraid he'd go after her and I'm stronger, you know, mentally than Charity. I thought I could survive better but she's been so quiet ever since, I worry about her now, too." Tear-filled gray eyes met Callie's. "I don't know how long he was doing that but then he got off me and left. We didn't sleep any more that night but left in the morning and never went back. I had your letter and went to buy the tickets. Then we came here." Faith finished with her voice a little stronger.

"So, you didn't try telling anyone else? Do you know this man's name?" asked Callie.

"I didn't want to get involved with anyone. I didn't want people knowing. His name is Dick Hansen, but I don't know anything else about him. I don't want to try to go after him. What if he said I was selling myself or had made promises or something? No one believes a woman over a man's words in these things. And Charity was positively broken. She didn't even talk for the first three days. She's finally opening up here, with Mary Margaret. She's almost like she was before it happened," Faith confided.

"But it did and you have to be helped to overcome the trauma, too," explained Callie.

"I may be with child. How do I over-come something like that? What would the Sisters at St. Michaels say?" she asked worriedly.

"I want you to go to see my friend, Rebecca, in town. She'll know how to help," Callie told the troubled young woman.

At the shocked expression on Faith's face, Callie went on quickly, "No, not that, never that. I'm a Catholic, too. We'll take care of the child, if there is one. I want Rebecca to talk with you, to help you know what to expect with a birth and the changes in your body. She's very down to earth. She'll understand and be a great help in the months ahead."

Faith sat there trying to take in what Callie was telling her. She had expected to be told she had to leave the ranch, leave Sweetwater. The relief that she wouldn't need to find a new position was one worry she wouldn't have to face. Not immediately, at least.

"I'll have Jamie take you into town. He'll be told to take you to Mary Elizabeth for a visit and she'll get Rebecca for you. Then Jamie will pick you up on his way back to the ranch. No one need know why you went except Rebecca. Will that be all right?" asked Callie.

"Yes, thank you Callie. You've been more than good to us and I'm so sorry I'm letting you all down," Faith said dropping her head in shame.

"You must stop thinking like that. You have no blame or guilt nor are you letting anyone down. Please try not to worry and we'll work this out together," Callie assured her.

CHAPTER 3

Jeremy looked in through the papered covered windows then tried the door finding it opened to his slight push.

"Hey, little brother," he called out upon seeing his young bother standing in front of a counter.

Jessie was tall but shorter than the rest of the Macgregor brothers and nowhere as wide. He had piercing blue eyes and blond hair sun-streaked to almost white in places. Jessie turned and in two strides was in front of his older brother accepting and giving a big bear hug.

"Jeremy, what in the blazes are you doing in Sweetwater? If I'd known, I would have met you at the train," the youngest Macgregor brother said showing real pleasure.

"Actually, I arrived a couple of days ago but finally got a chance to get back into town. I brought home the woman I'm going to marry. Well, I haven't actually asked her yet, but she's smart and has probably worked it out by now. Anyway, I brought her in to shop, mostly with Abby. I snuck away to visit my brother the practicing attorney and promising newspaper editor." Jeremy peered around the unfinished office. "Why do both?"

"I will have to do both until Sweetwater grows a little bigger. I need to support a family and there isn't enough work for a full-time attorney until local ranchers switch from using those in the big cities. And a weekly newspaper won't put out much income for a while, either."

"So, you're thinking of getting married, too? That will make all of us in the clan of Macgregor's. What a sad state of affairs but I guess it was bound to happen," Jeremy teased.

"I've been trying to convince this one girl, well, young lady, but she wants to be independent and doesn't think she can be married and have a career of her own. I'm trying to change her mind, of course."

"Clarissa, my intended, seems to want to do just the opposite. She, and I suppose my soon to be father-in-law, has my future all planned out. Run for public office in the capital and then in a few years run for a Federal senate position and finish out our lives living in Washington D.C. I think she has planned on two children, first a boy then a girl and both having an English nanny. Clarissa is willing to do everything to help me in my career, hosting dinner parties, attending the right social events, meeting the right people. I'm very lucky to have found her," said Jeremy happily.

"She sounds like exactly what you want. I'm glad you met her and are settling down. I had given up hope for Mac and then all of a sudden both Jamie and Mac are married, and both Mavis and Emily are expecting."

"I was a little surprised to see how they had, umm, blossomed since I had last visited. Jamie told me you were living here in town now? Over at the hotel?"

"No, right here. Let me show you the place."

They took the tour looking at the three offices besides the storefront, which will house the presses. Then they went out the rear door and up a set of stairs to the second-floor apartment. It had a kitchen with cooking stove and dry sink as well as a dining room and parlor.

Two bedrooms and a third used as a bathing room much like the ones found in the hotel. The partially furnished apartment would serve a growing family easily.

Jessie said proudly, "I own the whole building so if I ever build a house here in town, I can rent out the apartment or use it as part of the wages to a fulltime editor when I become a daily."

"I can't believe my little brother is becoming an entrepreneur. What's the next step?" Jeremy asked as they descended to the back stoop.

"I really can't say but I know I'll do whatever Mary Elizabeth wants me to do. Nothing means much if she won't marry me. I've been in love with her since I first set eyes on her and I'll keep trying until I wear her down."

"You'll get her to come around. After all, you're a Macgregor." They gave each other another hug as Jeremy explained he had better go and pick-up Clarissa before she bought Abby out of hats.

Once on their way home in the rented buggy, Jeremy said, "My younger brother seems to have gotten the marriage bug. He is setting up a nice apartment over his offices which should be a good place to start a family."

"What is it with you men out here? I mean there's this poor woman today with one baby on her hip and another on her breast. Can't the men around here hold back their baser instincts? Even your own sisters-in-law are breeding less than a few months after the wedding. I mean, men should simply go to a professional instead of putting their wives through all that sordid business," she said indignantly.

"Well, Clarissa, these things happen when two people marry," he said half-jesting.

"There are ways of handling such events. And the men can always go to a brothel or some such place. After all, that's what they are there for," she told him irritably.

"Clarissa, if we are to marry, I would remain faithful to my vows," explained Jeremy earnestly.

Reaching over, Clarissa patted Jeremy with her gloved hand. "I appreciate the sentiment but I won't expect you to give up your personal gratification merely to say you're faithful."

Jeremy drove the half-hour home in relative quiet after that. He kept replaying the conversation but each time he did, he didn't like the outcome any better. Was Clarissa against not only having children but also the act of lovemaking? What other things had Jeremy taken for granted because he thought they were normal in a relationship and marriage? What did he really want from his marriage? What did he really want from Clarissa?

His own parents had a good marriage and he never remembered a harsh word between them. He knew his mother loved all her sons but was disappointed when she never bore any daughters, as well. The quilts on all their beds as children had a story behind them about his mother making them for her 'girls' who never materialized. Instead, once she realized there would be no more children for her, she explained the Macgregor boys would need to wrap their wives in the quilts so as to bless their wives with daughters as well as sons. Smiling at the memory, he wondered if his older brothers had done that? Did they even remember the promise they all made to their mother to do as she had wanted?

What would Clarissa's reaction be to having an old quilt placed around her on their honeymoon? Would she think it romantic or simply some annoying country bumpkin idea? For some reason Jeremy didn't like his mother's wishes thought of as foolish. He would keep the story to himself and hope that Clarissa changed her mind once they were married. It was simply the talk of a virgin having her say such things. Once they had been intimate, Jeremy was sure she would change her mind and want him in her bed every night.

There was still a niggling feeling that some of what she said had been well thought out. She seemed to have certain ideas of her role in his life – and his in hers. This would be something they needed to sort out before either made a commitment but he knew she was simply saying what she had heard other women say. She didn't understand how married couples shared their lives with one another, their bodies. How he planned on sharing his with her.

Shaking his head, he chuckled at his own intimate thoughts. He had better remember they weren't married yet and he had no way of relieving any tensions he started in progress – even with his fiancée's permission to do so. Visiting Miss Lily's on this trip wouldn't be the best way to start his new relationship. Hopefully, after Clarissa agreed to his proposal, when he made it, they would consummate the union properly. He didn't want a long drawn out engagement, anyway.

Young Jamie Franklin, a last name he got to choose for himself once he became fourteen, pulled the buckboard up in front of the house Mary Elizabeth was living in while training as a midwife. Faith climbed down from the seat and smiled her thanks.

Jamie said, "I'll probably be a couple of hours. I have to drop off the mail, get supplies, and pick-up some more fence posts and wire. Will that be long enough for your visit?"

"Yes, thank you, that should be long enough. I'm just catching up with Mary Elizabeth," Faith lied, but didn't do it well. Jamie, being easy going, found no reason not to believe what she said. After all, it was pretty much what Callie had told him, too.

By the time Faith climbed the steps to the porch of the little white house, Mary Elizabeth had the front door open and a wide smile on her face.

"Oh, I do remember you, Faith." Then hugged the other girl to her. "I wasn't sure since you're a little younger and there seemed to be as many Faiths as there were Marys."

"I know, the nuns said they tried not to re-use the same name without at least three years separation, but I think some of them got confused and it happened. At least, I never heard of a Mary Faith." Both girls laughed knowing the possibility was there since the nuns had to come up with dozens of names each year.

"I'm trying to have people call me Mary Beth, it seems easier and I'll be working with a lot of new people."

Remembering her real reason for this visit, Faith said, "Callie sent me to speak with Rebecca. Is she here?"

"Just across the street. Let me run over and get her. Can I get you a cup of tea or coffee? I have the hot water ready and I can brew some coffee."

"No, thank you." Faith was becoming nervous as the time to tell a stranger about the night she left Three Rivers approached. A stranger who would judge her and her morals. Faith pressed her hand into her stomach trying to get it to stop flipping around. It had been doing that lately, it seemed. Another reason to think she was with child and she felt the weight of that reality added to her shoulders. All life was precious. It was what the nuns had drummed into the foundlings' heads and was accompanied, at the same time, by dire warnings for anyone bringing a child into this world without two parents. Most of those at the foundling home were such children. Abandoned, unwanted and left at the mercy of others to raise and care for.

She didn't want that to happen to any child of hers but could she face a world with a child brought into it through rape? Was it some sort of test from God of her faith and her commitment to Him? She couldn't see how what happened to her was any part of God's plan but the sisters were very sure of their faith. Everything is part of God's plan and we, mere humans, are not capable of understanding those plans. She must accept what He has given her to bear.

A pretty woman came in the front door. She was dressed neatly and wore an apron over her dress. She also looked several months pregnant but Faith didn't mention the fact.

"I'm Rebecca, the midwife. Mary Beth said you were, Faith? Nice to meet you. How can I be of help?" Her soft brown eyes peered closely at Faith.

At the younger woman's hesitation, Rebecca stated, "It's something personal that you have trouble speaking about."

Faith nodded and opened her mouth to tell this woman what had happened but no sound came out.

"This happened a while ago, before you got to Sweetwater?" asked Rebecca as the search to help this young girl continued.

Faith nodded.

"I'm going to hold your hand and you can begin whenever you feel able. Are you having thoughts that you may be with child?" asked Rebecca getting to the fact that brought most women to her door.

Faith finally was able to speak, "I think so. I don't know how to tell for sure."

"When was your last menses?" At the questioning look, Rebecca tried again. "Your monthly flow?"

"I, it should have been this last week and I've never missed a month, ever," Faith whispered as confirmation of her plight became evident to her.

"Is there a man in the picture, someone who would stand by you?" asked Rebecca in that same quiet manner that she used to sooth mothers giving birth.

As Faith thought about the question, tears filled her eyes and she trembled, finally letting the dam burst and sobbed into her hands. "I was attacked and I don't know what to do. I've been praying but nothing has brought me any peace." She tried to stop the tears now that the worse was over. She had admitted her fears aloud to this kind lady.

"You were attacked and were you hurt anywhere else? Do you need medical care, have you been bleeding anywhere, perhaps, just a little?"

"No, he attacked me and we fought." Faith left off Charity being present in case someone would think she should have done more to stop the assault. "And he shoved me onto my cot and kept pushing into me and then he left."

"Was there a lot of bleeding, are you sore or torn inside?" asked Rebecca more concerned with any internal injuries.

Shaking her head, Faith took in a shuddering breath. "I just had a lot of bruises. My breasts, my arms and my legs but they're about gone now. He was wearing boots and his buckle dug into me." She pulled up her shirtwaist to show yellow-brown splotches still marring her skin and scabbing over a cut.

"When did this happen?" asked Rebecca looking at the discoloration.

"About two weeks ago, right before we got the ticket money from Callie to come here. We were already planning on leaving. We just didn't get out quick enough."

"It's too soon for me to check for a pregnancy. There wouldn't be any strong signs yet so I would simply be guessing which isn't fair to you. It's going to be difficult but we need to wait a few more weeks before we can examine you internally."

"And if I am?" asked Faith tentatively.

"I don't terminate a pregnancy, not for any reason," explained Rebecca gently.

"No, I wouldn't want...I mean, Callie, told me already."

"We'll worry about learning of a full-term pregnancy later, when we know for sure." She stood-up and walked to the front door. "Now let's call over Mary Beth and have a luncheon. I'm starving already and it seems as if I just finished breakfast." The midwife laughed at her never-ending hunger.

Coming back from the churchyard across the street, Mary Beth started putting out food and made tea for the three of them. They would have at least an hour before Jamie would be there to pick her up. Faith may as well renew a friendship and make a new one. Life is too short to let one bad incident mar the whole thing. There would be time to figure out where she could go to have this child. A place she could hide the fact of its birth.

Mary Beth asked about Mary Margaret and how Faith liked working at the ranch. She asked about a couple of the cowhands and laughed at Faith's description of locusts and not a crumb left on the plates or table. By the time they heard the buckboard pull up in the front, Faith was feeling much better about everything. Perhaps what happened to her wasn't the worse thing in the world. Perhaps there was a plan she wasn't aware of being a part of.

The three women chatted all the way onto the porch and Mary Beth waved and spoke to Jamie for a couple of minutes as Faith climbed onto the front seat. Then with one last wave, the two of them drove off toward the ranches north of town.

CHAPTER 4

Matthew thanked Jamie as he watched the young boy run back across the street to the Mercantile. He opened the letter in his hand that Callie had sent him and read it with a grim expression. Abby, a slender brunette with bright brown eyes, came into the shop with Grace, almost one year old on her hip, saying, "I thought I heard the chime. Did someone come by?"

"Just young Jamie. He brought a note from Callie. She sent word about something she wants me to look into for her," he said folding the paper and putting it into his pocket.

"Do you need to leave? I can handle the girls so go if you need to," said Abby reasonably.

Matthew's mind went back to the day he found Abby on the floor of their kitchen, Grace crawling towards her mother. Abby told him she had been waiting until her contractions got stronger before making her way to the bedroom. She thought she would have plenty of time before disturbing Rebecca's day. When her water broke and the pains incapacitated her, they were so strong and coming so quickly there was no one to call out to. Matthew hadn't been due to come back for several days yet.

On that day, Abby decided she would need to deliver her own baby and keep their adopted daughter, Grace, safe at the same time. She had had a stillborn several years earlier but didn't have experience with actually giving birth. This time she would be on her own, unable to contact anyone to come to her aid. She had been going over, in her mind, everything Rebecca had told her. She had gathered a sharp knife and a leather strip she would tie off the umbilical cord with but was more than relieved when Matthew came in the back door of their dress shop.

In his typical take-charge attitude, Matthew put Grace into her crib and tried to get Abby more comfortable on their bed. Then proceeded to help deliver their daughter who they named, Hannah. After Abby and the baby were both clean and comfortable, Matthew ran down the street to get Rebecca to come back and make sure he had done everything correctly.

Matthew had, on that day, decided never to leave Abby alone. He would remain in the immediate area and never place his family in danger even to help others. He wouldn't leave her overnight again.

"Abby, you just had a baby and Grace wants to get into everything. You're getting too tired to be healthy and that's with me here to help you. Sorry, love, I'm here to stay. I can handle this from here, anyways. Now give me Grace and you try to rest before Hannah wakes up for a feeding. That's one thing I'm not able to help you with."

He leaned over and took Grace, kissing his wife who gratefully walked back through a curtained doorway to a waiting cot.

Finding a crocheted cap for Grace, he wrapped a lightweight blanket around her and took her out through the front door after turning the sign to 'close' on the door's window. Sheriff Mason was just down the street and Matthew needed to speak with him before they could send a telegram out to the sheriff in Three Rivers.

Matthew was on his way back from talking to

Mason when Mrs. Thomson, the wife of the dry-goods storeowner and mayor, stopped him. She had been the chairwoman of every social event held by the town since the town began. The dry-goods store was the first building built on main street even before Kansas was a state and she kept reminding everyone of that fact.

"Good morning, Mrs. Thompson." Matthew tipped his hat but planned on continuing back to the dress shop.

"Oh, Matthew, just the man I was looking for," Mrs. Thompson said in a booming voice that could be heard across the street.

"Is there something I can do for you?" Matthew hated hearing himself ask the question but knew Abby would think him a true gentleman for doing so.

"Well, actually more what your sister can do. I have a son, Thomas, Junior, who I would love see stay here in Sweetwater but with so few women of marriageable age, he is starting to talk about going to one of the larger cities." Holding Matthew in place with a stern glare, she continued. "Now this would be bad for the town - having our young men leave, I mean. And if Junior leaves then my younger son will also. He already has to go to school in another town since there still isn't one here for the older students, which has always been a thorn in my side, I'll tell you." Now she was really on a roll, Matthew thought. Could he make an excuse about needing to feed Grace but one glance at his undemanding daughter found she didn't appear uncomfortable in any way.

"I understand the problem of not having many young women in town and I appreciate the need for a school, especially when all these new babies start to get of an age." Matthew tried to commiserate with Mrs. Thompson, not knowing what else to say.

"I want you to ask Callie to bring more young women to town and then we can have, I don't know, maybe a church social or a celebration of some sort so the young people can get a chance to mingle. I mean, all the ranchers are grabbing up these women before the young men even know they're in town." Then after thinking about it she added quickly, "Oh, I don't mean you. Abby's been around for years and she is too old for Junior, anyways."

Matthew tried to think Christian thoughts and decided Abby would laugh at these comments if he was ever brave enough to tell her about them. So, he stood there shifting Grace onto his other arm and kept a smile pasted on his face.

Mrs. Thompson continued not sure she had made a strong enough point. "These young women are the life's blood for this town, Matthew. Young children are good and fine but the young men of this generation are leaving and making their lives elsewhere. Will you speak to Callie, please, and see if she will write to those nuns or something and get more girls sent to Sweetwater? They all seem like nice girls and they have no other family to pull them away from town. It makes perfect sense to bring them and then let them meet the fine young men who live here."

Matthew, being Matthew, said, "Well, Callie won't simply bring these young women out here to be bartered and sold like cattle, you know. They will all need a job and living space waiting for them. No pressure to marry. They are allowed to take the time they need to decide whom and if they wish to marry. Are you willing to furnish a job for a suitably qualified candidate? Maybe a bookkeeper at the lumber yard?"

"I think I can persuade Mr. Thompson into that," she said emphatically.

I just bet you can, thought Matthew. "I'll speak with Callie and see who she knows out west and looking for some positions. Will that work for you? It's all I can promise to do."

"I knew I could count on you, Matthew. Say hello from me to Abby." The woman seemed happy with his agreement of asking Callie about more young women and smiled broadly at the child in his arms. "And that little one is looking more and more like her Daddy," said Mrs. Thompson who had evidently forgotten Grace was adopted.

Matthew smiled and kissed his daughter as he carried her home to take care of Hannah if she had woken up, yet. He never felt happier in his life and he had his lovely wife and these two beautiful children to thank for it.

CHAPTER 5

The Macgregor clan had just sat down to a family dinner. For the first time in many years, all four Macgregor boys were sitting around the table at the ranch. In addition, there were the three women, two of whom were already Macgregor's and soon to bring forth the next generation. Mac looked over the group and felt a sense of pride that he had successfully brought his family to a new level, one that both his parents would have been proud of.

There was a large roast with some of the last of the root vegetables left in the cellar. Freshly baked biscuits with peach preserves and pickled beets as well as pickled watermelon graced the center of the table. The men all complimented how wonderful the food smelled and looked. Mac carved the roast and Emily passed the plates around.

Clarissa said, "Just a small portion for me. I'm still full from the wonderful luncheon at Julia's house this afternoon."

Both Emily and Mavis glanced guiltily at each other but remained silent. Both husbands stared at their wives but Jamie was the first to speak.

"You all went for a buggy ride to the Gregg's ranch? Have a nice time?" he asked smoothly watching the telltale blush on his wife's face.

Again, Clarissa spoke up, "Yes, Julia is such a gracious and refined hostess. She has one of those Mexican household help but she and Callie made the food. It was as good as the hotel restaurant in the capital

Jeremy and I always patronize."

Mac sat after finishing the carving and gazed at his wife saying quietly, "I thought we had an agreement you weren't to travel on these rough roads and especially not to do so when I didn't know you were out."

"Oh, I must say it was probably my fault. I had been a little restless, so Julia was notified and she invited us for the visit," confessed Clarissa and gave a little trill of laughter as if this would endear her to the husbands. It didn't.

Jeremy tried to defuse a possible family argument saying, "I'm sure Mavis and Emily were careful and it's only fifteen minutes or so on the road. And Callie was at the other end. She knows how to get help if they hadn't arrived on time."

Mac gave a look at Emily, silently telling her he was worried and would die if anything happened to her. Jamie took his wife's hand saying the same thing with his eyes.

Jessie, the youngest and the only one without a woman at the table, cleared his throat and said, "I was just out to Callie's and her son is sure growing fast. Did she bring him with her today?"

That broke the tension at the table and the family continued with the easy camaraderie that usually surrounded their dinners. Mavis told a funny story about Callie's son and Julia's daughter, just a month or so older, fighting over the same toy no matter what toy the little boy selected from the pile.

Finally, Clarissa, clearly bored with the talk of babies, said, "It's too bad there isn't entertainment in town, even an opera singer or pianist would do."

Jeremy volunteered an alternative. "Our mother

insisted we learn to play the piano. Mac is a fantastic pianist." At Clarissa's clearly unbelieving expression and both wives' expressions of surprise, he continued, "I always thought he should play professionally but he wouldn't leave the ranch."

Mac stated firmly, "I don't play anymore. Jamie's got a good hand, too, though." He rose from the table, kissed his wife, and went to the office by the front door.

Jamie held up his hands, saying, "Not me. I haven't touched the ivories in several years." Then he got up to help clear the table.

Once the washing-up was done and the whole family, except Mac, had joined Clarissa and Jeremy in the parlor, Jessie said, "All right, I'll be tonight's entertainment but if I hit a few sour notes I don't expect any complaints."

Jessie sat on the stool in front of the upright and exposed the keys, then began a lively modern piece that Emily thought sounded familiar. Jessie sang the words to one of the songs then trailed off either because he realized the words were less than polite in mixed company or he'd forgotten them. Either way, both Mavis and Emily tapped their hands on their knees. When Jessie finally brought the impromptu performance to an end, both wives clapped enthusiastically, teasingly asking for an encore. Jessie rose and took an exaggerated bow then sat on the sofa between the wives.

Jeremy had applauded also while Clarissa seemed to have plastered a half smile on her face and said tightly, "Well, that's the first time I ever heard honky-tonk coming from anywhere besides a saloon doorway. I hope your college experience wasn't a total waste."

Not to be cowered by a woman he didn't even like,

Jessie smiled and said, "That is just the lesser of my talents, I assure you. I spent a great deal of time tasting and grading beer, too. I can tell you where the best beer is sold if you ever get to San Francisco."

"I think I will be able to find more enlightening entertainments, thank you, Jessie," said Clarissa with more than slight derision in her voice.

Jamie piped in, "I might like a list of those places, Jessie. Mavis and I still have a trip planned once she can travel again and we both enjoy a good brewed beer." Which statement earned him a derisive look from Clarissa.

Jeremy tried to tease Clarissa into a better mood but she simply stood saying she was exhausted from the visit that afternoon and retired to her bedroom - alone.

Jessie said it was about time for him to ride back into town and kissed his two sisters-in-law goodbye then shook his brothers' hands. He called in on Mac before he left then went to saddle his horse for the trip back to Sweetwater and his own apartment.

The rest of the family went upstairs an hour or so later leaving Jeremy sitting in the dark, contemplating the telegram he had received that morning and his future over-all.

CHAPTER 6

Several days later, Jeremy found himself riding into town after having an argument with Clarissa, well, not so much an argument as it was a discussion. She had been hinting at getting the ring put on her finger so they could return to the state capital as an engaged couple. She thought it time to begin the campaign toward getting into some office, either within the capital or a state position, whichever opened up first.

Jeremy said he wasn't sure he wanted to do that so soon, possibly after spending a few years in Sweetwater. That's when Clarissa had set an ultimatum. Either make plans to return to the capital together or she would return alone and remain that way.

Tying his horse in front of the hotel, Jeremy brushed at the dust on his suit trousers. He gazed at the door, knowing his fate was going to be decided this afternoon then took a deep breath before heading up the step to the boardwalk.

After a two-hour meeting, Jeremy with a much lighter step, crossed the street hoping to find Jessie in his offices. Instead, Jeremy came upon a young woman, on her hands and knees, fanny in the air with a greasy wrench in her hand calling out instructions to Jessie who held onto a large piece of metal.

"Can I help?" called out Jeremy.

The woman answered, "No."

While Jessie said, "Yes."

Jeremy went to stand beside Jessie grabbing onto the same piece of metal, a crank of some kind, and pushed to see if he could get it in place with their combined strength.

"I've gotten it tightened, Jessie, you can let go of it now." The woman wiggled back out in a very feminine way that made certain parts of Jeremy uncomfortable immediately.

The young woman, a little smear of grease on her forehead, stood-up pushing her dislodged curls back on top of her head. Several tendrils fell loose drifting onto her shoulders.

Jeremy stood mesmerized while Jessie introduced the two, "Oh, Faith, you probably have never met my brother, Jeremy. Jeremy, this is Faith St. Michaels, my protective angel who is going to teach me how to operate this expensive piece of equipment I purchased."

"Nice to meet you, Miss St. Michaels. Wait, weren't you one of the girls, I mean, young ladies, Matthew was picking up when I came in on the train last week?" asked Jeremy, eyeing the pretty woman with light brown hair and gray eyes. She was slender but it was difficult to tell with the heavy leather apron, similar to ones he had seen blacksmiths wear, covering much of her body.

"Yes, sir. Charity and I arrived on the same train. I hope you're both enjoying your stay," she said smiling remembering he had not arrived alone, either.

Jeremy asked with a teasing smile, "Faith - Charity is there a Hope?"

"There's always Hope," she responded but Jeremy wasn't sure if she was teasing or not.

Jessie explained, "Mary Beth told me about Faith having worked in a newspaper for a while before she came here. So, when the man who was supposed to come along with this machinery got ill and backed out, I called upon her services. I got a real surprise because not only does she know how to run this thing, she knows how to put it together and keep it running. She may be my first editor." Blushing at his optimism, he continued, "As soon as I can afford one, that is."

"I don't know about editor, Jessie, but I can keep the press going and I can set type and proofread. You have to make the sales and that's what keeps it all going in the long run," she said, downplaying his need of her knowing she may need to leave Sweetwater when her pregnancy began to show.

Jessie turned to Jeremy saying, "Didn't I tell you she was great? I wouldn't be even half-ready to put my first paper to print this next week if I didn't have her help."

Embarrassed at such praise, Faith interrupted, "Excuse me, I think I better clean up. I know I've got grease everywhere it shouldn't be." Then she walked towards the back of the building, hips swaying in an unconscious way.

Jessie called his brother's attention back to himself. "Are you shopping again, Big Brother? What more could Clarissa possibly need?"

"I'm on my own and actually I came to see if I can strike a deal with you."

"I'm open, what did you have in mind?" Jessie asked while scrubbing at the black grease on his hands.

"I would like to rent one of your offices. I have won a commission to design and build a bank here on Main Street. Just as banks are closing all over the United States, First National is expanding. Something about never having backed any railroads and they're taking advantage of the banks that had which are now failing. They feel there will be a need of a strong bank for towns like Sweetwater that are potentially expanding. I wouldn't be here much but I need a place to meet with contractors and masons and such for a few months. If it works out, I'll build my own place."

Jessie let out a whistle. "Here in Sweetwater?"

"Yep. I made a decision. I don't want to be a politician. At least not now, not when I still want to build something. That's why I went to university, after all. Sweetwater is on the cusp of growing into the kind of place I want to raise a family."

"So, Clarissa's on board with all this? She's willing to stay a few years and then maybe move on?" Jessie asked doubtfully.

"I don't think Clarissa will be staying. We seem to have come to an impasse and I'm surprised at how unconcerned I find myself about that. She just seems different here. I don't know how, but I find I don't think I really know her and what I do know, I don't like. Does that sound like cold feet or do you think she changed?" asked Jeremy seriously.

"I think this trip home did what it was supposed to do. It made you look at her as part of your family and she doesn't fit. And I don't want to crush you or anything but she doesn't act like a woman in love. She has a plan, for herself, her life and she is simply trying to find a man who fits in with that plan. I don't think you're that man and I don't think Clarissa cares overly much. Another man will do as nicely." Afraid he might have hurt his brother's pride if not his feelings, asked, "Did I say too much?"

"No, I understand what you mean. I'm easily replaceable. Any educated man would fit into Clarissa's and her father's plans for a U. S. Senator. I was simply there at the time."

"Sorry, I know you were happy to be settling down, though. You'll find the right woman. I have and I wasn't even looking."

They were walking down the hall toward the office doors when Faith came out of a doorway and smacked right into Jeremy. He reached out to steady the woman and then let go of her quickly before she could shrug him away which is what he felt she was about to do.

"I'm, ah, I'm sorry. I should have watched where I was going. I thought you both were still in the press room," Faith stammered. "I'll just go and pick-up the tools to put them away." Then she scurried past the two men.

Jeremy followed Jessie into one of the open office doors, saying, "This would be fine, if you don't think you'll need it."

Jessie was quiet for a moment before saying, "I hadn't thought about Faith when you gave me the good news you were staying on in town. I gave her one of the other rooms to use as well as the kitchen upstairs in the apartment. I told her if she cooked, I'll buy the food. I can't cook beans, well, maybe those, but not much else and the hotel restaurant will get too expensive eating there every meal."

Jeremy asked, "And that's a problem? You aren't, umm, there's nothing else going on is there?" He wasn't sure why the answer mattered so much.

"No-o-o-o, oh, no. I think my being in love with Mary Beth is the only reason Faith even accepted the job. She has a position out with Callie if she wants it. I just forgot how skittish she is around men and I need her to stay. I realized there is a lot I don't know about that printing press."

"Can we ask her? I won't be here often. Mostly during usual business hours some days. I need a place where people can meet with me, go over building plans and submit bids. I'll stay out of her way," Jeremy explained again.

"Let me go alone. I'll make her understand the situation and I'll use the rent you pay me to pay her." Then Jessie left Jeremy standing in the empty room.

Jessie soon returned. "Faith says there won't be a problem. She knows you're engaged and going to be busy with getting ready for a wedding. I didn't set her straight and I think we should leave it at that." He looked hopefully at his brother for confirmation to the fabrication.

Putting out his hand, they shook on it. "I agree. It's not like I'm going to chase her around the desk or anything. Let her get to know me and then, if she finds I'm not engaged, it won't matter."

Jeremy didn't look forward to the conversation he would be having with Clarissa. But when he arrived home, he found she had packed her bags and was planning on leaving on the train the next day. Dinner was a solemn affair. Not so much because Clarissa was leaving but because all of the others were trying to be polite and not show their happiness at her departure.

In the morning, the family stood on the front porch and waved Clarissa off, wishing her a good trip and possibly a good riddance. Emily and Mavis looked at one another, then at their stomachs almost touching although they wanted to hug each other and laughed, right out-loud. A sound both husbands standing there realized they hadn't heard since Clarissa had arrived.

Their gazes met over the heads of their wives and they smiled, a sense of relief coming over both of them, too. Now they just had the up-coming births to get through and the household could return to normal.

Standing on the platform, having made sure the bags had arrived before them and were now stored safely in the baggage car, Clarissa pulled her gloves tighter onto her hands.

"If you come to your right mind, Jeremy, Father and I will be able to forgive this little hiccup in our plans, but don't take too long. I'm not getting any younger and Father has already been lining pockets to get a placement for a position in the capital," Clarissa informed her former suitor.

"Thank your father for me, Clarissa. I don't expect to see him again very soon." He almost went to shake her hand as if finalizing a business deal. Instead he took a step back and allowed the conductor to help Clarissa into the waiting train car.

Turning, Jeremy left before the train pulled out. He was anxious to see if the extra desk and cabinet he had borrowed from Mac's office had been set up. Next would be ordering a five-wheeled desk chair and a few other items but, for now, he was in business.

He had wired his old employer to send his personal drafting table by train as soon as he was able. It was all coming together and he couldn't wait to put pencil to paper and then make those drawings come to life as real, useful buildings. Something that would be here long after he was gone.

He walked through the door that now boasted in gold leaf that Jessie Macgregor Esq. and the Sweetwater Chronicle were both housed there. The room was neat with paper piled on a back counter and there was a front counter holding wooden pencils and small order sheets.

Faith turned from what she was doing and smiled a welcome. "Some men just left after delivering your desk and cabinet. I told them where to place them but I'll help you move them if they're not where you want. I figured there were more items coming, like chairs and lamps and things."

"Thank you, and yes, there are a few more items. I need to go over to the Mercantile and order other things I still need. I would like to get some stationary printed, also. Are your presses up to that?"

"I think we can manage." She gave him a quirky smile. "I have a selection of fonts here to choose from and we can print as few as you want to begin with. If black ink is all right. We don't have any gold and we can't emboss, yet."

"Black is fine. I don't want to look like I'm too expensive to ask for a bid. Maybe later." And he grinned. Then he realized he hadn't grinned in a long time and so did it again.

Faith watched the play of emotions cross Jeremy's face and thought he must be thinking of his fiancée, how proud she must be at his opening an office in town. She smiled, saying, "You can fill this order sheet out and would you like to place an advertisement for your services or announcement that you now have an office in town?"

"I see you not only fix and operate a press but you are a born salesperson. I'll have to recommend Jessie stay on your sweet-side." Then began filling out the order sheet.

CHAPTER 7

Mary Beth came out the side-door from the kitchen to the backyard, carrying two glasses of lemonade, although she didn't have any ice. She handed one of the glasses to Jessie.

"So, Faith is working out well with the printing press? I knew she was probably good. She always tried the hardest to learn new things, always worked harder than anyone else."

"I would have been up a creek without a paddle, that's for sure, without her. The press came in pieces and in several crates. It was like one of those Chinese boxes. You know, trying to get the right parts into the right slots. The printer who was going to help me with it sent a wire at the last minute saying he was too ill to travel. I'm not sure he ever planned on coming out here to set it up. Faith had done everything I planned the printer on doing plus she's given me a lot of help with setting up the business portion." He took a sip of the sweet, tart liquid and looked hopefully at the woman he loved. He wished she was able to see they could be good together, that he wouldn't hold her back in anything she wanted to do.

Mary Beth had become quiet and Jessie rushed to assure her, "Don't worry, I'm not attracted to Faith in that way. I think of her as your sister, part of the family. Really."

"Maybe you should look at her in a different way. You need someone to help you with your business and I'll never be that person. I owe so many people for my good fortune. I need to pay it back and that's through helping Rebecca bring babies into the world. She won't be able to go out to the ranches and farms much longer. That leaves only me and I've never attended a live birth, well, any birth. If Rebecca goes into labor early, I'd be helping her, following what she told me. It's a lot of pressure to be in charge of helping women have babies, being responsible for that infant to make it into this world." Mary Beth tried to explain why she couldn't be a wife, too.

"Rebecca doesn't expect you to learn everything all at once. It's like ranching. There are a lot of different parts that all have to go well to ensure the welfare of the ranch, but no one can learn it only from books. There's more than one part that needs to be done physically before you can understand it all. Don't put so much pressure on yourself. Rebecca took years to learn what she knows," Jessie said trying to help Mary Beth see his point of view.

"But I'm to be in charge of people's lives, their families. I can't start a life with you and concentrate on being a good midwife. I need to make a commitment to this community, just like Callie explained. 'We all have to give back to this world what it was so good as to give us'," she quoted, trying to explain the obligations she felt.

"But you don't have to give up your happiness, Mary Beth. No one expects that. Callie has a family," he reminded her.

But Mary Beth wouldn't budge from her conviction she owed more to others than she did to her own personal desires - and that meant Jessie was hurt in the process.

Matthew was sitting in Jeremy's new office when he spoke to both Jeremy and Jessie about his plans. "I need to have a job where I can stay at home at night. I don't want to leave Abby and the girls alone so much and I want to be there to help Abby raise our children. I've been thinking about this distribution business for months now, even before we got Grace and it looks better and better all the time. Right now, I sell an order and then wire it back east and they send out the product. Then I deliver it and get paid, take my commission and send the rest of the money back to the company. Sometimes I sell something only to find they're out of stock or can no longer procure the item. I have a couple of men selling under me right now and we can't keep up with the orders. We spend a lot of time hunting for where the products are, on a train or ship or whatever. If there was a distribution center closer, here in the west, the items we've been selling could be received quicker. Stick to the U. S. Postal Service and Central Pacific Railroad for deliveries."

"That sounds like a great addition to Sweetwater. Becoming a distribution headquarters for products going west into the Dakotas and Iowa. How can we help?" asked Jessie who was always looking for new adventures.

"I have my sources for products and I have my list of retail stores that have accounts with me that I want to continue to supply. Additionally, I would like to have a catalog so those people, women in particular who live too far from a larger town, have access to what they need. Order items and have them delivered in days not weeks. I need a building and maybe a little financial backing."

Jeremy thought about Matthew's needs. "I can help with the building, probably a post and beam to start with. It's the least expensive for the square footage and we can put in a loft to double the space. There's room right behind these businesses if Thompson will sell the land to us."

"He'll sell. When I bought this building, he made it pretty clear he wanted to sell off his holdings a bit at a time. He isn't sure his sons want to follow in his footsteps and he said he couldn't take it with him," Jessie told the others.

"What kind of financial help will you need?" Jeremy asked still trying to get all the facts of the project.

"I have enough for the building but then I might be short for the inventory. I'll have to buy in cases and then break those up to deliver them to mercantiles and stores that have placed orders for lesser amounts. I won't turn over some of the items for more than a month or two, depending on the item. I'll only stock things that have been selling well, items that aren't readily available right now. Focus on housewares for women now there are getting to be more families in the territories, farming implements now that the Indian's have been pushed north or moved to Indian Territory," Matthew told the brothers. "With the inexpensive Homestead grants and ex-soldiers being given land in the west, they will need all sorts of things to make a home."

"I'd be willing to go in on it with you." Jessie volunteered. "I can offer my legal services to set up the company with shares and filings and then be the business manager. Unless you prefer to do it. We may need to get an accountant to keep track of your sales, inventory and billings." Jessie thought of what he had needed to start a business from scratch.

Nodding his head in agreement, Matthew explained, "I'm more of a salesman. I'd like to set up the larger accounts and make sure I can supply what the customers want."

"I'll invest in some stock and supply everything you need for the building since I'll have the manpower on site. We can figure out a rent after I find out what Thompson wants for the land. If he's too high we may need to go out of town a little but it would be better to be closer to the train station to save time with deliveries," Jeremy speculated aloud.

"I agree, and close to the bank so we don't have to protect all that money by ourselves," added Matthew and all three men laughed. "You wouldn't believe the number of hats Abby has on order from a small advertisement she placed in one of the newspapers. The territory is starving for some of the niceties we take for granted in the east. Even that new easy-to-use can opener. It's selling like hot cakes. I'm having trouble getting enough of them. Every cowhand and farmer's wife wants one. I carry one with me when I travel." He showed the two brothers what he was talking about.

"I saw Faith had one. She used it without a hitch. I hadn't realized it was new. I know the one I use is dangerous, to be honest. Nearly cut my thumb off one time," Jessie said as he handed the opener back to his friend.

"Let's work on the numbers, Matthew, and if you can get us an idea of the amount you'll need for inventory, I think we can get a deal made," Jeremy told his friend.

Matthew rose and put out his hand to both men. "I appreciate your help with any of it."

That evening after dinner at the ranch, Jeremy asked to use Mac's office and Mavis and Jamie went up to bed early. That left Mac and Emily in the parlor sitting on the sofa alone.

"Mac, why didn't you ever tell me you played the piano. When I asked about it, you said it belonged to your parents, as if that's all it was." Emily questioned her quiet husband, a man who found conversation difficult.

"Well, that's kind of all it is. My Da was the one who played and taught all of us. Ma played, too, but not nearly as well and they spent many an evening with her sitting sewing and quilting and him playing. He did play beautifully. All of us boys were in awe, I think, watching his big calloused hands on these fragile ivory keys and hearing those lovely sounds emerge as the result."

"I think that's a beautiful memory. A family story to pass on to our children," she said and hugged his arm to her side.

"It's sad, too, though. When Ma died, he never played again. Every week he would have me play for him and the boys but I don't think he touched the piano again. Like his inspiration had died, too," Mac said sadly.

"Oh, Mac. That must have been hard on you, too. Reminding you that she was gone every time you played," Emily said to her husband knowing he was more sentimental then his brothers realized.

"Not so much anymore, *mo cridhe*. I have you and the baby and I understand how difficult it was for him when Ma passed. I don't know what I would do if I lost you." He leaned down and kissed his wife, reassuring himself she was a living, breathing woman.

"I think our child wants to hear its father play. Will you play something for me and the baby?" she asked quietly.

"Babies don't hear anything. You just want me to

make a fool out of myself. I haven't played in years," he said hugging her to his side with his big bear-sized arm.

"Rebecca says babies do hear and that mothers should talk to their babies to sooth them when they get restless. Even reading aloud can get a baby to settle at night if it's keeping the mother awake," Emily informed him.

"I'm not sure Rebecca is right about this, but I guess it can't hurt. Don't expect much, I haven't even tried to play in so long…."

"Do you want me to get some sheet music? I found some long ago in the breakfront drawer in the dining room," she asked as he headed to the piano.

"No, I never had much use for them. Once I heard a piece, I could pretty much play it." He sat down and lightly brushed his fingers from one end of the piano keys to the other. Like meeting an old friend and shaking their hand. Then he centered his hands and began a melody that Emily knew from her own childhood.

Mac played slowly at first but if he made any mistakes, Emily didn't hear them. She had risen when Mac had and now leaned against the end of the piano, watching as her husband's large long-fingered hands, somewhat calloused and rough, danced over the keys causing beautiful sounds to be emitted into the air, surrounding her and their child in beauty.

Emily was surprised by a hearty kick then another as the baby reacted to the piano's vibrations. She placed her hand over the spot of the last movement and realized she could feel the baby's foot push into her hand. She laughed and Mac stopped playing to find out what was happening in her womb as she placed his hand over the spot.

He looked in awe as he said, "Is that a foot? It has a foot already and can feel us feel it? It knows we're out here?"

Emily laughed and said, "I don't know if it knows it's in there. It's just where it has always been but, yes, it knows there is something else around. It hears my heart, my voice. I think our love making."

Mac turned crimson at that and Emily laughed saying, "Not like that. Just it moves sometimes when we're making love, getting comfortable, I suppose. Not so much now that we've been using Rebecca's suggested position. I think the baby likes it too, though. Seems to calm it, at least it calms me."

Mac stood and asked, "Then should we calm the little blighter? Maybe rock it to sleep, *mo gradh*?" Then kissed his wife, trying to seduce her into something she was more than willing to do.

"I think that would be the perfect end to this day," she said as they went upstairs to their room, which was crowded already having the added cradle and dresser full of baby clothes.

With long experience Mac undressed his wife, being careful of her sensitive breasts and pulling off her two-piece dress, letting the skirt portion fall to the floor once the ties were un-done. Laying her on the bed, he pulled off her shoes. She had dispensed with stockings the past couple of weeks as being too difficult to pull on.

Covering her so she didn't get chilled, he quickly removed his shirt, tie, and trousers. Sitting on the bed fully naked to pull off his socks, he then shifted to lay down beside his wife and take her in his arms.

He was always gentle, being a bigger than average man in all ways made him very aware of how much smaller his wife was and how much damage he could do if he were ever careless.

Emily was aware she was nowhere near as fragile as Mac thought of her and snuggled onto her side, her protruding belly like a third person in the bed. Pulling his head to her, they kissed, his tongue finding the warmth of her mouth, then nuzzling down her neck to the soft area under her ear. Emily giggled at the tickle and Mac continued his quest downward, stopping to kiss the now much rounder breasts but ending at the upward thrust of her stomach.

Mac drew circles on her belly and said quietly, "I know you're in there and I'm out here. We both want to see you but only when you're ready. I don't think I'm ever going to be ready, but your mamma says she'll be all right. I may not live through it. *Tha gaol agam ort*, I love you and your mamma so stay there as long as you need." Then he kissed her belly and brought himself up to her waiting lips.

Emily knew it was Mac's way of saying he was worried but was now more prepared to have her give birth. They both knew, that like their good friends, Callie and Seth, Mac was going to remain with Emily when she had this baby. Rebecca knew it, too, and was agreeable, a rare midwife indeed. Emily gave Mac one last long kiss then rolled in his arms, presenting him with her warm backside.

Mac nestled into her neck and found the womanly entrance he sought with his erection, sliding into the warmth and bringing Emily closer to his body. She moved to accommodate him and then the culmination of their lovemaking began. Mac brought his hand to the eager nub waiting for him and it wasn't long before both

Emily and Mac reached the goal of euphoric bliss with the calm rippling through them. Not as exciting as when they were first married but every bit as satisfying. Mac snuggled Emily and soon they were both breathing evenly as they slept.

CHAPTER 8

Faith was coming into the office area when she saw Jeremy trying to open the door and not drop the parcels he was carrying. Hurrying forward, she pulled the knob, catching a wrapped box at the same time.

"Thanks," said Jeremy. "I thought it was a goner. I think it's a glass ink well but I can't be sure any more. I might have gone overboard getting the office set up. Probably won't need half of this but Helen, you know, from the Mercantile, thought I would need all this and more. She's quite a saleswoman, too." He dumped the parcels wrapped in brown paper and tied with string on the empty desktop.

"If you need to, I guess, you can take them back or possibly it's something Jessie can use. Try them and let us know what you don't want."

"I'll try that. Thanks for the advice. Are you sure you've never set up an office before? You seem to have the knowledge."

"I've always been very organized, found the fastest way to do things with the least amount of waste. The nuns said it was because I was basically lazy, saying lazy people came up with the best ideas to make their own lives easier. I'm not sure but I know the nuns used many of my ideas even after I left St. Michaels."

"I never thought about it like that but you may be right. I'll take any advice you want to give me because in a few weeks, I think I'm going to get very busy." Jeremy began to place items onto the desk top.

"Do you think you're going to get more

commissions?"

"The Mayor asked me what I thought a school would cost and how long it would take to build. That's another pretty good-sized building and they want it to be able to expand, you know as the number of students increase."

"Do you know where they're going to build it?" Faith asked as she unwrapped a box of pencils. "In town, I take it."

"They set land aside for it on Main Street just the other side of the church. That way it's close to the ranches to the north and still has land around it for a playground and to graze any horses the children ride in to school. Then there's the need for a teachery, a sort of apartment for the teacher to live in. They don't want to have to board her with a local family or rent a house so they thought this would be perfect. No need for a horse or stabling either since it will be part of the school building."

Jeremy was drawing out some rough plans on one of the brown papered packages.

Faith was watching his long fingers quickly make sense of the lines and then offered a suggestion. "If you make the building a couple of steps higher, wouldn't there be enough room in the basement to have a civic center, you know for town meetings and voting and such. It could have half windows at ground level which would appear at normal level from the room side."

Jeremy, his tongue touching his lower lip, drew in the higher stairs saying, "That would cover two birds with one stone, saving money and giving the town something, it needs. There will need to be a beam and supports but otherwise a fairly open space."

"And then divide the upper room in half this way, placing two doors side by side but with enough space between them," Faith suggested taking the pencil from his hand drawing what she was thinking of for the entrance to the building at the top of the steps.

"And we can either put in the central dividing wall or leave it until it's needed," Jeremy finished for her.

"But you need to plan on that. A central chimney will work for both the rear living quarters and the stove to heat the schoolroom. I think a second should go on this side, too, so that when its divided, there will be a heat source on both sides." She added the little square to reflect the chimney.

"The basement can be heated by a larger stove sharing this chimney." And more lines were added to the brown paper.

"Oh, and there could be either a cellar door or a trap door of some sort so the fire wood or coal can be stored in the back area under the house portion of the building. The rear of the building could be set up with a garden and all the privies going on this side, closer to the front doors of both upstairs rooms. You'll need a cloak room that can be used for the students during the day and activities in the civic room in the evening with a set of stairs going down to the lower room." Again, she added the lines as she spoke.

"I think we have a good plan, Faith. I might hire you for advice when I get stuck," Jeremy said with admiration.

"I think you would have gotten there on your own. I merely became excited thinking about the building. I was trained as a teacher at St. Michaels but then went a different way once I left there. Charity needed me and she didn't have the training I did. She had kitchen experience and found work in a laundry in the last town we lived in," Faith explained.

"I need to draft this into proper building plans and then a rendering. Maybe some elevations to show the city fathers what it will look like. That will give the mayor something to show the others. I'll have to get bids for the windows and such. The mayor wants me to buy from our local merchants whenever possible, so I should be able to get prices from them easily." Jeremy stared down at the rough drawing while thinking of his material list. His excitement had grown with each mark of the pencil so now he was as anxious to see this project through as he was the bank.

"Well, I'll leave you to do that. Jessie is out selling advertising and I'm going to see what kind of typesets I have that may be used for those ads. If you need anything, simply let me know."

Once Faith left Jeremy, he felt subdued. Having had so many ideas flowing through him had been exhilarating. After getting it all down on paper so none of the features would be lost, he missed the rush of ideas and thoughts. He could probably ask Faith if he couldn't remember everything later. Possibly he should run the final draft past her before he gave it to the mayor.

Turning away from the drawing on the brown paper, he set the packages aside. Then taking out a large sheet of paper, he put down his ideas for the bank's building now that he had the parcel size. It was several hours before he realized it was getting dark.

Jeremy went to the livery to get his horse and ride home, using the moonlight on the wide road to guide his way to the ranch house. He thought he better bring clothes back to town so if he needed to stay at the hotel he would be prepared. Or if Jessie would let him use the second bedroom, Jeremy wouldn't need to worry about working into the night. He'd ask Jessie tomorrow if he could leave clothes upstairs.

He realized on the trip home he hadn't thought of Clarissa since she had left. Hadn't thought of her father or their plans for his political future, either. And he was relieved. Sweetwater was where he felt the happiest. Close to family and friends and helping the town grow to the potential his father always knew it would get. His Da would often say that the town was on the cusp of expansion even before the railroad decided to include it and ignore so many other potential towns along the tracks.

The ideas of how to help that happen was buzzing through his mind and he made sure to pay attention to where his horse was going in the pale moonlight. Still, he couldn't stop thinking about Faith and her excitement as they discussed plans for the new schoolhouse. Even if the town council didn't like the plan, Jeremy thought he could sell it to other small towns needing to grow within a budget. He would ask Faith how she thought the best way to do that would be. She seemed to have some good ideas to do with business and marketing.

In the morning, when Jeremy came into the pressroom, he was met with chaos. There were large sheets of paper wadded up and thrown on the floor everywhere. Buckets and jars, lids off, lined the counter next to the press. The smell of oil and ink and paper filled the air, as did his brother's cussing. Jessie was wearing a leather apron with ink everywhere. Jeremy looked at Faith with her hair tied back at her neck and hanging in a soft swirl. Escaping, curling tendrils clung to her damp temples.

She turned to face Jeremy straight on and Jeremy about gave his brother a facer. Right there, in plain sight, was a large ink handprint over Faith's left breast, the apron almost covering it but not quite.

Faith became flustered saying, "I better get changed. You'll get the gist of it in time Jessie. It just takes some practice."

"Oh, I'm sorry Faith but I got ink on your sleeve. I'll pay to replace it," Jessie said sincerely as he wiped the sweat out of his eyes leaving even more signs of grease.

"No, don't worry about it. I'll simply dye the whole thing. When I worked in the newspaper before, more than half my clothes were dyed black. It looked like I was in mourning all the time." She scurried down to her room.

As soon as she was gone, Jessie tried to clean his hands with a solvent from one of the jars but it wasn't really removing the ink. Jeremy watched his brother nonchalantly going about his cleansing as if he hadn't been caught out.

"What the hell do you think you're doing?" raged Jeremy, unable to hold his temper in any longer.

Jessie glanced at his brother and said, "What's it to you? I don't work for you, you know. I don't answer to you, anymore. I'm my own boss and you're merely a tenant. If you don't like the way the place looks or smells, I suggest you move on."

Using a harsh whisper in case Faith could hear them, he spat, "I meant, what the hell do you think you're doing with Faith? I thought you found the love of your life. Mary Beth, wasn't it?"

"I still love Mary Beth but she won't come around to my way of thinking. If I ignore her a little, show her I have other interests then I'm hoping she'll change her mind," explained Jessie still wiping ink marks from the counter.

"And then what will happen to Faith? Is she simply someone to amuse yourself with until this Mary Beth comes into her right senses?" asked Jeremy, inflamed that his younger brother was so callus with a girl's reputation and heart.

"Faith will still be here, right down the hall as always. What's your beef, Jeremy? I'm not doing things that much differently than you or Jamie." He stopped working to look closely at his brother. "Why are you so angry? What did I do to provoke you so early this morning?"

"You man-handle a sweet, gullible girl and then tell me it was only to show the girl you really care about there are other fish in the sea," Jeremy said, his eyes steely with anger.

"There are no other fish in the sea for me. It's Mary Beth or no one. I don't understand what you're talking about." Jessie stopped cleaning and stared at his older brother, his obviously angry older brother.

"I'm saying leave your ink-covered hands off of Faith. She's too vulnerable here and I won't stand by and have her hurt or worse. You forget, Seth stands behind all of the young women Callie brings here and he's not going to appreciate you manhandling Faith," declared Jeremy trying to get Jessie to see reason.

"Jeremy, you've got to get more sleep. You're seeing things if you think I'm interested in Faith in that way. Hell, Faith and Mary Beth were at St. Michaels together. They're like sisters. Mary Beth would kill me if I made advances toward Faith. If I made advances toward any woman. I'm not stupid. I'm simply waiting for Mary Beth to figure out what she really wants from life. I know I'm it." He wadded the last of the ink-covered rags. Tossing it into a wastebasket along with all the others.

Faith came back looking a little tidier and said brightly, "All right, Jessie, the next step is to make sure that the print set will come out crisp and clear. Are you ready?"

"As ready as I'll ever be. I don't know why I thought I could do this by merely reading a few pamphlets," he said as he stood at one end of the press with a clean sheet of paper.

Jeremy stared at the two then shook his head in amazement. They were both acting as if nothing had happened. What was wrong with the woman that she would allow a man to touch her and then act like nothing had been going on? He walked down the hall towards his office but saw the rumpled shirtwaist on the floor of Faith's room as he passed the doorway. He bent down and picked up the garment, holding it out in front of him to see the damning evidence once again.

He jumped when Faith said over his shoulder, "Jessie didn't even realize he had touched me. His gloves were so covered with grease and ink his hand slid off the press and smacked into me as I came up beside him to help. It was the back of his hand and he was wearing gloves and concentrating so hard on filling the rollers. He's unaware of the event. Believe me, I'd know if it were intentional. And he'd be wearing a bucket of ink dumped on his head so there would be no doubt as to my response. Callie and Rebecca set me straight on how to protect myself."

Jeremy felt somewhat guilty that he thought so poorly of his brother and, in a way, of Faith, too. "I'll take this to Abby so she can use it for a pattern. He still owes you a blouse." Taking the ruined material with him, he left quickly through the rear door.

At the dress shop's alley entrance, Jeremy knocked and then saw Matthew wave him in. His friend was sitting back in a rocking chair with two babies, one on each shoulder, dozing. "I've got Grace and Hannah both sleeping so I couldn't get up. Do you need to speak with me? I haven't got all the figures for the building together, yet."

"No, I have an order for Abby if she has time," Jeremy said, lifting the wadded-up blouse in his hand.

Matthew pointed through the curtained doorway. "She's in there and I can hear the machine whirling so go in and ask. I stop at the sewing portion of the business."

Jeremy ducked through the curtain and called out quietly to Abby so he didn't startle her.

"Why, Jeremy, this is a surprise. What can I do for you? Some new shirts or perhaps a waistcoat?" She smiled up at her old friend in welcome.

"I need to replace this." He held out the blouse while Abby took it from him and studied the handprint then studied Jeremy.

"I didn't do that, no one did that. I mean, Jessie did it but he didn't know he did it. Is there a way you can make another like it, I mean, less the handprint?" Jeremy asked flustered at the curious gaze Abby was giving him.

"Certainly, and Jeremy, that's a handprint probably

wearing a wide glove. Don't be too hard on Jessie, he didn't feel anything more than possibly bumping into an immovable object," she explained, reading her old heartthrob too well.

Jeremy relented. "I can't believe he's that stupid but, I guess, if everyone involved says he didn't know he did it then I have to give him the benefit of the doubt, too."

"And I know you. If this had been your handiwork, there wouldn't be a spot of white left on the front of this blouse and several other pieces of clothing as well," Abby teased now Jeremy had calmed down.

"Maybe I should check that out. I didn't do a complete investigation," he said teasing in return now that his better nature was in charge.

"Is this Faith's blouse? That's her name, right? I haven't met her, yet, although she's only down a couple of buildings. I never get much time to socialize anymore. I hardly get time to socialize with Matthew." She laughed at her own daring to say such a thing. "I'll have this done in a day or so. Mason's wife, Victoria, is still working with me caring for the children and taking some of the fine stitching home. That way she doesn't feel she isn't taking proper care of Mason."

"Good, send the bill to Jessie, but I'll pay for another one in a different color, something soft and maybe shiny or silky. I'll leave that up to you. And can you sew a skirt, too?" he asked, his brows raised in question.

"I can sew, anything, but how tall is she?" Abby asked thinking of the practicalities of sewing for someone she had never met.

"She comes up to here on me." He placed his hand level with his chin.

"That helps but I may be able to sneak down and

look her over. I take it these are to be a surprise?"

"Yeah, just in case I ruin anything and have to replace it." He laughed at Abby's knowing expression. "No, I owe her for helping me think some things through. I think I can get her to accept the clothes but not cash. She is very conscious of what it takes to start up a new company. She's been a great help to Jessie, as well."

"You be careful around those St. Michaels' girls. Matthew and Seth are like big brothers of the scariest kind when it comes to protecting them. Callie is no slouch, either, so that's fair warning," she cautioned her old friend.

"I think I have the best of intentions," he said and tipped his hat as he went back out the curtain. He waved farewell to Matthew who was still holding a babe in each arm and still sitting in the rocking chair.

Entering by the back door, Jeremy went directly to his office to work but could hear the rhythmic sound of the press and the swish of the paper as it was taken from the machine. Every once in a while, he heard Faith's soft voice encouraging Jessie and Jeremy would grit his teeth and try not to picture them standing close together or Jessie having his arms both sides of Faith as she lifted the finished sheets off the press.

Jeremy knew these scenarios probably weren't happening but they were a way of torturing himself for not letting Faith know he was attracted to her. The way he was acting, half the town would know before he let on to her he was interested in her.

Finally, the press stopped and there was no talking going on, either. What were they doing? What could they be doing? Well, if it were him with Faith, he knew what they would be doing. Rising from his chair quickly, he went to the front of the building to find the pressroom empty except for the damp papers hanging to dry from wires strung across the room. Both Faith and Jessie were gone. Jeremy went back to his office and slumped onto his chair. He was going to need to do something about this distraction or he wouldn't get the bank building done on time.

Jeremy was still sitting there half an hour later when he heard the front door open and someone call out. The train depot's ticket clerk and telegraph operator stood in the open doorway, "I have a delivery for you, Jeremy. It looks like some kind of dresser and a table with funny legs and things."

"It must be my drafting table and the other holds blue prints once they're complete. I'll come and help carry them in, Tom. I've missed using them but this should get me back on track." He followed the deliveryman out to get the office pieces.

Faith returned after passing out the dried newspapers and stuck her head into Jeremy's office. She found him bent over a table with a tilted top and attached shelves on both sides holding lit lamps. Jeremy was so focused he missed the slight noise her stopping made.

A little later, Jeremy lifted his head and was surprised to find it dark outside his window. He looked down at the paper on the flat surface and smiled, pleased with the amount of work done on the interior of the bank building.

Faith came in with a plate of food placing it on the desktop along with a cup of hot coffee. "I thought you were in need of a meal. I hope you like coq au vin, I learned the recipe from Callie."

"Well, it smells delicious so if it tastes half as good,

I'm a lucky man." Unwrapping the flatware from the napkin, he tucked into the food with a hearty appetite. Faith looked on with a smile and then she saw the drawings. Thinking it was the school, she walked over and stood in front of the interesting maneuverable tabletop that could be slanted to any angle.

"This must be the bank. I like the layout inside. Looks safe and secure, interior doors that lock." She looked closer at a drawing in the corner. "Is this a door you would like to use?"

"I'll have those made. Extra thick, I think, and the bars set in between boards so there are no visible screws to remove to get inside. It will take a while to cut through them and I am having special hardware and locks made. Probably slide bolts, too, one top and bottom," he explained between bites of the delicious meal.

"That should cover the doors but what about the windows?"

"I have them higher off the ground from the outside and then there will be fancy iron work on the inside but fastened in several places on all sides of the window. I've seen some beautiful wrought iron work in New Orleans and I'm looking for something like that. Decorative, yet secure."

"I look forward to seeing more as it progresses." Faith stood upright and took the dirty dishes.

"I'll clean those up, Faith. In the Macgregor household, the cook never had to do the washing up. And besides, I'm going to have to spend the night. There's no moonlight showing so it would be rough getting back to the ranch," he told her stretching his shoulders after being hunched over the drafting table for so many hours.

"Funny, Jessie never explained the rule about the

cook not having to clean up. I'll have to discuss that with him." Then laughed because she never would expect Jessie to do the washing up. After all, he was letting her live there for free and she felt that cooking and cleaning up afterwards was fair. "I'll see you tomorrow then. Good night, Jeremy."

"Good night, Faith." He listened as her skirt swished down the hall the few steps from him and then the click of her door latch. Jeremy sat there a moment longer then shook his head to clear it turning down the wicks before going upstairs.

He had placed the now clean plate he had eaten from on the draining board when Jessie came into the apartment, looking disheveled and despondent.

"No luck convincing your lady to marry you?" asked Jeremy half-seriously.

"No luck convincing her of anything, I'm afraid. She's so worried about letting the rest of St. Michaels down or some such malarkey. I already told her she could continue being a midwife or whatever but she says she can't ignore her vow or something. I don't know what I can do to convince her we belong together and everything else will work out. Maybe I should ask Jamie for advice," Jessie said as he plopped onto the sofa.

"I wouldn't do that if I were you. When I was first at home with Clarissa, I went in to ask Jamie something while he was with the horses and he about bit my head off. Saying things like 'why did we all think he knew women and who did we think he was, Casanova, and if we couldn't handle our own women why did we think he could'. Hell, I just wanted his opinion on which horse I should use to get back and forth to town. I still don't know what I said that set him on such a tirade but he really doesn't want to talk about women."

"I don't know why he wouldn't want to share a few of his secrets. I mean, take it from someone who lived in that house with those newlyweds for months - it wasn't easy to sleep at night. And whatever Jamie does to Mavis she likes it, she likes it a lot. Mac, being Mac, goes about things quieter. I think everything gets done properly but both Mac and Emily are more reserved in their encounters," Jessie told him remembering how embarrassing living at the ranch was back then.

"Don't tell me anymore. I still sleep there remember? I don't want to put pictures to sounds. It's like thinking about our parents having sex. You know they did but you want to pretend you were found under a cabbage leaf," Jeremy said with some discomfort.

"Let's just forget about it. I don't think I can change Mary Beth's mind by compromising her. That would probably put the final nail in the coffin. She has pretty strong convictions. Raised Catholic, you know," Jessie needlessly explained.

With no answer to that, Jeremy told him, "I'm staying the night in case you haven't figured it out yet. No moon." Then picking up the suit jacket he had taken off so he could wash the dishes, went back to the second bedroom for the night.

CHAPTER 9

The next day began innocently enough. The brothers awakened to the smell of coffee brewing and ham and eggs frying. Faith told them as they each entered the kitchen to help themselves. She was going to finish setting some type for the second edition of the Sweetwater Chronicle and hurried down the stairs.

Jeremy went to his office upon entering the lower floor and Jessie continued on to the pressroom. Everyone was busy with their own work when Faith put her head through the doorway of Jeremy's office saying, "I'm going to pick up some porkchops from the butcher. Are you planning on staying for dinner?"

"Thanks for the offer but no. I need to pick up some clean clothes and talk with Mac so I'll be leaving in a little while," replied Jeremy. He finished calculating the number of board feet he would need for the bank and the estimated number of bricks. These would need to be ordered soon if he wanted them all out of the same drying lot and delivered by train car.

Picking up his suit jacket from the back of his desk chair, he shrugged into it. He wanted to talk with Mac about the expense of the school and to see what he thought the ranchers could contribute in this down market for beef if the city council approved the plans.

As Jeremy was walking to the livery to get his horse, the mayor hurried over to him from the sheriff's office. "Do you have a minute, Jeremy? I'd like to run something past you."

Several hours later, Jeremy emerged from having a

nice meal with the mayor at the hotel's restaurant and excited about the news he had received. He knew he would need to stay at Jessie's again that night since it was too late and too dark to try to make it back to the ranch. Taking the stairs to the apartment two at a time, he spotted Jessie's jacket on the back of a chair as he entered. Jeremy turned the wick all the way down on the dimmed lamp and was on his way to his room in the dark when he saw the light coming from under the bathing room door.

Turning the knob on the door, he pushed it open, anxious to tell his brother the good news. "Jessie, I…" And came to a dead stop. Faith, evidently just getting out of the tub with sudsy water sliding over her hips and down her slim legs, splashed quickly back into the copper tub. The small towel once wrapped around her breasts floating on the water in front of her.

Jeremy turned away saying, "God, I'm sorry, Faith. I thought Jeremy was in here. His coat is right outside the door." When Faith didn't respond, Jeremy snuck a peek at the glistening wet back and then looked away again, ashamed of his lack of control.

"I, ah, I have a clean towel in my room. Let me get that for you and then I'll leave you to it." Jeremy shut the door, thinking what a dumb thing to say. Did he think Faith would invite him in to help her dry herself or something? Striding quickly to his room, he pulled the towel off the shelf and returned with it.

This time he knocked. "I'm opening the door but not looking. I'll just toss the towel in." And he did just that. Jeremy returned to his room and closed the door nosily so Faith would know where he was and lit the lamp on the dresser. He sat in the chair, trying not to envision

Faith getting out of the tub, water streaming down and over her womanly curves. Trying not to think how the towel would be used to stroke her entire body until it was pink. Trying not to remember how the warm moist air of the bath smelled like flowers and lemon and Faith. He was trying but not succeeding.

Finally, after thinking he heard the backdoor latch close, Jeremy took a tentative peek out to the living area and saw the glow of a lamp turned low and went out in his socking feet. As he passed the now open door to the bathing room, Jeremy looked in noting the wet towel wrung out and hanging over the side of the tub. The metal tray under the tub catching the few drops of water as it dried. Jeremy's towel was hanging over the bar and he reached out pulling it to his face. It was still warm, damp from her skin, smelling of that damn flowers and lemon and Faith. A scent he was sure would be haunting him all night.

Hanging the towel back up, he resisted the urge to take it to his room and sleep with it. His throbbing erection was going to be enough torment and he had no way of assuaging it's need. Well, there was one but he had giving that up as a teenager and wasn't about to resort to it again. He could get over this with a little self-control - and by not remembering what had caused it. He didn't fool himself into thinking it would be easy.

The next morning Jeremy woke to noises in the kitchen again. He wanted to talk with Faith or at least see if she would talk with him. She hadn't said a word last night so he wasn't sure of his welcome. Jeremy entered the kitchen and pulled the chair out, making sure the legs dragged a little to let Faith know she wasn't alone.

"I've made some hash and I can add a couple of eggs

if you want," she offered not turning from the stove.

Jeremy wasn't sure if she knew it was him or Jessie so answered, "That sounds great. I'll take some of both."

Faith, never missing a beat, continued, "Jessie got called downstairs by a young man I don't know. I thought he would be right back up."

Just then Jessie burst through the door still in his shirtsleeves, a little winded but very excited. "Andy was sent over to get me. Rebecca wanted to know if I would drive them out to the ranch. Mavis is having her baby. I'm going to grab some clothes and I'll be back after the baby's born." Then turning to Faith asked, "Can you take care of everything here?"

"Yes, of course. Go on and be there when your first niece or nephew gets born," urged Faith. "It will be Mary Beth's first birth, too, so she'll need some moral support."

Jessie turned to Jeremy and asked, "Will you be coming out, too?"

"Of course, someone is going to have to talk Jamie into rational thought. Mac will just disappear and you'll be more worried about Mary Beth. I've got a couple of things to do but I'll catch up since I'll be riding."

Jessie declined breakfast grabbing the rest of his clothes and left.

Faith put a full plate in front of Jeremy who tucked into it. "You look a little tired. Neither you nor Jessie are very early risers. It must run in the family."

Since she was the cause of his loss of sleep, Jeremy merely grunted through his food. Sounding a great deal like Mac even to his own ears, he continued to clear his plate. Standing, he wiped his mouth on the napkin and thanked Faith for the breakfast, ignoring the Macgregor rule about not making the cook clean-up and hooked his suit jacket from the back of the chair.

"Jeremy, I'm taking some things for Jessie over to the Chinese laundry. Did you have anything you wanted to go with them?"

"I'll get them for you." He got the sack of clothes he was going to take home to the ranch and set them on the kitchen floor. "Thanks again, I owe you." He said a quick goodbye to Faith as she washed the dishes while he went down the stairs.

The Macgregor ranch was unusually quiet as Jeremy pulled his horse to a stop outside the front porch. There was normally a greeting party by now but Jeremy was glad to see the rented buggy pulled up beside the house. He waved a ranch hand over to take care of both horses while Jeremy went up the porch steps and pulled off his boots, leaving them on the mat beside the door.

There was an inaudible conversation going on in the kitchen and Jeremy wasn't surprised to see all of his brothers sitting around the table, cups of coffee in front of them.

"What did I miss? I take it there's no baby, yet?" asked Jeremy trying to gauge the mood of each of his kin.

Mac, usually the more constrained of his brothers, said, "No. Mavis started having pains last night but didn't want to bother anyone so didn't say anything till, umm, her water broke this morning. Said she wanted everyone to get a good night's sleep because it was going to be a long day."

"She's always planning everything out. She should have told me so we could decide together when to send for Rebecca and Mary Beth." Jamie shook his head as if lost to a woman's thinking. "And she's the one going to have a long day of it."

Jeremy raised his eyebrows in surprise. "You'd think she'd be more worried than that. I mean having your first baby can't be easy."

Mac looked up from his coffee cup in surprise and then Jamie told him, "Mavis is a widow. She lost her husband and young son to diphtheria a few years back. I think that's why she felt she could determine when to call in the midwives. I swear she'd have had it alone if she had to. She told me 'to stay out of the way', is how she put it. Doesn't want me to worry. Hell, what else am I going to do down here besides worry?"

Jeremy watched his next older brother then said earnestly, "I've heard nothing but good things about this Rebecca. And Mary Beth seems bright, too. I don't suppose Emily has any experience?" But as Mac shook his head, Jeremy continued, "Mavis is in the best of hands."

Up until now Jessie had remained silent but wanted to both support Mary Beth's abilities and reassure Jamie. "Mary Beth is ready for this. Rebecca has had years of experience and Mary Beth has been trained and has studied additional research into everything. They know more than a doctor does about birthing and taking care of newborn babies. If there's a problem, I know those women can handle it."

Just then Mary Beth came into the room and when all four pair of eyes swiveled to her, she said quietly, "Everything is progressing as it should be. I'm going to get some water for tea. Mavis can drink clear fluids and the sugar will sustain her energy. The other water I'm heating will be used to bathe the baby so it needs time to cool down after it comes to a boil. I will continue to keep you posted since the other ladies are, um-m. It's a little difficult for them to navigate stairs easily."

That's when it dawned on the Macgregor men that Mary Beth was the only female in the house not possibly giving birth within the next twelve hours and an unusual quiet came over those at the table.

True to her word, Mary Beth came down every half hour with a report, even if it was to say 'no change' or 'progressing satisfactorily'. The men all looked at her, hungry for information, although they all simply wanted to hear that a healthy baby was born and the mother was doing fine. It started to look as if that wasn't going to happen that day.

Mac had started a stew earlier in the day and was mixing up biscuits when Mary Beth came down in a rush, "She's here, I mean the baby. It's a girl and she's beautiful. Mavis is fine and strong and did everything right on the spot." Then she turned to Jamie who was getting up and heading toward the stairs saying, "They'll both need to be cleaned up but then she's waiting for you."

Jamie continued on his way to his new family and the smile of relief on his face was a pleasant change from the tight mouth and worried expression that seemed to have been there all day. After Jamie and Mary Beth left, Mac sat heavily in a chair and said softly to his two remaining brothers. "I won't be able to do this again, not be this worried over Emily."

Jessie, the youngest and most optimistic since most of his life's trials have been small so far, said, "She'll be fine, too. Now Mary Beth has experienced a real birth, she'll be able to handle another. And if Rebecca isn't there, Mavis will be. She's gone through two births now and Doctor Winters can be called in if that makes you feel better."

Mac continued to stare at the table envisioning all the problems that can occur during a birth, things he had seen go badly with a calf or foal. He should have protected Emily from that, for a while at least. Why had he been in such a hurry to start a family? After all, he had Emily and that's all that should have mattered. As if his fear had conjured her up, Emily came into the room, her bulky stomach entering the doorway before the rest of her.

"Oh, Mac, it was so beautiful. Well, not all the messy part but having that infant come out and become a little person…it is truly a miracle. It's a little girl, did you know? They're going to name her, Aileen, after your mother. She finally got her girl in the family." And then Emily wiped a tear out of her eye but more formed quickly behind it.

Mac stood and went to his wife saying, "*Mo cridhe*." Lifting her in his arms, he took her into his office where they could be private.

After dinner, which Jamie ate upstairs with his wife and daughter, Mary Beth said that she would stay and help with the baby since Emily needed her rest, too. Jessie said he'd stay but then Mary Beth reminded him he needed to drive Rebecca back to town and her waiting husband.

"I can drive Rebecca home and drop off the buggy to the livery," volunteered Jeremy knowing Jessie was trying to get some time alone with Mary Beth, well as alone as anyone can be in this house.

Rebecca, happily fed and on her second cup of

sugared tea, said, "That will be fine. I don't care how I get home, but I don't want Daniel to worry that I'm working too hard. He sleeps better with me beside him."

Jeremy went down to the stable and with a ranch hand's help soon had the buggy and his horse ready to take the trip back to town. He drove the rig over to the front porch of the big stone house and Jessie helped Rebecca down the steps with her medical bag and into the waiting buggy. They all said farewells. Jeremy and Rebecca had a nice drive home with Rebecca asking a lot of questions and Jeremy giving a lot of answers.

They spoke mostly of his architectural work and the newspaper and how well Faith was doing. And how Faith had helped him with the plans to the new school he had won the commission to build. That had been the big news he wanted to tell Jessie the other night. Was it only last night? Anyway, he had imparted the news earlier to his brothers trying to get them to think of something besides what might be happening upstairs.

It worked for a while but then thinking of the school led to thinking of children and that brought about the reality children had to be born and they all ended up morosely thinking of the danger of childbirth. This time he and Rebecca could remain on a lighter note. Rebecca was very enthusiastic over having a school built in town and one so close to her home and work.

Jeremy dropped off Rebecca to a very relieved Reverend Daniel and then took the buggy and his horse to the livery. He tipped Andy and headed home, well, Jessie's home. Maybe it felt like home because Faith was there. He had spent a good deal of the day thinking of Faith and how he would feel if she were the one giving birth. Would he have been as quiet and calm as Jamie had been? Probably not, he was more apt to be right outside the door or, more than likely, in the room.

Hell, Matthew delivered his own daughter and he had no training at all. If Matthew could do it then Jeremy certainly should be able to stay at his wife's side. Mac was planning to and Seth had helped deliver his son and let everyone know how wonderful it was.

How had he come to be thinking these thoughts anyway? He didn't even plan on getting a wife anytime soon. He had just gotten rid of one woman wanting to tell him what to do. He certainly didn't want to shed his freedom so soon for another.

Opening the door to his bedroom, Jeremy found a pile of freshly laundered clothes including the towel Faith had used last night. Damn, he had wanted to keep that towel as it was, smelling sweetly of Faith. He would need to steal one of her towels later. Replace it with another and maybe she wouldn't notice. He picked up the cloth and covered his face, inhaling deeply. He put it back on the pile disappointedly. It held not a whiff of Faith anymore.

In the morning, Faith was in the kitchen portion of the apartment when Jeremy came in and said, "Good morning, Faith. It's just me for breakfast. Jessie stayed out at the ranch."

Immediately there was a change in the atmosphere. Jeremy looked worriedly at Faith's back as she began to move slowly. She didn't respond as she usually did to his good morning.

"Is there something the matter, Faith? He'll be home soon, I'm sure. He wanted to stay with Mary Beth and she had to stay to care for Mavis and her new daughter. The first daughter in our family for three generations. It takes a lot of pressure off the rest of us, that's for sure." He laughed at the family joke.

"That's nice. I'm just heating the hash from yesterday. Nothing special," she said still not glancing toward him.

Thinking that after a day to consider it, Faith wanted to talk about his bursting in on her in the bath said, "I'm sorry about the other night. I'm so used to an all-male household I didn't think to knock and wait for a response. I promise it won't happen again. I learned my lesson, believe me."

"Umm, it's not that, not really. It's not anything you did," she admitted quietly. "I always get nervous around men, I guess."

"But not Jessie? You don't get nervous around him?"

"Jessie is different. He's practically engaged to Mary Beth and I don't get the same feelings from Jessie as I do, ah, other men," she confessed.

"You don't trust me, you mean. You think I'd harm you?" He was indignant and angry at her unspoken accusation.

"I didn't say that. It's just me. I don't feel comfortable around single men even if they are engaged. I didn't think I still felt that way. It seems so long ago now that I should be able to be alone in a room with a man. Perhaps it's where you sleep, I don't know…" The last words were almost a whisper.

Jeremy had come closer to hear Faith's words but then she realized he was right behind her. Turning quickly, she gave Jeremy a shove so she could get past him after finding him between her and the door. Putting out his hands to prevent himself from falling, the contact between them seemed to cause Faith more agitation. Tears rolled down her face and a sob escaped as she searched frantically around for a weapon.

Jeremy read the wild expression on her face, then said calmly, "Look, I'm sitting down. My hands are on the table. If you need to go out that door, I'm not going to stop you but I think you owe me some explanation for this reaction. I'm not a threat to you. I promise you that whether Jessie's here or not."

The panting of fight or flight was beginning to ease but Faith said nothing, her wide-eyed gaze moving from Jeremy to the door as if measuring the steps.

"One of us has to move that pan from the stove or we'll have a fire in a minute," Jeremy stated calmly.

The reminder of a daily chore had Faith thinking rationally. With the help of her apron wrapped around the hot handle, she moved the food off the heat to a safe resting place on the warming shelf. She turned back to Jeremy realizing she trusted him enough not to attack her while she was dealing with the hot pan and sat at the table across from him. The door was right behind her and she thought she could get out it quickly if she needed.

"I'm sorry," she started out saying.

"You don't need to apologize. I'm only trying to figure out what happened to make you so frightened of me. You've never shown fear of me before so - what did I do?" Jeremy asked trying to figure out what he needed to change so they could return to the easy comradery they shared before.

"It's not you, really, but suddenly I was reminded of something from before, something that happened before I came to Sweetwater. I thought I had forgotten it, that I was over it but then a strange feeling came over me. I got mixed up and I frightened myself. I'll be all right now, I promise." She forced a smile on her face as their gazes met across the table.

"Well, it appears you were afraid of me. I'm not sure but that you would have jumped from a window to get away from me and I wasn't moving towards you. You need to do something to help you over these fears." Jeremy remembered how Jessie had told him she was skittish around men. "Have you had these fears before?"

"Only at night, when I'm alone in my room but then I remember Jessie's up here. I could scream if I needed to and he would hear me and come down," she admitted now that most of the panic was out of her system.

"Is Jessie the only one you'd trust? Do you think I wouldn't come down and help, too?" questioned Jeremy.

"It isn't like that. I have one plan, one idea to save myself, and I've been able to stay here because of that. Finding out Jessie wasn't going to be here threw me off for a moment. I'll be fine, maybe go to Mary Beth's… Oh, wait, she's with Jessie…." Her voice petered out.

"When did these panics begin? Maybe we can find the cause and work out a better solution than living in a room beneath Jessie's," Jeremy said trying to be of help.

"I know what caused my fear," she told him defensively. "I'm not insane."

Jeremy felt he was walking on eggshells here, so said, "I never meant to say that you were. I know that if you talk out a fear, it becomes weaker until you can over-come it by yourself." He tried to connect with her in some way. "When I was a child and woke up after a bad dream, my mother would put me back in bed and we would work out what I could have done to protect myself if I hadn't woken up. You know, slay the dragon with a magic sword I found in a rock or get my Da with his gun to shoot the lion coming to eat me. It made it easier to go back to sleep. I almost looked forward to that bad dream returning since I had a plan to put an end to whatever had frightened me."

"Both Callie and Rebecca said the more I talked about it the less power it would possess. Maybe they're right and I was covering it up but it was there all along, waiting to strike at me again. I need to be free of it, not only for myself."

"I'm a good listener. I'll be your sounding board if you want."

Twisting her fingers together, Faith made a bold decision to tell a man her worst nightmare come to life. "I was sleeping in my room with Charity. Do you remember, Charity?" At his nod, she continued, "And a man, a very vile, mean, drunk man kicked in the door and attacked me."

This wasn't what Jeremy had expected at all. He took his hands and put them under the table because he felt himself want to ball them into fists, to pound the bastard who had hurt Faith and made her so frightened.

She didn't notice the movement and continued, "I tried to fight but I couldn't and Charity tried to pull him off me but she's smaller than I am and we had no weapons. She hit him with a shoe but he slammed her into the wall so hard I was afraid he'd killed her. I yelled for her to stay where she was and the man finally got up and left."

Jeremy, sensing the story wasn't complete asked, "And was that the worst of it? He didn't return or anything?"

"I don't know if it's the worst of it but I may be with

child." She glared into his eyes daring him to say anything about that.

Concealing his real emotions, Jeremy said, "I'm glad you trusted me with this information. I'm glad you felt strong enough to say the words out loud. I'm sorry something like that happened to you and I have no other words to make it better." Jeremy laid his hands back on the table, opened palms, wanting Faith to place her hands into them.

She did. He squeezed her hands lightly and she smiled squeezing his in return.

"I do feel better. It must be true the more times I relive that night the lighter my soul feels. The nuns told us there was a reason for all things and I will have to wait to find out the reason for this, too."

"I wish I could help but other than being a good listener I don't have much. When the child's born, I may be able to help then. After all, I just went through it with Mavis." He smiled trying to lighten what must be the hardest thing a woman could face.

"I have to wait, Rebecca says, before she can be sure. I have been thinking about one thing, over and over. When a woman gives birth it's usually a culmination of a happy event, of making love with her lover or husband. I don't want to give birth remembering how that infant began its life. I want to remember a loving union, if not that then a safe, quiet union I can think of as this child's beginning. Do you think that's sinful?"

"I can't see that it's sinful to want a child's creation to be one of peace and joy. I just don't see how that can be accomplished now," Jeremy admitted.

"I've been feeling if I can make love to someone I like and trust then I can remember that time in my life when I give birth. If I did it before Rebecca pronounced me with child, I could pretend, in a way, the infant was from the second union." Faith glanced up embarrassed, realizing how personal her confession had become. "I'm sorry, that's not part of my fear. I'm rambling now." She went to stand.

Jeremy held on to the hands she had placed in his when they first began this conversation. "Wait, I don't think what you want is wrong or sinful. I can see by bringing in another memory it can lessen the more brutal one you have now. I can see myself helping you if you allow me to stay with you until at least the baby is born. Then we can decide what to do next."

Faith's face first lit up but then shook her head. "I appreciate the offer, I think, but you don't have to feel sorry for me. I mean, it's my problem and I have to find a way through it."

"What if I'm the way through it? What if fate or destiny or whatever placed me here at this time in your life to help you?"

"What will your fiancée think or say when you tell her what we plan on doing? I can't be part of anything like that." Faith pulled her hands away from Jeremy.

He grasped her hands again, saying, "I've never been engaged and Clarissa went back home before I moved into the office. We decided we didn't suit one another. She wasn't what I thought and I evidently wasn't what she thought. She wasn't broken-hearted by any means. Neither of us were," he confided.

"I will have to think about the other, then. Pray on it. I wish there was a priest nearby. I need someone to unburden my soul to, someone who has God's ear." Standing, she left him to return to her room.

Jeremy thought back on what they had discussed. What was he thinking to offer to bed this young woman after she had unburdened herself to him about the most traumatic occurrence in her life? How could he convince her he had feelings for her before this? He should have told her the truth about his non-existent betrothal sooner. Once he felt she had accepted him in the office, in Jessie's home. Now he seemed as if he had taken advantage of her uncertainty, her need to feel close to someone, so that she could accept what was going to happen later, when the baby was born.

And there was the infant to consider. Did Faith expect to keep the child or place it with the nuns in New York, as she had been raised? He knew his preference but he really wasn't part of this equation. He didn't have a voice in her decision.

What he did feel and what he did know was that he could care for the child as his own. As Matthew did with Grace. Jeremy would soon forget the child's conception, especially if Faith could and he felt Faith would soon accept the child as a blessing from God, not a vile act of a worthless male.

Now how did he go about convincing Faith she could trust him to be there for her, with any decision she had to make?

CHAPTER 10

Jessie was helping Mary Beth wring out wet clothes through the manual wringer placed over the tub. "I thought after you had helped with a birth you would feel more confident, more like you were able to handle both. I know being a midwife is important to you but you can be married and still help women."

"I don't want to have to choose between my husband and my patient. I'm here because Rebecca is expecting, too, and if I were in the same condition, I don't know how these women like Mavis would go on." She repeated the same argument Jessie had heard multiple times.

"You wouldn't have to get with child right away, there are ways to prevent that from happening." Jessie knew immediately he had said the wrong thing and tried to undo the damage. "I mean, if one wanted to that is. I mean, we could just wait and see what happens."

Mary Beth in all her indignant glory said, "Jessie, that would be a sin, a sin for trying to alter God's plan. And it's a sin for a wife to deny her husband her bed so I don't see a way around sinning if we married."

"I wouldn't demand my, ah, husbandly rights all that often. I can control myself," Jessie tried to explain.

"That is a sin, also. Husbands and wives have a duty that must be met. We cannot marry while planning on committing a sin," Mary Beth said shaking her head while taking the clothes to the line to hang.

Jessie took the basket from her and followed. "I don't get you Catholics. On one hand having children seems to be the whole point of life and then on the other the nuns and priests deny themselves the same activities and say that's for a higher order. Which is it?"

Mary Beth turned on him, red from the neck to the top of her pretty brunette hairline. "Jessie, you don't know anything about my faith so I would suggest you leave. I am busy doing a job I intend to keep doing and you need to find someone else to tell these sinful ideas to." Then straightening, she clipped nightgowns and sheets to the line.

A day later Jessie returned to town saying Mary Beth had sent him home after telling him she had a job to do. He said he was bored not having the paper to run but Jeremy noticed a difference in his attitude. Now Jessie talked and thought only about the paper.

Jeremy had been staying the nights in the second bedroom of Jessie's apartment when he was awoken by yelling outside their door. One of the men hired in to work on the bank was pounding on the door and it was barely daybreak.

"Hans, what is it? I can't understand a word you're saying," Jeremy said standing back to let the man enter. Hans was half dressed, shirt unbuttoned and trousers pulled on with only one suspender in place, his balding head bare.

"Sorry, boss, I just got so excited I did not know I was not speakin' English. Tiz' just dat we just scared off some guys tearing down dah bank," Hans explained between deep breaths.

"You're still not making sense. What do you mean, tearing down the bank? The two walls we got secured yesterday, you mean?" asked Jeremy still trying to make heads or tails from his foreman.

"Yah, dey had tied some ropes around dah braces

and den rode away, dropping dah ropes but too late. Dah walls went over and splintered to pieces. I dink maybe dey do more. I came here to you," the man said trying to calm himself enough to relay the story.

"I'll be right with you. Get the other men to search for any other ropes or booby traps. It seems that not everyone is happy about having a new bank in town." Jeremy headed to his room to get dressed while Hans went back to the tent city to get the rest of his men moving.

Surveying the wreckage in the breaking daylight, Jeremy shook his head. Not only had the vandals torn down the only two standing walls but they broke some of the tools. It would take a day to fix or replace the tools and then a couple of days to repair the broken studs and raise the walls again. A loss of at least three days.

Jeremy swore, "Damn it to hell, why would anyone do this? It's just plain vandalism from what I can see. It's going to slow us up a bit but nothing we can't fix given a little time." He confided in Mason, the tall blond sheriff about his same age who was a close friend with his older brother, Jamie.

"Well, I heard the commotion so I headed over but the riders were already gone. I asked Andy over to the livery if there were any strangers getting their horses early this morning or if he's seen anyone new around but with all the construction going on there are a lot of men coming in to fill your jobs," Mason explained the lack of potential culprits apprehended.

"I doubt it was any of my men or even potential employees. There's a bonus pay for finishing each portion on time. This certainly wouldn't add to the job availability. I mean, the crews get larger as the building progresses. There's a family of Italian's coming in to do the marble work once we're ready. No one else knows how to work with the stuff."

"Do you think it's motivated by the immigrants working on the site? You know, like the problems with the Chinese working on the railroad?" asked Mason concerned for the peace of his town.

"I don't see how. I'm the only one who knows they're coming. They'll probably set up in the tent city behind the bank construction site. They're not really planning on staying unless I get a commission to do more marble but I don't see that happening here." Jeremy rubbed the back of his neck trying to ease the headache he was getting.

"Well, I'll check the groups camping by the river and see if anyone got disturbed by riders early this morning. Otherwise, you might need to put a guard out each night to watch over the project," advised Mason.

"I'm hoping this is a onetime thing. Maybe they have it out of their system and they'll be satisfied with this mess and go back home or whatever." Jeremy was still confused by the senseless destruction.

Not satisfied with the answers he was coming up with, Jeremy questioned Hans about any of the men who may have been turned down for work on the site.

"No, I got no problem wid any of dah men. Some are waiting at dah river for dah next crew to start but no one looked suspicious to me. I not fire anyone. Everyone so far looks like a good worker," Hans told him.

"Then I can't find a reason someone, well sounds like more than one, would want to keep this job site from moving forward. It just seems strange," Jeremy said as he walked back towards his office.

More strange things happened. The lumber Jeremy ordered to finish the bank building and start on the school was never loaded on the train car or the car itself was sent to another town on a different train. After hours of sending and receiving telegrams, the missing car was found in the Kansas City rail yard, the lumber still neatly stacked inside.

Arrangements had to be made to send it on to Sweetwater but due to overloaded trains already, the car in question would not be in town for another week. Jeremy, his frustration over the entire mix-up making him feel like he had steam coming from his ears, went back to his office. He placed his head under the pump and ran a few gallons of cold water over it.

Jessie saw him come in and laughed. "The building business more than you can manage? Want to let Faith handle it? She seems to be able to smooth out the wrinkles for me."

"Yes, she does, doesn't she? No, I better learn to do these things on my own. Not every job runs smoothly and this is merely an example of what I should expect, I guess," Jeremy said morosely. He had not been able to get near Faith since their private talk upstairs. She conveniently found other places to be whenever he came in to the office.

"I'm writing a little article on it. I have to mention something or people will think I don't know what's going on. Do you have any quotes for me?" Jessie asked, notebook in hand.

"None that are printable. Just put it down to a couple of boys with too much spirit, or spirits in them, depending on their age. I don't think there was any real menace in them but it did set the job back a few days,"

Jeremy explained without telling his brother about the missing lumber.

Jeremy put on a nightguard to make sure no one got near enough to the building site to cause any problems. After a week of quiet nights, Jeremy told Hans just to make sure all tools were put into a tent that was close to the men's sleeping quarters. He didn't think the vandals were going to return and had probably moved on with their nighttime antics.

The Italians arrived and were helping with the bricks and mortar part of the building. The two brothers and their sons, a five-man team, were going to be responsible for most of the interior finish of the marble walls and floors, a large undertaking and a type of finish unknown in the rural west. Dom, and his two adult sons and, Nick, along with his grown son, were experienced in all sorts of marble work as well as specialty plaster molds. Jeremy had taken a chance these men would be able to do the finish work since there was no one else anywhere near Sweetwater to do the work as he had designed it.

The Italians, although speaking very little English, were well liked among the other workers. They were always willing to share a meal or wine with anyone wanting or needing either. Dom had a hand-held Contadina that he played after dinner most evenings. The young men of the family would break into song, many sounding possibly rowdy and randy, not that anyone else understood but every man within earshot would try to mimic. Everyone would applaud when a song ended, slapping the young men on the back and laughing.

As soon as the nightguard was removed there were more problems at the job site, which had only begun to catch up to its original deadline. The tents the Italians slept in were set on fire while everyone was off working on the building and only an observant worker on the trusses saw the smoke but didn't see anyone in the camp area. Most of their personal items were burned but the squeezebox was salvaged as was the case of wine.

Jeremy replaced most of the lost items sending the men into the Mercantile with an open account. Then he and Mason tried to figure out who could have targeted the Italians and why the friendly immigrant group had caught someone's wrath.

The Italian's didn't take it to heart. They didn't feel they had been singled out for this damage. They simply accepted that burning their tent was a random act. It could have been any of the many tents in the growing number of living quarters in the area nick-named, Tent City.

Mason stood looking over this tent city as Jeremy told him, "I don't understand it. Their tent wasn't closest to the outside edge or the furthest away from the workers. I think it had to be a targeted attack on these men. I hate to think there are people in Sweetwater who are willing to resort to such lengths simply to keep immigrants out. Heck, most of us were immigrants at one time. My parents hardly spoke English when they settled in the territory, facing down the Indians and the weather."

"I haven't heard anyone talking, even when they're drunk in the saloon and that's where I get my best information on the kind of men who would pull this intimidation bullshit. I even sent away for any information on men as far away as Preston but got nothing back. So, they must be local. I mean it's been days between the incidents so whoever is doing this is staying in the area. I'll look closer at the groups of men by the river. See if any of them get antsy when I talk with them this time," Mason told Jeremy as they walked back toward the jail.

Jeremy headed back to Jessie's apartment. He hadn't had a lot of time to talk with Faith when they could be alone. Jessie was home most nights so it was the three of them for dinner and then Faith went downstairs to read a while before going to sleep but time was running out. He finally forced a meeting with her when they could talk.

Faith had time to rethink her plans and had decided making love with Jeremy would put the past out of her mind forever. Not that she wanted him to feel obligated to her or the baby but she could think of this time with him as the conception of her child. She had also decided she wouldn't be able to put this infant up for adoption but would tell her child about a wonderous night when it was conceived with a man, she held very strong feelings about. For all purposes, Jeremy would be this child's father - at least in Faith's mind and heart.

Jessie was out selling advertisements and had gone over to Preston for the night. It would take him much of the morning tomorrow before he returned. This seemed like the best time for Jeremy and her to be together without interruption. The closed sign was placed in the window and no one would be looking for Jeremy.

Faith wanted to complete her plan so she could think of the baby as coming from a good memory, unblemished from any reminder of her attacker. She met Jeremy in the hall outside her bedroom wearing a thin muslin nightgown and bare feet.

"I don't think this is a good idea, Faith. Please wait

until you speak with Rebecca, at least. I want to help you through this but I'm not an unbiased participant. I want to make love to you, to show you what it's really like between a man and a woman. I'll stay with you, take care of the baby but please reconsider this decision. Until we know for sure that you're pregnant."

"I must be with child. There's no other explanation." She peered up at him through the dim light. "I can't wait. I can't stand it any longer knowing it will soon be too late to pretend, to think of it as being anyone else's. I want to wipe that night from my mind, from my memories." There were tears running down her face. "You can't understand, it's a type of pain, something I keep trying to hide from but, then when I least expect it, it pops up in front of me and it's like it's happening all over again."

He took her through the open door of her room and to the narrow bed there. Jeremy couldn't say no to Faith. He loved her, he wanted to protect her from something that had already hurt her so badly and he could only do that by helping her as she asked him to. He began by kissing her tears away and when she began to respond, he placed his hand gently on a breast.

"Just do it. Please, Jeremy, I can't wait," she said as she tore her mouth away from his.

"We do it my way or we don't do it at all. I can't disrespect you, Faith, I love you. Don't try to make me like that other man. Let me show you how it will be between us," Jeremy protested.

"I'm sorry. I'll try to relax. I'll calm down. I don't mean to make this difficult for us. I think I love you, too, but I'm still not sure I will ever be able to live as your wife," she confided knowing she felt as if she should not, could not, be part of a loving marriage. She felt devalued as a woman and unable to be a good wife to any man.

"Let's worry about that later. Right now, let me show you how much I love being with you." He began kissing her lips again, finding the warmth and silently asking permission to enter, finding her tongue welcoming his. Then again, he placed his hand on her breast and was rewarded when the nipple hardened to a pebble and Faith unconsciously pushed into his palm. He gave the same attention to the other peak impatiently waiting its turn.

Jeremy pulled the nightgown up and over Faith's head to free her for his mouth's exploration, following the same trail his hand had recently covered. As his mouth paid homage to her breasts, his hand stroked down Faith's still flat stomach to end at the mound covered with soft curls. Jeremy savored the feel of such an intimate area and yet it wasn't enough. His hand slid between Faith's legs, searching and finding the most intimate of female openings, feeling the slickness that told him more than the moans, more than the writhing, more than the quickened breathing, Faith was ready for his body to enter hers.

Placing himself over Faith, he asked between kisses, "Are you sure? I can still stop this until you…."

"No, please Jeremy, you promised. I want you," she said and pulled him down towards her body.

Placing his knee between hers, he nudged her legs to give him room and then placed himself at her enticing entrance.

"Look at me, Faith. Keep your eyes open. I want you to know this is me and that I love you and we are committed to one another." He pushed into her waiting warmth.

Faith buckled with the pain that flashed in her eyes as Jeremy looked on in consternation. He pulled away and quickly held Faith to him, saying, "I'm sorry, God, Faith, I'm sorry. It shouldn't hurt. Something didn't heal or something. It shouldn't have hurt."

Faith caught her breath. "It didn't hurt like that before, not there. I don't know what's wrong. I'm sorry I got you involved in this whole thing."

"Shhh, it's all right. Let me make it all right. Do you trust me? Trust me not to hurt you again?" At her agreement, Jeremy placed his hand where his most private part had been and brought her to a climatic conclusion, easing her into, then through, the natural culmination of their lovemaking.

Faith fell asleep soon afterward but Jeremy worried about what had occurred, how he had caused pain when he only meant to make things better, to help Faith work through the trauma of the attack.

Jeremy woke to an empty bed and a bright sun shining against the building next door. He got up and dressed then went in search of Faith. He found both Faith and Jessie in the pressroom, both busy at the front counters. Jeremy went to Faith and placed his fingers under her chin, lifting her head so that their gazes met.

"We have an understanding," he stated. Then gave her a quick kiss right on her surprised mouth.

Two ladies were entering the door and witnessed the kiss. Jeremy, still holding his hat, tipped it toward the two customers before placing it on his head. "Morning, ladies. I was just kissing my fiancée good morning. Have a good day." He left through the still open door.

Both ladies changed direction from Jessie's counter

to Faith's, trying to get all the information they could so they could then disperse it throughout the town. The kiss would have been bad enough but to announce another Macgregor betrothal was going to make this information worth listening to.

Jessie went back to proofing the article but then thought about not hearing Jeremy come in the rear door and realized he may have come from Faith's room. Jeremy's office had been empty when Jessie passed it not half an hour ago. He smiled as he realized that both Matthew and Jeremy wear clothes that are so similar from one day to another, no one can tell if they are the same ones from the day before or not.

He was just figuring out how that may be a good thing. No one could be sure you hadn't made it home overnight. And when had Faith and Jeremy gotten close enough to become engaged? He had a lot of questions for his older brother but little confidence they would ever be answered in his lifetime.

The ladies finally had to finish their ordering and get about the business of spreading the news in their own fashion. Faith excused herself saying she was going upstairs to put on some soup stock and quickly left before Jessie could ask any questions of her.

Jessie could have told her not to bother running. He would get his information from Jeremy or not at all, but he felt Faith needed some time alone and let her leave undisturbed.

Jeremy took the set of porch steps two at a time and found himself facing the door with his hand up to rap on it - then stopped himself. How was he going to approach this topic of concern without exposing Faith and himself? He really wasn't worried about what anyone thought of him but he didn't want Faith's reputation to be tarnished.

Rebecca opened the door. "Did you need to see Daniel, Jeremy?"

"I will later, ma'am. I came to speak with you."

Confused, a bachelor not being her usual patient, she stood and waited for more information.

"I need to tell you about something and I don't want you to judge her, anyone to judge her," he said and was trying to say what he needed without disclosing Faith's name but couldn't find any way of doing so.

"Jeremy, when you know me better, you'll know I never judge. It's not my place to do so. Who is the 'her'?" Rebecca asked.

He stood there on the front porch of the parsonage and told Rebecca about the night before. He ended with, "I hurt her. I was wearing a Goodyear condom and I couldn't feel anything strange. But I've never been with a virgin so I'm not experienced enough to know if I did something wrong. If I should have felt something that I missed." Then he said, "I love, Faith St. Michaels. I don't think she can be with child. I don't think she was, that she was, you know."

Rebecca started to argue with Jeremy but then he said, "I know she was attacked but I don't think he entered her. I think she was too innocent to know the difference. She had just gone through a traumatic experience, didn't really know what was happening."

"I think I need to see her. Speak with her and maybe we can find out what happened last night," Rebecca told him.

"I'll send her to you. Will today be all right? I don't want her worrying more than she has to about being -

about having a baby," Jeremy explained.

"I know she was worried but I think we can get to the root of her concerns now. I'll be at the house across the street," Rebecca said without any other explanation.

"Is Daniel home? I want to discuss a wedding," he said making sure Rebecca understood his seriousness.

"He's in his office in the back." Then opening the door to her home, said, "I'll take you to him."

CHAPTER 11

Jeremy returned to the newspaper and found Faith hiding in her room. He rapped and then entered without permission.

"Faith, we need to talk but not until after you see Rebecca. I told her I would send you back to her. She'll be at Mary Beth's. Will you go and see her? I already told her about last night and she said she never judges. Please go and see her."

Faith stood and went into Jeremy's open arms, leaning her head against his warm chest, and asked, "When will this end? I need to feel at peace and I can't seem to do that."

"I asked Reverend Walters if he could get a priest for you. He said there was a Father Manuel who has held services in the church here in town and has done marriage services with him. Callie and Seth and then Matthew and Abby had him officiate. I would be willing to do that. I just need you to agree to marry me," Jeremy told her holding his precious gift to his chest.

"Oh, Jeremy, I need to talk with a priest. Please find out where he is, for me." Tears formed in her eyes, she was in such need of solace and forgiveness that only her faith could provide.

"I'll find him, I promise." He kissed her lightly then walked her to the door. He wanted to accompany her but knew better and stayed in the office until she disappeared toward the north of town before crossing the street to speak with the sheriff.

Rebecca was waiting as Jeremy had said and she

welcomed Faith into the back room of the house and onto the high examination table located there.

"Jeremy told me about last night and his concerns. How about you telling me what you experienced last night," Rebecca said.

Faith told Rebecca everything as she remembered it and then asked, "Did it hurt because of the baby? Did we hurt the baby?"

"No, nothing you did would hurt the infant this early. May I examine you to see why it was painful?"

At Faith's agreement, Rebecca proceeded to explain what she was doing each step of the way, making sure Faith was agreeing to each procedure. Rebecca sat back.

"I can see no sign that you are with child. I think you were traumatized by the attack and your body shut down, simply stopped working as it always had done. I think in time and maybe with you being able to relax, your body will continue its normal schedule."

Faith began to cry with relief and soon Rebecca was sitting next to her on the cot holding her hand. This was not the first time a woman who thought she was pregnant cried when she found out she wasn't but this was a good cry, a good cleansing and Rebecca didn't try to stop it.

When Faith finally seemed cried out, she asked, "What hurt last night? I know Jeremy wasn't expecting it to hurt and he stopped as soon as it happened."

"I think you were still a virgin and Jeremy broke the hymen, the maidenhead. It's natural to cause pain for the woman. Something that has to occur to make love or make a child. Neither of you did anything incorrectly. It shouldn't hurt the next time," the midwife explained to the younger woman.

"I was a virgin with Jeremy? How can that be?"

"The man who attacked you…. You said he was drunk and that he was still dressed? Many men can't function properly when they've been drinking a lot. I think he was too drunk to do more damage than bruise you. It was a horrible attack and the man should be sent to prison because his intentions were what really matter.

"For some reason, you were saved from the worse that could happen and now you have to decide what you wish to do. You can make up your mind any way you want. You don't owe Jeremy anything more than what you've already given him. He'll understand if you need to be free, to reconsider your life's choices," explained Rebecca, looking after the interests of her patient.

"I'll think about what you've said, Rebecca. I owe you so much," Faith said earnestly.

"No, I'm merely telling you what I can see has happened. If I had done a physical exam at the time you came to me, I might have been able to tell that you were still a virgin. But you were so sure you were with child. I focused on that and knew it would be too soon to tell about a pregnancy. I feel partly to blame for you lying with Jeremy," Rebecca confessed.

"Don't feel badly. I might have been with Jeremy anyway, well, soon anyway. I think I love him and I'm sure now that he loves me. It's happened so quickly I find it difficult to believe it can be true. After all these years to come to Sweetwater and find the love of my life. It's a little unbelievable."

"I know how that feels, Faith. I've been here less than a year and have found the love of my life and had to prove it to him. Daniel wasn't the same man then but I loved him anyway. We both realized what we had and made the decision to love and live together forever. As

107

you see, we are about to add to Sweetwater's population. We should never turn our backs on love. I sincerely believe we don't get too many chances at true love," Rebecca said, remembering the misunderstandings and hurt feelings she and Daniel went through.

"I believe Jeremy may be my soulmate but am I ready to be his? I don't have any experience in life and these last few months shook my faith. I need to regain that before I can be what Jeremy needs," Faith said wisely.

"Maybe you are more what he needs than you know, Faith. I wish you the best and if you need me at any time, you can always come back." She patted the younger girl's hand hoping to encourage the young woman she was meant to become.

Jeremy waited impatiently for Faith to return, pacing back and forth in his office, unable to concentrate on his work. He looked at the watch in the small pocket in his vest and found it was less than ten minutes from the last time he had looked. He thought he heard the front door but waited where he was, not wanting to rush Faith or force her to talk with him if she wasn't ready to do so.

Faith found him and closed the office door. Jeremy was holding his breath and leaned back against the desk, keeping both hands on the edge giving Faith the option of reaching out to him or keeping her distance.

"Rebecca says I was a virgin until last night," she stated baldly.

Jeremy's heart sank. "I'm sorry, Faith. I should have known. I should have made you see her before we went that far."

"I'm not sorry, Jeremy. I enjoyed last night with you. I'd like to enjoy more of the same but I need to make sure I'm ready to be anyone's wife. I made some decisions under wrong assumptions so now I need to make decisions based on whether or not I should marry, that my emotions are not clouded with other feelings, with other things that are not what I thought," she told him quietly, feeling she would know when the time was right for them to be together.

Jeremy nodded his head, accepting her verdict but added, "I'll give you all the time you need but I won't let you shut me out, not completely. My feelings have always been strong for you, have even surprised me in their intensity. I can't throw that away. I'll fight for you, for us, because I think what I feel for you doesn't come to everyone and I feel blessed that I found you."

"I believe you. You have been nothing but kind and generous and you are a sincerely good man. That makes it harder for me to find myself in all that has happened. I must be sure what I feel for you is real, is what we need to have a life together. I need to be sure it's forever." Staring into his green eyes, she asked, "Am I making any sense to you?"

"It sounds like I may have a chance and I'll settle for that now. Please don't lock me out and I'll wait, maybe impatiently, but I'll wait." He smiled in relief it wasn't as bad as he thought.

"Thank you, Jeremy."

"I sent someone to see if Father Manuel could come to Sweetwater and speak with you. Take confession, possibly help you find some peace finally," he told her as she had her hand on the doorknob.

"Thank you, again. You don't know how much that means to me." She left to go to her own room and contemplate all that had happened.

Father Manuel came to the little white church the next day to take confession and to christen Abby and Matthew's daughter, Hannah, later that day. Mary Beth went to confession first and then Matthew, leaving Faith to go last. She spent a long time with the Father and he helped her understand how there is a plan and that plan is known only to One and that there is always an answer to our prayers if we listen for it.

Faith returned from the church with a much lighter heart, a weight removed she hadn't even known was there. She didn't need to feel badly for feeling relief that there wasn't to be a child. That decision had been made by someone with much more power than she had. The fact she had been accepting she would give birth was what mattered. She had no sin, only the man who forced himself on her had to face his maker with that sin following him. Faith had left the small church feeling cleansed and fresh and new.

That same morning Matthew had gotten word from the sheriff they had found Dick Hanson, the man who had attacked Faith. Matthew was unsure whether to bring it up to Faith directly, let Callie know, or tell Jeremy. Abby advised him to tell Jeremy and he could tell Faith when he felt it was the right time.

Matthew went to the newspaper office knowing Faith was at the church to give Jeremy the updated news, that Dick Hanson was dead and had been in the ground for several weeks. He had fallen off his horse while drunk and was found with a broken neck on the road between Three Rivers and Preston. No one claimed the body so they buried him on boot hill. Matthew left it up to Jeremy to tell Faith and anyone else who needed to know.

When Faith returned from the church, she was a happy young woman, more so than when she had been told she wasn't carrying a child. She smiled when she came into the apartment, going straight to Jeremy and giving him a hug while he leaned down and found her lips, covering her mouth with a passionate kiss, welcoming this new Faith into his life.

She was wearing the clothes Abby made so many days ago and Jeremy had finally given her. A peach colored blouse trimmed with satin ribbon and lace and the tan skirt with a slight bustle emphasizing Faith's naturally slender waist. He looked at Faith, her bright smile beaming at him in her delight of what she assured him were the most beautiful blouse and skirt she had ever had. Jeremy was already planning the other items he was going to order for his soon-to-be wife. He was sure Faith was ready to accept his proposal.

That afternoon, everyone went to the church to help celebrate the christening of Hannah, with Father Manuel presiding over the sacrament. The men were all wearing their Sunday best suits and hats while the ladies were in their best finery, festive hats perched on their heads. As they walked toward the white church, they joined others heading in the same direction forming a steady stream of people.

The church pews filled quietly, many people in awe because the Father was in front at the pulpit rather than their own Reverend Walters who was sitting near the front with his wife. Also, in the front were Abby and Matthew alongside Callie and Seth Harrison, who were to be Hannah's Godparents. The congregation settled and Father Manuel began the ceremony that would bring Hannah into the protection of the church.

There was a reception held at the parsonage where several desserts and platters of canapés had been set out by Mary Margaret and Charity. As soon as Charity saw Faith, looking so lovely and loved, she ran into Faith's open arms and cried. Rebecca found a quiet room for them to go to where they would have some privacy to speak of things better kept to themselves.

"I'm so glad to see you, Charity," Faith said as she wiped the tears from her face. "I was worried about how you were doing out there by yourself."

"I felt so guilty. I was so well taken care of and then not knowing how you were doing…. Not having anyone to ask." Charity asked carefully, "Are you with child?"

"No, and I found out I was actually still a virgin. That man, that Dick Hanson, was so drunk he couldn't, he didn't…." And she stopped, not having the words to explain to her dearest friend.

Charity patted Faith's hand saying, "I understand and I'm so thankful you didn't have to go through that, at least."

"I'm sorry I didn't know sooner. It would have saved me and others a lot of worry. At the same time, what happened to me forced us to come to Sweetwater when we had been hesitating to leave our positions," Faith said remembering their earlier indecision.

"I, for one, am very glad we came. I found a man I think I shall marry. Do you remember, Will? He's been wonderful with me. I told him what happened. I hope you don't mind. I was sick with guilt and worry and he helped me understand what I could and couldn't control. I came to forgive myself for failing you and then I could learn to love," Charity confessed. "That I was worth love."

"I never felt you failed me, Charity, never. I once

wondered if I had done something to make God angry but then I remembered the nuns telling us about man having free will to choose to be good or evil. I felt then there was a message in all of this for me and I kept moving forward waiting for Him to let me know what He wanted me to do."

"I'm glad you are doing well. You look wonderful - healthy and happy, I think," said her old friend staring at her flushed face.

"I'm all those things. I love a wonderful man, Jeremy Macgregor, and he seems to love me. I am looking forward to a marriage with him and staying in Sweetwater. I want to remain close to you, to see you married, as well."

"I think that will be sooner than we realize. Will has already asked me and is waiting for me to feel I can move on with my life. Knowing you are in good hands, I think, will allow me to give him my answer." Charity confided, "Callie has already given me her blessing."

"That's wonderful. Now let's get out there before all those pretty little cakes are gone." The girls stood up and arm in arm went to the parlor to give the happy parents all the good wishes they deserved.

People began leaving to return home for the evening. The Harrison ranch group, including baby, Warren, left first since they had the farthest to travel. No one from the Macgregor ranch attended nor did Mary Beth who returned to the ranch right after confession to care for Mavis and the new baby there.

Jessie was becoming antsy. He had been hoping Mary Beth would travel to town but also realized she would feel an obligation to her patients. Jessie spoke to Jeremy and then headed toward the livery. He had decided he was going to spend a night or two at the ranch and try to get some time alone with Mary Beth. He didn't have any new arguments to boost his cause but being able to talk with her would lessen his frustration.

Jeremy walked back to the newspaper building with Faith and went directly to his office. "I ate so much. I think I'm going to pass on dinner. I have some ideas I want to get down on paper about the school so I'll see you later?" He raised his brows in question.

"That's fine. I'm going to take some work upstairs and proof it for next week's paper." She stepped away heading towards the back door.

Unsure if this was the best time, he said, "I need to speak with you about something important that Mason told me. It's about that man who attacked you." He waited for any sign she didn't want to listen to this news but she had stopped and turned toward him expressionlessly.

"He was found dead a couple of weeks ago. They think he was drunk and fell off his horse breaking his neck. You'll never see him again. He'll never come after you or be able to harm anyone else," he told her watching for any sign of fear, hoping to see less anxiety.

"I, I…thank you, for telling me. I didn't ever want to find him watching me from across the street or something. I don't know what I'm feeling right now but I think it's mostly relief." Seeking some sort of answer, she asked, "Should I feel sorry a man is dead? I don't. So, does that make me evil? Or sinful?" She shook her head slowly. "I think I want to be alone for a while to see how this really affects me."

Jeremy felt conflicted, wondering if this news would push Faith into moving on again, leaving him before they could forge a relationship. "You know I really would rather go with you, anywhere, but I'm not sure I can be trusted right now. There was something about being around Abby and Matthew so happy with their new family and then seeing Seth with Callie and Warren. I had the hardest time not claiming you in front of everyone. Bringing you back here until I was sure you wanted me as badly as I want you." Shrugging, he continued, "Anyway, I'm hoping work is the answer to having me spend less time thinking of you and your body."

Faith stood in the doorway, unsure of what she should do, either accept Jeremy's offer or leave and take herself out of his focus.

"I'll be fine, Faith. We can't appease my appetites so I may as well get used to controlling myself. I love you." He so wanted to take her in his arms but knew he didn't dare. Didn't think it was how he should go about things. Instead, he forced himself to stay behind the desk. "Now go upstairs and I'll get to work."

Faith moved to do as Jeremy had asked. "I'll try to make a decision as soon as I can. I need to be sure."

"Don't rush into anything. I want you comfortable with any decision and we have the rest of our lives if that's what it takes." He looked down at his work as if his attention was on the drawings.

After Faith left, Jeremy shook his head and thought, damn, I hope it doesn't take the rest of our lives to come to a decision. He was having a difficult enough time staying away from her. To give her time but he may need to move back out to the ranch to keep from breaking his word.

CHAPTER 12

Jessie arrived at the ranch just as all hell seemed to be breaking loose. Jamie was rushing water upstairs and Mary Beth was shouting out orders. Emily had her water break while she was downstairs and Mac had carried her to their room. But it hadn't been set up as a birthing room, yet, because Emily wasn't due. Or at least they thought she wasn't but as Rebecca had taught Mary Beth, babies have their own time line.

The extra sheets and towels were placed under Emily and there were pillows for her shoulders and head. Mac, his eyes looking large in his face was controlling his need to yell at someone because his wife was in pain, ones that kept getting harder as her contractions increased at what he felt was an alarming rate.

Jessie stood outside the door. "Should I get Rebecca?" At Mac's growl and Mary Beth's request, he rushed downstairs and jumped back onto his horse. It would take more than an hour to get back to the ranch and that was if Rebecca could move that quickly.

Mary Beth made Emily as comfortable as possible after feeling the baby through a contraction and then checking to see if she could see the top of the baby's head. She could during the contraction but what she saw, concerned her. She didn't have the experience Rebecca did but Mary Beth was pretty sure the baby wasn't in the right position.

She went over everything she knew in her mind, all the possibilities of a dangerous birth, while at the same time trying to keep Mac and Emily calm. She watched once more as Emily stiffened through a contraction warning Mary Beth, she felt the need to bear down, push the tiny new life out of her.

"Mac, keep reminding Emily to breath during those contractions. She needs the air and so does the baby. I don't think this one is going to wait for Rebecca so we will have to be extra brave."

Mac became alarmed and asked hoarsely, "What are you doing with that knife?"

"Emily and I have gone over the need for the cut if it is necessary and I feel it is. It is better than tearing. I can suture her and it will heal in a few days," Mary Beth said, doing the procedure with a slight twinge to Emily, which at that time went almost unnoticed due to another contraction beginning.

"Emily, Emily." Mary Beth tried to get Emily's attention over the contractions now rolling like ocean waves taking over her body at increasingly closer times. "Don't push, don't bear down. After the next contraction I'm going to have to turn the baby, it's facing the wrong direction. Remember the diagrams, the position the baby needs to be in?"

Mac asked hesitantly, "Is it breach?"

Emily nodded to Mary Beth's question and then gritted her teeth as another contraction took over her body.

"Not breach, facing up. I have to push it back and turn it carefully before the contraction can do any harm. All right, Emily, one, two and three…."

Emily's stomach actually could be seen rising and then Emily relaxed onto the bed. Mac was still reminding her to breath, telling her he loved her, telling her she never had to give him another child no matter what.

Emily shushed him, saying between breaths that she was fine, that they had to worry about the baby, not allow the baby to die.

"I think the infant's back into position." Mary Beth took a deep breath. "Now the contractions can do their job. It may not be as painful and I think we will have this little one here in a few more pushes."

There was more of a respite between the pains and Mac kissed his wife's forehead, whispering prayers, which Emily told him were unnecessary. She was prepared for it all after having seen Mavis go through it.

Mary Beth stayed at the end of the bed. Emily was half-sitting being held up by pillows and bolsters and Mac. Mavis brought in the cooled bathing water and asked if there was anything more, she could do.

"We're pretty much there I think, Mavis. This one is anxious to become part of the family even if there was a small directional change needed," Mary Beth said without further explanation.

"Now you can push, Emily. Keep breathing and then bear down when you feel the pressure." With an almost silent swish, Mary Beth held the baby and cleared out its mouth, allowing it to bellow as loudly as it could. Wrapping the baby after wiping most of the amniotic fluid off, she handed him up to Emily to discover the sex.

Mac and Emily both grinned at each other saying something about not holding the quilt tightly enough. Mary Beth continued with the duties needed to ensure Emily was kept healthy and then did the few sutures needed to repair the cuts.

Mavis had gone to the head of the bed to admire the new Macgregor and when she asked if they had a name was told this son would be named after his grandfather just as Mavis's daughter had been named after the grandmother.

Mac said cheerily, "Meet Elliott Joseph Macgregor everyone. He'll be the best rancher the State of Kansas has ever seen."

Emily entered into the conversation. "He'll be the best at whatever he chooses to do, Mac. I won't have you brow-beat him into something he may not love as much as you do." She petted the tuft of red hair on the top of her son's head.

"Well, it looks like the Macgregor family traits are strong in this one, too. Soon we'll have a whole county full of red-heads," teased Mavis since her daughter looked like she was to keep the blue eyes and red tinted hair of the family, also.

"I think Elliot's eyes will be green, like Mac's, and always full of mischief. I hope you've gotten over those promises you were making, Mac. I want Elliott to have brothers and sisters to keep him grounded," Emily told her husband happily.

Mac's usually bright eyes clouded over. "I meant them at the time but let's see how things go before we worry about siblings for this one." Then he kissed his wife. "I'm going to go down and let Jamie and the others know. We have much to be thankful for. Especially that Mary Beth was still here. You didn't give us much warning, Emily. All in all, that was a quick birth."

Mac stood and stretched. "Is there anything I can get for you, love? How about some tea with sugar?"

"That sounds wonderful, Mac, and then I'll try feeding our son."

Mac's chest seemed to swell with the pride the word 'son' evoked.

Mavis helped Mary Beth clear up the extra sheets and towels and then watched as Mary Beth cleansed the baby and checked the cord was still tied tightly. Once clean, Elliott was handed back to his mother and Mary Beth went downstairs with the discarded bedding.

The midwife arrived about an hour later. Jessie at the reins and a very pregnant Rebecca huffing to climb the stairs as people informed her the baby had been born and was healthy with the mother doing fine.

Rebecca checked everything and complimented Mary Beth on the fine suturing before saying, "Well, we'll have to move you into town for the next birth, Emily. You're not one to give notice it seems and a little early to boot. I bet Mac was fit to be tied."

Emily responded, "I'm not sure he wants to go through it again too soon but I think he was pretty good considering he's Mac. I actually think now that he's seen it once he'd be able to deliver the next one like Matthew did Hannah." All three women laughed now that the birthing was over.

Mary Beth, once almost homeward bound, was now staying on to help Emily and Elliott get started. Mavis was still recovering from little Aileen's birth. Although the husbands were dedicated to their families, Mary Beth was able to keep the meals and laundry going as well as give advice on child care that Rebecca had instilled in her. Mary Beth having worked with the infants at St. Michaels was experienced with everything but the suckling and Mavis had experience with that so the three women worked together very well.

Jessie tried to catch some time with Mary Beth before needing to drive Rebecca home to the rectory. "I was headed out here to talk with you about coming back to town but that looks like it will need to wait a little longer."

Mary Beth said, "I told you, babies set their own schedule. Emily wasn't due for a couple more weeks, yet, here he is. I have to be able to go when I'm needed."

"But being here was just a chance of the draw. I mean, you can't be everywhere all the time. People plan on finding you at the house or at least nearby. Right now, both Mavis and Emily needed you but how many times is one household going to have two babies within a few weeks of one another? You can't stay with one mother for very long. At some point she will have to take care of the baby by herself or get some kind of home help, like Callie has with Mary Margaret and Maria." He was trying to be reasonable.

"I understand that. Rebecca was trained to stay with the mother's while her own mother returned to the family, that's what I am to Rebecca," explained Mary Beth.

"Well, then I don't see why you can't get someone to take over after you deliver the baby. I know Doc Winters never stayed to care for a woman and infant."

"I'm not Doc Winters. Now you better get ready to take Rebecca back. I've got work to do." She left Jessie standing alone.

Damn, that hadn't gone at all as he planned. He thought if he showed up at the ranch, he would get to stay a few nights and have plenty of time to convince Mary Beth of what he wanted for them. How good they could be together. The urge to marry and start his own family was eating at him and the woman he wanted was willing to let him go. He thought it rather unfair since he was willing to let her keep being a midwife if she wanted.

Turning down dinner, Jessie waited on the back-porch rocking until Rebecca was ready to return to town and then drove home morosely. Not even the knowledge that Emily had made it through without too much difficulty and that he had a nephew to go with his niece kept him from the doldrums.

Hell, why did loving someone need to be so difficult? Why did he need to love a woman so set on her own goals? He would have confided in Rebecca but she seemed to have fallen asleep and was leaning against the side of the well-sprung buggy.

Then a truth came to him as if a lightning bolt had landed next to him. His main concern was getting his businesses started and making plans for his future, including having a wife and family. But he wasn't anywhere near the age some of these other men were. Hell, he had just graduated with his law degree. There wasn't a rush…not really. Sure, it would be nice to have someone to come home to and sleep beside but he could postpone having that. He could live with a little discomfort as long as he could see and talk with Mary Beth when she was in town and not with patients.

Why was her wants and desires less important than his? Why was any woman's ambition thought to be less important than being a wife and mother? Abby was both and she seemed happy, as did Matthew. Of course, she had years devoted to getting her business going and Jessie would need to allow Mary Beth the same chance. To do the work she felt was important. And he wasn't denying the importance or her reason for doing it.

Damn, it probably seemed that way to her, though. His saying he would allow her to continue as if granting her permission. As if he had any right to grant or withhold such permission. One thing he should have realized watching his older brothers and their wives. They all gave up something to their partners willingly. No one trod on the other. No one abused the other's ideas or contribution to the marriage.

If he thought back, he could see where he sounded as if he would control Mary Beth after they were married. Words like 'allow' or 'let' or 'for now' shouldn't even be in his vocabulary. Her wants and wishes and dreams were equally as important as his were to him. He needed to make her dreams as important, no, even more important, to him than his own. She shouldn't have to alter any of her plans.

Bearing children would be a simple alteration in Mary Beth's schedule just as it was in Rebecca's. She had no plans on quitting the profession to become only a wife and mother. And she didn't even have a home help at this time. Jessie would be able to afford someone to help Mary Beth with things when the time came if he couldn't do so himself. Most of his time was his own. His job was more or less eight to five and he would enjoy taking care of any children they had. The way Matthew took care of his two.

Feeling better now that he thought of them working as a team and that he didn't need her to make up her mind immediately, brought him a sense of ease. Pulling to a stop in front of the parsonage, the reverend came out as Rebecca woke. The other man helped his wife down from the buggy and took the black satchel with one hand while holding onto her arm with the other.

"Emily didn't wait but Mary Beth did fine. I'm not sure Rebecca needs to go out every time any longer," Jessie said to the other man deciding he may as well help

Mary Beth rather than try to get her replaced.

Fully awake now, Rebecca said, "I'm not sure I can make it out anywhere any longer, Jessie. I am glad Mary Beth is such a smart girl and willing to take over the practice for a while. Good thing I'm the only one left to need her services." She waddled up the steps as the men looked on.

CHAPTER 13

Mason rode his horse closer to the campfire and the three men sitting around it. "Evening gents," he said as he dismounted, startling the men into jumping up and facing him. "I understand you've got a beef with the bank that's being built in town?"

The three men, none of them wearing clothes that didn't look as if they'd been made for a smaller man, stared at Mason, his broad shoulders and the badge on his shirt. The biggest of the three, a gold tooth prominent in the front of his mouth, said, "Got no problem with the bank. Jist the guy buildin' it."

"Macgregor? You've got a problem with Macgregor? Why?" asked Mason surprised by the man's answer since no one had a bad word to say about the man. Besides, Jeremy had been gone from town for at least the past six years. Hard to believe anyone held a grudge for that long.

"Cuz we're paid to." With that the gold-toothed man peered at his friends and they all chuckled.

Mason thought a second then asked, "And who's paying you?"

"Wouldn't you like to know," said the first man again, evidently the chosen spokesman for the group.

"I'm going to give you fellas another chance to talk with me out here before I take you in to the jail cell." Before Mason could barely finish the sentence, the big man lunged at him taking them both backwards to the ground.

Punching wildly, the man left himself open for

Mason to bring a punch to the man's jaw that knocked him off and out. By then the other two men thought they could get some punches in, but Mason got to his feet. Then there wasn't a chance for the two shorter men.

Mason placed a punch to one man's middle and while he crumpled over into a fetal position, turned to the other. Mason landed two punches, one to the torso and a follow through to the jaw sending the man straight backward and out cold.

Looking around at his handy work, Mason sighed. He still hadn't gotten the information he wanted, yet. Walking over to his horse standing patiently waiting through the fight, he retrieved his rope.

The two men finally woke up groaning only to find themselves hog-tied to each other. As they realized there wasn't any way for them to get lose, one of the men who had remained quiet said, "I'll tell ya everything. I just don't want to go back to Leavenworth."

Mason sat watching the men. "I'm listening."

The leader, tied separately, snapped, "Shut your mouth, Benny, or someone else will do it for ya. We got paid to do a job and part of that job was to keep our mouths shut."

Mason, seeing a weakness, said, "Well, then I'll just get a group to help me take you all to town and from there to Leavenworth."

"No, no, don't do that. We were hired by Timothy, out of Chicago to keep the bank from getting built so that Macgregor would be sent packing when he couldn't fulfill his contract," said the man who didn't want to be sent back to prison.

"Timothy who?" Mason barked.

All three men stared at Mason as if he were from

Mars. "Dick Timothy, he's a boss out of Chicago. Runs the whole damn city and everyone in it. Got the last two governors elected and a lot more," supplied the man who up to now had been quiet.

"So, a political boss from Illinois wants Macgregor to fail and then what?" asked Mason still trying to see who was at the bottom of this scheme against his friend.

"Hell, we don't know that. We were told to queer his deal here so that he would go back to the capital. Topeka, ain't it?" This information from the second man.

"All right, we made a deal. Give me your names and I'll untie you. But I better not hear that you're still in the area tomorrow or I'll chase you to ground again and next time I won't be so lenient," Mason told them before untying them and sending them on their way.

Mason stood at his kitchen sink washing the blood off his knuckles when Victoria came up behind him with a jar of salve asking, "Is that blood yours or someone else's?"

Without looking up, Mason confessed, "Probably a little of both. I had to convince the men who were harassing the bank worksite they should be moving on to another town."

"Men, as in more than one? Why must you always take on a gang? Why can't you simply arrest them one at a time?" she asked dabbing the salve onto the knuckles and then wrapping them with a light piece of gauze before tying it off.

"I do fight them one at a time - well, mostly. And if they come at me in gangs, I have to fight them in gangs," explained Mason leaning against the kitchen table and pulling his wife between his splayed legs where she leaned into his body awakening his strong shaft. "And because then, honey, I come home and you feel sorry for me and try to make me feel all better. Cause it's working already." Mason kissed his wife trying to unbutton her blouse using one wrapped hand.

Victoria removed her mouth from his. "You are absolutely the worse husband. You miss a perfectly cooked supper and then come home in a disreputable condition of dirty trousers and, look, you've torn another shirt." She asked innocently, "What am I to do with you?"

"I could give you a few suggestions but I find I like what you come up with on your own, honey," he replied not so innocently.

Victoria knew when it was a lost cause. She was happy to have him home and in one piece, so she said, "Drop your clothes here and I'll take care of them in the morning. I'll meet you in our room when you're done." She left him, slowly unbuttoning her blouse as she went.

When Mason entered the bedroom, naked as the day he was born, Victoria was laying in the bed, covers folded down and a wide smile as she watched her virile husband come towards her.

"I think you've had a rough enough night. Why don't you lay down here and let me administer some well-earned rewards," she cooed.

Smiling at the invitation, he did as Victoria suggested, allowing her to run the lovemaking any way she wanted. "This isn't going to include using the jail cell and my handcuffs, is it?" Mason teased with one of his favorite fantasies.

"Not this time, big boy. I'm simply planning on doing most of the work to let your hands rest up a little. You can run things tomorrow," she promised.

Victoria kissed her husband, letting him wrap his arms around her and then kissed her way down his body stopping at the part of him that still intrigued her, how it becomes the benefactor of her passions. Taking the velvety tip in her mouth she lavished all her attention until a slight hiss from Mason told her he was beginning to like this game too well and it was time to move on to other things he liked just as much.

Kissing her way back up to his mouth, Victoria invited Mason's tongue to enter hers while his hands rose to cup her breasts. Victoria pushed his hands back to each side of his head and whispered, "No hands tonight, remember. You're injured."

Then she straddled his hips and allowed the protruding shaft to slide into her womanly warmth. They both hesitated to move more as they enjoyed their joined bodies. Victoria raised then lowered herself on his rigid shaft as she and Mason began the age-old dance of lovers. It wasn't long before both of them were stiffening with a euphoric culmination and then drifting down to earth.

Mason rolled to his side sending Victoria tumbling unto the mattress as he whispered into her ear, "A man could get real used to coming home to this, honey. I sure feel lucky to be coming home to you." Then he nuzzled into her throat beginning the dance all over again.

CHAPTER 14

Jessie rolled the ink evenly across the press like the professional he was. Faith had recently finished the proofreading and it was ready to go. He said, "I don't know why I put the birth announcements in the paper. Everyone knows all about it within a few hours and I feel like I'm more of a historian than a news man."

Faith replied, "Well it was news for most people that a First National Bank was being built right here in Sweetwater and being designed by the famous Jeremy Macgregor, architect. And you let the cat out of the bag about the new school and civic hall that will be financed by the local ranchers as well as the town."

"I know. I guess I thought the paper would be full of more exciting things, like bank robberies and train derailments," he laughed at his own folly.

"Then you better start printing ten cent fiction books. I never heard of anything like that happening here in Sweetwater and I hope I never do. This is a pleasant town. I don't want it dirtied up with bank robbers or crooks," Faith said emphatically.

"I know. I'm just nervous since this is the first edition I was going to charge for. The advertisements are where the money is but people have to read it to make it worth the advertiser's investment. I can't keep giving the paper away so I'm hoping people will be interested enough to buy it."

"It's always slow at first. I told you that and it takes word of mouth to get the outlying ranchers and farmers used to picking one up at the Mercantile or dry goods store when they're in for provisions. All we can do is keep the information fresh and the picture advertisements appealing. So far, I think you have done well with both."

"I liked the promotional ticket drawing for the spring hat from Abby's. They all will look quite fetching for the Easter Sunday sermon. And having a contest with an award certificate for the hat that gets the most votes was just short of genius," he complimented her.

"I have an award all printed up. We simply need to add the lady's name. Abby was offering to give her some silk flowers to add to the hat or to make up another. I think any woman would be pleased to win."

"What do you think the reverend will think about us turning his church into a beauty contest of sorts? Is he going to damn us all to perdition?" Jessie asked half-seriously.

"If he does, that will be the next week's headline." Faith laughed at the astonished expression on his face. "Never leave a good headline laying in the street. Use everything to entice the reader into picking up your paper. We don't have any local competition but that doesn't mean other papers brought in by the train won't out sell us, especially with national news. We may need to pay for a news service to wire us important news from around the country."

"This week will tell us whether we need to add more items of interest. Let's hope it goes well. I plan on taking some out to the ranchers when I visit my brothers. It seems Callie always knows what's happening before anyone else but hopefully she'll enjoy the paper anyway."

That night, the Macgregor family sitting around the

dinner table included Mary Beth and both new mothers, the babies sleeping in the parlor area close to the adults. Mac, as usual at the head of the table, was grumbling with pride about having changed his son's diaper in the night before handing him to Emily for feeding.

"Not one of you warned me that a boy will spray you as soon as he feels cool air on his bottom." He shoved a fork of potatoes into his mouth.

"I didn't think to warn you, I guess, because I never envisioned you changing a diaper," said Mavis. "I've been christened more than once." She chuckled at fond memories of her son, now deceased for several years.

"I didn't know they did. Thanks for the warning for my next one," Jamie chimed in smiling, too.

"I'll let you practice with Elliott, then, if you want. Make sure it's a cool night," Mac said smiling though he didn't slow down his eating.

Emily added, "Well, I thank you for getting up in the middle of the night. It makes it easier for me and I still find I'm tired all the time. I thought that was all over." She tried to cover her yawn with a hand.

"That will fade after a while. Remember to sleep when the baby sleeps, drink extra fluids and eat plenty of meats. You both need to rebuild your strength and keep it up while feeding these little ones. They take a lot of nourishment," Mary Beth reminded the mothers sounding like Rebecca without acknowledging the fact.

Jessie felt his face warm but no one said anything. Mary Beth was as comfortable talking about these personal things as Mac and Jamie were. Then he realized this was simply more of life. What happens day to day on a ranch, with his family, and he relaxed knowing this was Mary Beth's life, too.

Saying goodnight to Mary Beth on the front porch, he took her into his arms and was grateful when she leaned into him, not pushing him away as sometimes used to happen. "I'll try to be out here in a couple of days to visit everyone again," he told her against her ear.

"Rebecca didn't think I would need to stay here too much longer saying the husbands were so good about helping and Callie was sending enough food to feed everyone for days. Maria's sister is coming for the laundry and that leaves me with very little to do. And I want to get back with Rebecca in case she ends up coming due sooner than she had planned."

"I'll check with her and then probably come and pick you up in a day or two. It will be nice to have you back in town. I miss our daily talks." He kissed Mary Beth as if she was the only woman in the world - and for him she was.

Returning home, Jessie went upstairs from the rear door only to discover Jeremy and Faith locked in an embrace while sitting on the sofa. He wasn't totally surprised but wasn't sure what he had interrupted.

His brother welcomed him saying, "Faith and I have decided to get married. Probably as soon as Daniel and Father Manuel can coordinate their schedules. I've already told Faith to select a dress and shoes for the wedding but she can choose whatever else she needs." He gazed toward his intended with passion-filled eyes.

"You don't have to do that, Jeremy. You're just starting out and I can wait," Faith said firmly

Both men looked at her, surprised at her words.

Jeremy said smiling, "Neither of us are impoverished, Faith. I have invested my share of the ranch's profits the last few years plus I made a very good salary from the architectural firm I worked at in the capital. I'm not in need. I plan on starting the design for our house as soon as I secure the lot here in town which I've already placed a deposit on."

When she turned accusatory eyes at Jessie, he raised his hands up saying, "I never told you I was poor. Only that I needed the paper to make its own profits. I wasn't running a charity for the town's people and I intend to charge for my legal skills when and if I ever get a client, too. I can fall back on my savings and my investment from my shares of the Macgregor ranch. I've been living a student's life for too long. I can afford to start living like an adult and I intend to.

"When Mary Beth and I are married, she'll keep working because she wants to - not because she needs to. I may even hire a housekeeper so she can continue working with Rebecca without feeling she is letting me down at home or feel under pressure to do too much."

"I'm not sure Mary Beth knows that Jessie. Not that she needs you to hire a helper but possibly you should be more forthright with your financial standing. It won't mean she'll marry you but it might ease her concerns of letting you down as a wife," Faith told him.

"I guess I thought she knew. I never said I was in need of money. I simply don't need much personally to live. I'm not much for dressing showy or anything but I don't mind paying for anything Mary Beth wants," Jessie continued.

Faith looked self-consciously at Jeremy and Jessie, then said, "I'm going to go back to my room. I never meant to stay up here this long and it sounds like it may be a busy day tomorrow. I'll be up to make breakfast as usual." She slid past Jessie before Jeremy could put up an argument.

Jeremy waited till he heard the door downstairs open and close, then told Jessie, "I haven't told Faith, maybe I never will, but Mason found those guys who were vandalizing my building site. They were some bullyboys sent by a political boss out of Chicago. Clarissa and her father set them on me to try to convince me this isn't the place for me to settle down. I guess she didn't take my telling her I wasn't interested as well as I thought. And her father seemed to think making my work difficult here would have me running back to them."

"They actually paid men to come all the way here just to make your life miserable? What about Faith? Was she in danger, too?" Jessie asked enraged that Clarissa would endanger his friend.

"No, evidently Clarissa wasn't aware of my feelings for Faith. That might have been the one thing that would have had her backing off. She wouldn't want to think she was second choice. That would really be a sore point with her. Mason roughed them up a little when one of them went for him and then told them if he saw them around here again, he'd throw the lot of them in jail for trespassing and vandalism. Then he told them I was married and I wasn't planning on moving anywhere," Jeremy finished telling Jessie the whole of it.

"If I were you, I'd forget what Mason told me. It won't make you any points with Faith and it's better to let it get lost in history," Jessie warned his brother.

"I agree. It's over now and I can relax a little around the building sites. I actually feel better that it had been those out-of-towners. It's good to know it wasn't any of the men I brought in to work here."

Walking down the boardwalk to Abby's dress shop,

Faith looked admiringly in the window filled with lovely spring hats, parasols and white kidskin shoes. There were subtle samples of perfume bottles, silver hairbrush sets and other feminine frippery for sale as well.

The little bell chimed a welcome as Faith opened the door and for the first time stepped into Abby's store, a world of feminine needs if there ever was one. Corsets with pink ribbon ties were on sewing mannequins next to piles of silk. Satin stockings with delicate clockwork going up the sides in various colors of pink, peach, white and pale blue were in protective packaging. There were hatpins and barrettes with precious stones and some with real pearls set in gold and silver.

Abby came out, pleased to see who it was in her store. "Why Faith, how nice to see you again. Are you browsing or can I help you with something special?"

"Jeremy sent me to buy a dress for my wedding but I don't have any idea what it should be. I want to be able to wear it more than once, you know what I mean?" Faith said, ever practical. The years of living fugally would not be overcome simply because her future husband said he had money.

"Certainly, I have a few drawings of ones I've done and there are some in this book out of New York that I thought would be lovely on a younger lady. I've been itching to find someone who needed something like these. Do you like them?" asked Abby. She held up a book open to a page with a light-blue day dress. There was white lace around the high collar and tight cuffs as well as an underskirt in a darker blue and white stripe. A bustle was swept back from both sides and held in place by dark-blue ribbon bows.

"I'm not sure about the color but I like the way it

drapes in the front and then is pulled up into the bustle. The bustle looks a little cumbersome, though…. But what do you think?" Faith turned toward Abby who inspected the bustle on the dress in the drawing.

Nodding, Abby agreed. "This bustle may be a little grand for Sweetwater. We want stylish but it still needs to be practical. I can take it down a little so you can feel the bottom of a chair when you sit but will still give you the statuesque silhouette that is all the rage. This has a jacket that can be made to go with it so it can be worn both for summer and winter."

Abby pulled a bolt of cloth out from a pile saying, "I've been saving this for one of my red-haired friends. You have the red highlights and I think it does wonders against your complexion. See how creamy your skin looks now?" They both stared at the new face in the mirror.

"I can't believe the difference a color can make. I always thought it was due to the style and material, not the color. I don't have anything near this except for that blouse Jeremy ordered. I wear white a lot."

"You probably should wear more pastels but not blue, that seems to bring out shadows under your eyes that aren't there with these other colors. This yellow would be good on you, too. Creamy butter, I think we should call it, don't you?" She tucked a piece of the bolt under Faith's chin.

"Now I don't know which to choose," Faith fretted.

"I know, Jeremy, and he would love to get you both." Picking up fabrics and laying them next to one another saying, "Now I think this for the dress since it has a better weight to it for the bustle and jacket with the creamy butter for a blouse, which will also go with your tan skirt. Let's see about another skirt in this rust colored brocade and another peach blouse but I'll make it from an entirely different pattern than the one you have already." Abby went on to explain the choices and how to make them look like several different outfits.

Faith was trying to keep up with all that Abby was saying as the seamstress pulled bolts of cloth out and then rejected them for something prettier.

"I don't want to spend too rashly right now since I'm not making much at the paper. Not until it gets more established," Faith told Abby honestly. "I've never had so many new things at once and never so many nice things."

"Well, then, I'm on the right track. Jeremy said to spoil you when you came in." She turned and began making a pile of lingerie. "You will need some stockings and let's get these white ones for the wedding day and here are some pretty peach ribbons to tie them up with. I have some shoes that will be perfect for these, too. Soft kid but stained a fawn color. I can have some made in your size and they will be here in a few days. I simply wire the size to Preston and a man there makes them to order."

"Oh, Jeremy will have my hide if I order all these things." Faith seemed worried.

"No, he won't. He tried to buy most of these things for you before and I warned him people might misunderstand. And Callie or Matthew would have come down on him. Possibly even convinced you to return to the ranch," Abby explained the previous conversation with Jeremy.

"I wouldn't have accepted anything like that from him, you were right. I mean, I had a difficult enough time to accept the skirt and blouse he ordered but then he said I could pay him back in installments as I got paid so, I took them. I really didn't have the right clothes to represent the paper to customers in the office. I already paid him some back but I think he lied to me about their price. I was going to ask you what they cost and then repay the correct amount."

"I know he was happy to buy you something you'd like. It's better than wasting money on hot house flowers or imported chocolates although those are nice to get, too," Abby confided.

Faith made her final selections and Abby said she would start on the dress that afternoon, promising all would be ready before the week was out.

CHAPTER 15

Mary Beth and Jessie were finally on their way back from the Macgregor ranch. He had gotten talked into staying for the midday meal and to meet and visit his new nephew. Most babies seemed the same to him. Too little to be good conversationalists, yet, and he never knew what to do with one when someone placed it in his arms. He nervously held Aileen until he found one of the fathers to palm her off on and then they all laughed knowing the baby would elicit just such a result.

"I know I've asked before and I promise from now on I'm only going to ask once a week until you decide to marry me. Here it goes - Mary Beth, will you marry me?" he asked as he effortlessly handled the reins of the buggy.

"Yes, Jessie, I will marry you," Mary Beth answered primly.

Jessie almost dropped the reins he was so surprised by the answer. "You will? Right away, I mean?"

"Yes, I will - right away if that's what you want," she said just as primly as the first time.

"I'm not complaining or anything but why are you finally saying you'll marry me?" he asked still not quite believing his good luck.

"I've been staying with your brothers and their wives for weeks now. Neither knew each other very well and the women took a big chance answering the letter Mac sent in response to their advertisement as a mail-order bride. Even if Mavis married Jamie, Mac found Emily and they are extremely loyal and loving to each other. If they could form this kind of commitment in such a short time, then we should be able to do so, too. After all, we've known each other for a lot longer than they did before getting married. Maybe there is such a thing as love at first sight or at least having a special attraction to someone at first sight. But we've been attracted to one another for almost a year." She tried to explain her change of mind but she wasn't sure of why she could no longer stand behind her refusal of him and marriage.

Much of it had to do with her staying with his family. Not that he was like his brothers but Jessie had bits of each of them in him. She could see Mac's strength of character and hard work ethic. Then there was Jamie's ability to grin and make everyone feel good and welcomed along with Jeremy's drive for the future and the potential it held for everyone. Jessie was all of his brothers and then none of them. He was his own self, as well, and she loved him for it.

She also knew from watching his brothers that these men knew their woman and allowed them the freedom to be what they needed to be. Just because Mavis and Emily wanted to be housewives and mothers didn't mean their husbands had ordered them into those positions. Mary Beth could see the women loved those roles and their husbands adored them. But she also thought the husbands would have adored them as well if they had wanted to do something else such as open a store in town or become a midwife.

All the things Mary Beth kept putting in the way of her happiness with Jessie were merely roadblocks which weren't needed. She didn't need protecting from Jessie. She was protecting herself from what she thought a husband would demand. Seeing Jessie as the man he is made her realize she was the only one keeping them apart.

During a rare time alone, Jessie confessed, "I knew that moment I saw you in the kitchen at Callie's, I was going to be your husband or die trying. I can't tell you how many times I confided in Rebecca, sitting on the side of that riverbank. At first, I didn't tell her who I was rhapsodizing over but she knew it had to be someone out near the ranches. She told me to keep trying, keep talking to you and never let too much time pass between seeing you."

"Well, I think you followed her advice to a T. Sometimes I felt like I was being haunted but I knew you were sincere and I finally believe you mean what you say. I could keep being a midwife and I could love you, too. They don't conflict. It was only in my mind that I couldn't have both, couldn't be that happy. To do good, I thought I had to sacrifice and you were my sacrifice but now I know I can do good deeds and not need to forfeit my life. A good Christian, a good Samaritan and a good wife." She smiled at him happily as she finally felt she had aligned her worlds.

"I should stop and pull off to the side of the road but I don't want to slow down. Kiss me and I'll get us back to town in time to talk with Reverend Walters. You wouldn't mind a double wedding with Jeremy and Faith, would you? They're having Father Manuel preside over their wedding ceremony."

"Let's ask Faith, first. I don't want to take anything away from her wedding day," Mary Beth said feeling as if she were on top of the world.

"I don't think they'll mind since they've teased me unmercifully about getting married on the same day.

This will make them think harder next time they try to goad me." He leaned over to give Mary Beth another kiss while maneuvering the team over the ruts.

The double wedding brought people in from all around, including the Harrison ranch. Charity acted as the maid of honor for both Faith and Mary Beth. Jamie was the best man since Mac refused to leave his wife's side and it was too soon after the birth for the new mother to make the trip to town.

Both Reverend Walters in his collar and Father Manuel in his black cassock and white Alb stood at the front of the church, the three brothers standing side by side next to them.

After Charity walked solemnly to the front of the church, Faith came down the aisle wearing the dress she had Abby make for her. Her smile was more beautiful than anything else as she saw her husband-to-be and walked to him as if in a dream. Mary Beth came next and she, too, wore a lovely dress sewn by Abby with a confection of a hat and a short veil. Her eyes glistened with unshed tears as she walked ever closer to the priest and her soon to be husband.

What could be better than to be married with her St. Michaels sister and both of them marrying Macgregor brothers? It would be a wedding of the season that was for sure.

After the ceremony, a very expectant Rebecca welcomed everyone to the parsonage for a celebration that Callie had furnished along with a lavishly decorated cake for each of the couples. Cakes that Charity admitted to being the main artist on. After a few hours both of the newlywed couples told the group they were leaving and Jeremy warned them there should be no shivaree or he would swear to get every single participant back in spades.

Jeremy and Faith walked back to the newspaper while Jessie and Mary Beth went to the house across the street from the little white church with the steeple.

Mary Beth was self-conscious until the last of the buggies pulled away and she knew there would be no one stopping by to give them congratulations one final time. Jessie sat on the sofa and pulled his bride down to his lap saying, "There, now we are all alone. If I knew this was going to make you nervous, I would have booked a hotel room for a couple of days."

"No, that would be worse. Everybody looking at us in the morning, knowing, ah, knowing, you know...." Mary Beth said, words fading into embarrassment.

"Mary Beth, married people do things with each other. That's why there are so many married people." He pulled her close, trying to ease her fears. "We can wait till you're more ready. My goal has been met. This next step can wait if you need it to."

"Thank you for understanding, Jessie. I really love you. I really want to be a wife but I'm afraid." She nestled into Jessie's chest as he sighed leaning back.

Jessie made little circles with his thumb on Mary Beth's arm and said thoughtfully, "Is it because you've seen childbirth that you fear the act? You know, the act that causes the babies?"

Mary Beth thought about it. She had a similar conversation with Rebecca when Callie first recommended Mary Beth as a possible replacement or helper for Rebecca when she and the Reverend married months ago.

"I don't think so. I mean I'm not linking the two

separate incidents. I think I'm afraid of giving you that much power over me, giving up my independence," she told him truthfully.

"Well, do you feel independent enough to kiss me? Right here, right now?" he teased.

Smiling shyly at him, she said, "I think I can manage that." She leaned in to kiss his mouth. Jessie held up his end and soon they were mouth to mouth, his tongue entering her warmth and receding. Her tongue mingling with his as he continued dueling with hers.

Jessie couldn't stop his hands from claiming the breast that was teasing him with its perkiness and he asked if he could take off the dress so it didn't get wrinkled. Mary Beth smiled at his offer and accepted, wanting to be more intimate with Jessie than she had ever been with anyone in her life.

Allowing Jessie to remove everything except the camisole, she tensed when he went to lift the bottom edge and he acquiesced to her unspoken request. He had discarded all but his shirt and trousers then sat back on the sofa, gently pulling Mary Beth's hand until she was back on his lap and laying against his chest once again.

"There, that's better, isn't it?" said Jessie settling into his role of husband.

"I'm sorry, Jessie. I know you've been so patient with me and you have these needs and I'm making you wait longer. I should never have married you." With tears in her voice she said, "It was a mistake."

"Mary Beth, if we've ever done anything right it is that we got married. Everything else can wait until you're ready. Don't worry about all the things you think you know. I know what is best for us, for me. Don't make decisions on what you think I need or want. I love you and what I wanted was to be married to you. Everything else will happen at its own time. You are in control, I promised you would be before you accepted my proposal," he said bringing her mouth back to his.

Jessie tentatively covered the breast and then leaned down and caressed the rosy tip with his lips, sucking it into his mouth and tonguing it to pebble hardness. Mary Beth accepted this attention and Jessie moved on to the neglected breast as she moved to accommodate his reaching the needy peak.

She had both arms around Jessie's head, holding him to her breasts letting him suckle one than the other. Her breathing increased rapidly and she was soon covering Jessie's mouth with her own, thrusting her tongue into his mouth while he accepted her ministrations glorying in the attention, she was bestowing on him. She moved so she could free Jessie from his still buttoned trousers.

Jessie in a daze of need prevented her hands from getting to their destination. "Mary Beth, are you sure? I can still stop if you give me a break. Let me calm down."

Mary Beth continued undressing Jessie, letting his erection spring free only to be grasped as she clutched the sheathed strength in both hands. "I want to feel your heart next to mine, your body next to mine, your body in mine." She positioned the velvet tip to her feminine entrance as she straddled his lap.

Jessie held his breath, unsure if he should be participating yet unable to turn Mary Beth away from what he wanted so badly. She covered Jessie's mouth with hers and lowered herself onto him, a soft moan filling his mouth as she settled onto him fully.

Unbelieving the intense emotions flooding through

him at being surrounded by his love at that moment, he closed his eyes. He felt every muscle in the warm satin channel. Mary Beth raised and lowered her body until Jessie thought he would lose control. As she finally stiffened, Jessie knew he could no longer hold back and poured his seed into her womb. His mouth covering Mary Beth's swallowed her cries of ecstasy.

CHAPTER 16

Jeremy and Faith sat in the apartment that would be their home until a house could be built on Second Street across from the rectory. He toasted his new wife with a glass of Champaign and she took a small sip from her glass, not used to drinking anything as fine.

Having taken off his coat, shoes and tie, he relaxed in his shirtsleeves and was comfortable being alone with Faith. They had already consummated their union but it seemed different now that they had said the vows. Consummating this wedding night was a very important part of their life together, forming the basis of their union.

"Are you afraid of me now, Faith? You've been on the move since we got home and I need to know," Jeremy asked quietly, urging Faith to confide in him.

Faith smiled, then said honestly, "I guess, I am. I mean, why should I be nervous of you? We've been together, the worst is over as Rebecca would say. I don't know why I feel as if you were a stranger." Her eyes pleaded for his understanding. "I don't mean to be difficult, Jeremy, I really don't."

"I hate the thought of you being frightened of me. No one cares what we do tonight as a couple and if all I get to do is sleep beside you in the same bed, the same room, I'll be happy," he said smiling, trying to relieve the worried expression from her face.

"Really? Sleep in the same room and you'll be happy?" She gazed at him doubtfully.

"As long as I can be close to you, I'll be content until

you want more. I trust our love. Trust you will want more eventually. I've been waiting all this time for you and I'll continue to." He raised his glass to her in a toast once again.

"Let's go to bed, darling, and possibly I can be persuaded to change my mind." She stood and led him to his bed where they undressed one another taking their time to learn each other's bodies.

Jeremy stopped to kiss every inch as he uncovered it. Faith took her time in studying and touching her husband noting what he seemed to like and enjoying his touching and kissing her. Faith soon knew they would be consummating this union this evening. All fear and coldness gone to be replaced with a heat and need to join with this man - soon.

Leading Jeremy to the bed, Faith lay on the new sheets pulling him down next to her. Jeremy didn't want to have Faith feel forced into doing anything, her previous attack present in his memory. He would let her lead and he would follow. He felt Faith had come to a conclusion but wasn't sure what his part was to be, at least not that night anyway.

"Faith, tell me what you want, honey. I want to please you but you need to let me know what you expect of me."

"Come and be my husband. I can't see us being anything else, darling. I'm sorry I started to panic and I can't fathom why, now. I guess it's true about bridal jitters but I thought that was before the wedding not after." She laughed into his chest.

Jeremy smiled knowing Faith was going to be all right and they were going to be good as husband and wife. Relaxing, he began to take more of a lead, to show

Faith how wonderful it could be between them. He continued to kiss her mouth and cupped her breast, kissing one to a peak followed by the other. Each time he was rewarded by Faith's eager pulling on his shoulders to be closer so he obliged.

He rolled onto Faith and was met by her spreading her legs as he rested between, his erection nestled at the apex of her thighs. Jeremy held his breath and moved to finally join with Faith - sliding into her moist, satiny passage. Faith's sharp intake of breath stopped Jeremy's forward motion immediately but she hugged him to her. Lifting her hips, she urged him to continue the rhythm he had begun.

Together Faith and Jeremy created a breathtaking meeting of their bodies culminating in a crescendo together. He felt Faith's internal muscles milk his seed from him as he spent into her.

Jeremy moved off his wife taking his weight from her but stayed tightly to her side. "Oh Faith, you're going to be the death of me. I'm not sure I can take too many of these nights, honey. I can't catch my breath, even yet." He rolled toward her and kissed her lips, pouty with passion.

"I didn't know it was so all consuming. I can't believe I was afraid of this, of you. I love you, Jeremy, and I'm sorry I wasted so much time." She pulled him to her once again.

"I think we were paying our penance but not any longer. We are bound to one another for the rest of our lives and you are part of my family, part of my life. I couldn't be happier, believe me, Love."

"I like the sound of that. I now have more family. I didn't give up anything. I gained. I love you, Jeremy, and

I always will. I am so glad I came to Sweetwater. I would have missed you if I hadn't." She clutched at Jeremy to make sure he was staying with her.

"I would have found you, honey. Somehow, somewhere, I would have found you." Kissing his wife, he knew it to be true.

There's Always Hope

CHAPTER 1

Matthew spotted the young woman moving along the Sweetwater depot's platform as he waited for a delivery. She wore a sky-blue two-piece dress with fashionable bustle trimmed with satin ribbon and lace around the tight collar and at both cuffs, which were buttoned tightly up to her elbows. He noticed these things because his wife, Abby, was a dress designer and he had sold ladies fine under-apparel for years.

He watched the pretty, blue-eyed blond with a sweet smile that lit up her face. Her hair was piled high on the top of her head with golden curls spiraling down the back of her neck and topped by a small hat with imitation sweet cherries perched on the brim. Lace gloves covered her hands and a beaded reticule bounced up and down as she joined and hugged two other squealing, young ladies about the same age.

The two welcoming ladies were nicely dressed, also. One in a stylish peach satin shirtwaist and tan linen skirt. Her golden-red hair tucked under a hat except for a few soft curls that escaped appearing more stylish than any in San Francisco. The other waiting woman wore dark brown curls on top of her head, a wide smile and a rose-pink dress with a waterfall bustle, round neckline trimmed in lace with pearl buttons down the bodice. Her hat wasn't much more than feathers and netting but it looked charming bobbing up and down as she talked excitedly with the other two.

Matthew watched the three women and smiled, enjoying their apparent pleasure of being together again. He tipped his hat as he passed but was more interested in the young boy, he was now ushering in front of him. The boy, a mulish expression on his face, twisted away from Matthew's hand on his shoulder and stomped down the steps of the train platform.

Matthew said, "Behave yourself. You could have stopped and talked with the young ladies. They're practically your sisters."

"I don't have no sisters," the boy said belligerently.

"You don't have any sisters," corrected Matthew.

"That's what I jist said! Don't have sisters. Don't need any." He walked in the direction Matthew again steered him.

The three girls were giggling and Hope, the newcomer, teased her oldest friends. "I can't believe you are both old married ladies now. Remember when we all decided we would stay together always and never do anything so mundane as get married, Faith?"

Both Mary Beth and Faith laughed, then Faith said conspiratorially, "Well, Charity, is joining the matrimony group, also, if I'm not mistaken. She met and fell in love with a very nice man who works for Callie at the Harrison ranch. I met him when I worked out there as a cook before I moved into town to work at the newspaper."

"Will is one of the nicest of men, he will be very good to her. He's very much in love with her and I was jealous until I realized I had a man as crazy in love with me," admitted Mary Beth.

"So, you really married brothers? Are they alike?" asked Hope.

"Not really, but they are both handsome and tall and charming in their own way." Faith explained the husbands as best she could.

"And tenacious," added Mary Beth.

"And set in their ways," concurred Faith nodding making her curls bounce.

"And controlling, used to getting what they want," included Mary Beth.

"And we wouldn't have them any other way," said Faith as they all laughed.

The young woman, new to town, turned to walk with her friends and the image of perfection was lost. A large purple birthmark appearing like wine splashed across her otherwise porcelain skin covered the right side of her face from her eye to under the high collar of her dress.

Her two companions didn't notice the disfigurement that made others turn away in repulsion or even repugnance. Such actions only made the young woman pull herself up taller, draw on her self-confidence once again and give herself the talk the nuns gave her to explain why God made her the way she was. There was a plan and a reason – His plan. *'For I know the plans I have for you, declares the Lord, plans for welfare and not for evil, to give you a future and a hope.'* Her name wasn't Hope without a reason. She was part of the plan.

"Let's get Hope to her temporary residence until the schoolhouse is done in a few weeks. I'll send Andy back for your chest and boxes later," Faith said.

The three walked down the dusty Main Street toward the buildings lining both sides making up the fast growing town, past the construction site of the new bank and then onto the wooden boardwalk. Faith explained the dress shop was owned by Matthew St. Michaels' wife,

Abby, and they had two adorable daughters.

"Will they be attending the school in the fall?" asked Hope.

"No, one is less than a month old and the other is less than a year. One is adopted but they say they can't remember which one," Mary Beth told Hope chuckling. "Anyway, I think that the little ones are what may be called job security in your profession. More children to teach in the coming years."

"I know from what Callie wrote there seems to be an abundance of babies being born and the town and surrounding ranchers were interested in getting the school set up now, before they all get to school age. Besides, a town this size and growing as it seems to be should have a school, maybe even one to prepare students for college," Hope said wondering where the children went to school now. She hadn't had much information before accepting the position. Callie's letter arrived at a most serendipitous time and Hope thanked her guardian angel and her namesake saint for coming to her aid when she was in need.

"There are some of the teens attending classes in other towns. I know all the Macgregor's went to college except Mac. He's my oldest brother-in-law and stayed and ran the ranch so the others could get further education in fields that interested them. He's quiet but one of the main supporters of the school. Even with beef prices depressed, he has contributed a lot of money already and his son is only a couple of months old," Faith imparted more family information.

"And he was one of the men who paid to have a midwife brought to town. Paid her way here, gave her a house to live in and paid her a monthly salary," imparted

Mary Beth.

"But I thought you were the midwife, Mary Beth?" Hope questioned, perplexed.

"I'm training under Rebecca Walters. She's due to have her first child and I've already been at one delivery with her and then delivered one on my own," Mary Beth told her friend with pride. "Actually, they were my two other sisters-in-law. I spent weeks out at the Macgregor ranch and both women are wonderful as are their very loving, protective husbands."

"My, it sounds like everyone gets married here and immediately starts a family," Hope said quietly.

"Yes, so don't be surprised when the men start lining up to court you," chuckled Faith.

Hope put her hand up to her face, blushing, and said, "I don't think that way anymore. I think I was made to teach other people's children. I'm happy to do so."

"I think you'd make a wonderful wife and mother. As the sister's said at St. Michaels Foundling Home, there's always hope," voiced Mary Beth.

Then Faith laughed. "Especially if they had a Faith and Charity to name at the same time." Referring to the habit of the sisters that ran St. Michaels to name any three girls the trio of saint's names whenever they happened to cross the orphanage's doorstep at the same time.

"When will I get to see Charity? Does she ever get into town?" asked Hope.

Mary Beth explained, "Will is bringing her in tomorrow so we can have dinner together and share a long talk. At some point, we'll get to take you out to the Harrison ranch where you can see Callie again and meet her husband, Seth, and her young son, Warren - another future pupil."

"We're here, home sweet home. At least until they finish the teachery attached to the schoolhouse." They stopped in front of a large window proclaiming it the home of the Sweetwater Chronicle and office to Jessie A Macgregor, Esq. Attorney at Law.

The three women entered the front room of the building and went through the short swinging door between the two front counters. There was a large printing press on one side and stacks of paper and cans of ink and grease on the other. The smell of ink followed them as they continued down the hall and stopped at the door on the left while Faith opened it for their viewing.

"This is where I was staying when I first came to town. Jessie let me have it as part of my wages for working on the paper with him. Now Jeremy and I live in the apartment upstairs but I expect you to feel free to use the kitchen and bath anytime you want. Meals are with us, of course. I'm sorry it doesn't have much room or privacy," Faith apologized as her gaze moved around the small room with single bed, dresser, wash stand and chair.

"I just came from a position where I shared a room with the daughter of the house, so this is privacy I haven't had in a couple of years. And the family I boarded with…the poor woman couldn't cook at all. I offered to help with the meals but she refused. The whole family is skin and bones, I swear, due to the poor tasting food, that which she hadn't burned to charcoal. I know the nuns taught you better than that, Faith." They all laughed with commiseration at Hope's past plight.

"Even better, Callie taught me so much in the few weeks I was there cooking for the ranch hands. I merely need to remember not to start with ten pounds of flour for biscuits and I have it made. Mary Beth was a cook there, too, so we share recipes," explained Faith as Mary Beth nodded in agreement.

"If you live upstairs, where are Mary Beth and Jessie?" asked Hope knowing Jessie owned the building they were standing in.

"I have the house that went to the midwife. Jessie and I live there but as soon as Jeremy gets time, he's building him and Faith a new house on Second Street across from the parsonage and one for Jessie and me next door," Mary Beth explained excitedly.

"There is so much going on. I thought I'd be going to a sleepy little town in the west and, instead, I get a growing metropolis," said Hope trying to keep track of all that was new and interesting.

"Not quite but we are growing in a good way, I think. We still have little crime and we have a big handsome sheriff if any banditos do try to come in," teased Faith.

"Faith, behave yourself." Admonished Mary Beth. "She's referring to our new friend's husband, Mason. His wife, Victoria, is new to Sweetwater and we all live here in town. Victoria's been helping Matthew and Abby take care of the two babies. Especially when Matthew goes out of town with his job as a travelling sales man. We'll have to visit Abby's dress shop. She has some lovely materials and all sorts of things I never thought to own. It makes me light-headed even to go in and sniff the air. It always smells of some sort of exotic flowers and spices," Mary Beth explained.

"And she has beautiful underclothing. I had never even seen some of the things before. The sisters would definitely have made me pray if they knew I had even thought about buying them. Actually, Jeremy did." Faith blushed as she realized what she had revealed.

Hope straightened and said sagely, "Well, I have a feeling I am much better off down here than upstairs. Newlyweds need their time alone or so I've been told." She smiled at her closest friend and then they both blushed a little and giggled.

A tall man with auburn hair and the greenest eyes Hope had ever seen came up behind the group placing a welcoming kiss on Faith's lips as she turned her head toward his in a similarly familiar greeting.

The two stared into each other's eyes a little longer than appropriate, sending silent messages between them when a discreet cough from Mary Beth shattered the interlude and Faith, blushing brightly, introduced her husband. "Hope, this is my husband, Jeremy, and the man responsible for getting you into your own home this summer."

"It's nice to meet you, Jeremy. I'm glad you make my friend so very happy," Hope acknowledged honestly now understanding why her friend seemed so besotted. This man was so attractive it made Hope almost wish she would meet a man who could love her.

"It's nice to meet you finally, also. And I'm glad to make your friend so very happy," he said smiling that devastating smile that showed off some hidden dimples. "I came in to pick up some plans for the school that I need to go over with the foundation diggers. You're more than welcome to come and visit the site but I warn you it may get a little dirty."

Jeremy waved goodbye with a sheaf of papers in his hand and left through the rear door.

Hope looked at her friends and said, not hiding her admiration, "And you got the brother, Mary Beth? I don't suppose there are any more?"

"Well, not unmarried. There were four and in less than a year they're all married. That's what I meant when I said there was always hope. None of us thought we'd be wed within a few months of arriving here. Mary Beth held out the longest but there are so many good hard-working men wanting a wife and family," Faith explained to her friend.

"So many that they'd even consider me, you mean," said Hope as she gazed at her reflection in the mirror, seeing the two-faced Roman god, Janus, that she was. One side of her face unblemished, perfect actually, while the other covered by a large red stain beginning under her right eye and covering her cheek, running down her neck to disappear under the collar of her dress.

Faith touched Hope's arm to get her attention from the mirror and meet her gaze. "I never meant that. I know you find it difficult to believe but I don't see you as the woman with the birthmark. I see you as the beautiful woman you are. Your birthmark is the same to me as your height or color of your eyes. A feature but it doesn't define you to me. You are so much more than that mark. I think there is a strong possibility a man in this town will think the same."

"I agree with Faith. Once someone knows you, the birthmark becomes secondary, not something of note," agreed Mary Beth.

"Then you didn't warn Jeremy about my face?" asked Hope anxiously.

Faith drew her eyebrows down in thought and said, "It never crossed my mind to do so. I mean, it's not something I thought about when I was telling him about us. The three of us growing up like three peas in a pod."

"Yes, but one of the peas has a worm," stated Hope bluntly.

"Hope, I know you won't believe me but only a fool would be stopped from seeing the real you by your birthmark," added Mary Beth.

To get the conversation back to a less worrisome note, Mary Beth said, "Let's go to my house. We'll pick up some ice from the butcher and have cold lemonade. Hmmm, I can almost taste it already." She slipped her arm through Hope's turning her toward the front door and the three ladies continued back out to the boardwalk.

CHAPTER 2

Matthew, still ushering the young man in front of him, called out as soon as he entered the shop full of ladies' fripperies and feathers. The young boy looked around in wonderment and awe but tried not to show it on his face. Seemingly, he tried putting on a blasé expression at the unexpected beauty and luxury surrounding him.

"Abby, I have a surprise for you," Matthew called to his ever-patient wife. Instead, Victoria, the new wife to Matthew's friend, Sheriff Mason, came through the curtained doorway blocking off the dressing room from the rest of the shop. She had light brown hair and grey eyes and was wearing a stylish shirtwaist and skirt that he knew Abby had sewn for her. She was carrying his oldest daughter, Grace, who squealed and held out her arms toward him.

He took her immediately, smiling at her and kissing her chubby baby cheek, giving her a loud smooch and making the baby laugh with glee. He turned to the young boy and introduced the two, "Victoria Maxwell, this is Thaddeus St. Michaels."

"It's jist Thad," he said as acknowledgement to the introduction.

"Is Abby out, then, or napping with the baby?" asked Matthew ignoring Thad's bad manners.

"She's across the street at the Mercantile. Some new trim was due in the mail and she's been checking on it daily. Hannah's napping but will be awake not too long from now. I think Abby will be back, anytime. She's had enough time for Helen to talk out all the gossip she has. With the newspaper printed each week, Helen feels she isn't listened to as often and wants to be the first to impart the news every day." She smiled at Matthew who lifted one brow, evidently glad it was his wife and not he who has to talk with Helen.

Just then his lovely brunette wife came through the front door wearing a vibrant ruby-red gown with a waterfall of bustles trimmed in black lace and black onyx buttons from the high collar down to the narrow waist. Her expression immediately turned into a wide welcoming smile as she saw Matthew standing in the middle of the shop. Carrying in two small packages, she set them down before greeting her husband.

Taking-in every detail about him in hungry exploration, she sighed. A tall, handsome man with black hair that curled onto his forehead much to his chagrin, wearing his typical three-piece black suit, white silk shirt, and black tie even in the heat of the day and donning a black wide-brimmed hat. His dazzling blue eyes fringed with thick black lashes returned her admiration.

She reined in her welcome in front of the others. "Oh, you're back early. How nice. I was missing you and Grace seemed to be, also. She kept looking toward the door and saying the same word." Abby went directly to her husband for a kiss and hug from his still free arm.

"I brought a surprise." He turned so Abby could see Thad standing at the side of the room. "Abby, this is Thaddeus St. Michaels. I brought him home to stay a while."

Without a moment's hesitation Abby extended her hand, saying, "Welcome, Thaddeus, I'm so glad you can stay with us."

"It's jist Thad," the boy said but with less hostility than before and self-consciously shook Abby's hand.

"Then I welcome you, Thad. I've a room upstairs for you but I'll need to move a couple of things off the bed. I always have so many projects started, I kind of sit things here and there," she explained.

Thad bent his head slightly. "That's all right, Ma'am. I'm not used to much so I can make do."

"I appreciate you being flexible, Thad. We have two young babies and they can disrupt the normal routine so that meals and bedtimes sometimes get postponed," Abby told him, liking the boy she thought she saw under the armor he wore for protection.

"I only eat once a day so it's no problem," the thin boy told Abby and a shy smile came across his face.

"Well, I make three meals and you're more than welcome to eat with us at every one of them," she told him, hiding her sympathy for his past plight. This was the first young boy her husband had brought home and she wanted to make him feel welcome.

Victoria began to open the packages and lay out the new ribbons and thread bobbins to be placed in a special rack Abby had made years ago. Thad came to see what was in the packages and asked Victoria a couple of questions which she answered in her friendly open way.

Matthew and Abby went towards the door leading to the kitchen downstairs and began talking quietly when a loud SLAP! ricocheted across the room. Both of their heads swiveled toward Victoria and Thad who had his hand up to his reddening cheek.

Victoria, with tears forming in her eyes, said, "I'm s-s-sorry. I've never hit…." And then she remembered fighting with her abductors, swinging at them with all her might and she broke down, sobs rending anything else she tried to say meaningless.

Matthew turned accusing eyes toward Thad who was now watching Victoria with a sad expression.

"Did you deserve it?" Matthew asked the boy.

Thad stood a little straighter and nodded, waiting for the additional blows he felt were also deserved for causing such pain to this pretty young girl.

Matthew, his lips tight with anger said, "Then apologize. Now."

Thad looked at Victoria, not totally understanding her distress, and said, "I apologize for my bad manners. I never meant to so disrespect you." Then he stood there completely unable to comfort the woman he had shown such bad manners toward.

Abby was able to quiet Victoria, reminding her that no one was ever going to get close enough to hurt her again. That Mason and Abby and Matthew and many others could always be counted on to come to her aid.

Victoria asked if she could go home and clean up but said she would come the next morning as usual to help with the babies and sewing. Abby agreed readily and they walked to the door together.

After she was gone, Abby turned to Matthew and said, "You had better explain to Thad a little of the past. I'm not sure what he said but it brought it all back to her with a vengeance." She took Grace from Matthew and went behind the curtain to where Hannah was still sleeping.

Matthew looked at Thad, a bright red handprint visible on his cheek. Matthew told Thad to follow him outside and Thad went warily, still unsure if he was going to get a beating for his poor choice of entertainment.

Once out back of the building, Matthew chose his words carefully. "A few months ago, Victoria was abducted twice by a gang of thugs that wanted to kill her and pass her body off as that of the gang's female ring-leader. So twice, on her own, she was left to deal with men who were the worst kind of evil. Both times the sheriff, who is now her husband, rescued her but not until she had been terrorized. Whatever you said brought that all back today. She had to relive that fear all over again. And as you can see, she's not completely over it." Matthew watched the young man's expression to see if he understood and if he empathized with Victoria's fear.

"I didn't mean anything. I was just, I don't know, trying to flirt, get her to like me. I didn't think she was that much older than me. She looks young even to me. I think she was all right until she slapped me and then she got scared. Before that I think she was just mad, reacting to my rudeness. It was after the slap that she kind of got so sad and cried," Thad said trying to make sense of Victoria's reaction.

"That may be but you have to learn to read people better and stop trying to flirt with married woman for God's sake. You're only fifteen," Matthew said exasperated.

At that, Thad jutted out his jaw and said, "I've been with a woman. I've been with plenty of women. I'm as much a man as you are," he threw out as a challenge.

"You're as much of a man as I was at your age but that's a little different from what I am today. I learned to read people and to know how far to push them unless I wanted to get a facer. I grew up fast and I know what you don't yet, so believe me when I say you don't need to prove yourself with anyone here."

"I was doing just fine in the streets. I can fight and I take care of myself. I don't need you to tell me I'm a kid," Thad said belligerently.

"I didn't say you were a kid. I said you still had some growing to do, both physically and emotionally. I'm giving you a chance to do that in a better place than I had. You left St. Michaels to be a man. Now show me you know what that means," Matthew told the young man standing in front of him. "Let's get cleaned up for the meal Abby's been putting together for us." He led the way to the sink in the back room of the shop.

Thad stood thinking for a moment and then decided Matthew had treated him as an adult and there wasn't going to be any other physical punishment. It was something that happened and it was done with. Thad would have to mull this conversation over as he got used to his new environment.

The next morning after breakfast, Abby went downstairs. Matthew told Thad, "I just heard Victoria come in. She helps Abby with some of the fine embroidery and baby clothes she sells. I'm watching the babies right now but you can go out if you want to investigate the town. Be careful around the construction sites, I don't want you getting hurt or in the way."

"Yes, sir," said Thad because it felt like it was what Matthew wanted him to say.

Once downstairs, he went into the shop where he could hear Abby and Victoria talking. Victoria was sitting in the chair, a small pile of cloth at her side and a needle in her hand.

"Good morning, Mrs. Maxwell, I hope you, er, feel

better today," he said hesitantly.

"Thank you, Thad. I'm much better today. I'm sorry for my outburst and you may call me, Victoria, unless someone told you otherwise." She looked towards Abby who gave a little shake of her head to indicate no one had.

"Matthew said I could go and look over the town," explained Thad not sure how he was supposed to treat these new people in his life but wanting to please Matthew for some reason.

"That will be fine, Thad. If you happen to go into the Mercantile will you ask Helen, she works behind the post office counter, if there is any mail for us? Oh, and while you're there they have a nice selection of readymade items including overhauls. I noticed you didn't have much luggage so if you find something you like, please feel free to have it put on our account. I can sew a few things for you later but, right now, I have all these garments needing to go out to the ranches. Their babies are growing as fast as mine and it's beginning to be an all-day project simply to keep up with them."

Thad mumbled his thanks and went out the front door to the main street. He saw the Mercantile across the way but hesitated going there. He had to think about accepting more charity from Matthew than he already had. Maybe there was a job he could do at the building sites or something to earn some money to help repay Matthew.

As he passed the newspaper office, he stopped and went in to ask if there were any jobs posted there or if they needed any help. When he entered, he recognized the woman behind the counter as one of the three at the train station. Now he was sorry he hadn't stopped and

171

been introduced. It would have made this a lot easier.

Faith looked up from the drawing she was doing and asked, "May I help you?" A warm bright smile lit her face.

Thad felt himself smile in return. "I'm new to town. My name's, Thad, and I was looking for work. I thought maybe there was a job posted in the paper or somewhere."

"Well, not actually in the paper. We're fairly new and still kind of small but let me ask my husband. He's in charge of the construction going on around here." She went down the hall behind her disappearing through one of the doorways.

Jeremy came out of a back office and looked Thad over, then asked, "Do you have any experience in the construction fields? Masonry or lumber?"

Thad felt disheartened but answered truthfully, "No, sir, but I'll do whatever you need me to do. I'm a fast learner and don't mind working long hours." He tried to look taller than he was.

Jeremy said, "I have some work you may be up to doing. You're going to get dirty but they're clearing the lot for the school at the north end of town and they could use another man to help move the dirt, pushing wheelbarrows and emptying them into a wagon. Maybe piling the bricks for the masons once they get here for the basement walls. Other jobs like that."

"I'll be glad of the work, sir. When do you want me to start?" Thad asked anxiously.

"Tomorrow morning, about seven. That will give me time to let the job foreman know you're coming." He stuck out his hand for the boy to shake.

Thad shook the proffered hand and smiled his

thanks. Once back outside, Thad couldn't believe his luck and continued down the street to look over where he would be working the next day.

In the newspaper office, Jeremy turned and asked Faith, "Are you sure he was with Matthew yesterday? He seems a little rough and tumble but he did speak well."

"Yes, Dear, I'm sure it's the same boy. He got off the train with Matthew and then they walked to Abby's shop." Faith assured her husband. "I'll stop by there and get more information but I know he's probably one of Matthew and Abby's orphans. I have a debt to repay for my good fortune and helping Thad may be one way."

Mason, the town's sheriff and Victoria's husband had been watching the dark shadow leaning against the building next door. Finally, tired of waiting, he got off the chair tipped against the jailhouse wall and walked over to the path between the two buildings.

Mason began friendly enough. "What's your business here, Wilder?" Then waited for the man dressed in all black, including the leather vest with silver buttons, to speak. His black Concho hat had several braided strings around the brim hanging down with weighted silver tassels. A shiny black revolver was holstered low on the man's leg, tied with another leather strap.

Wilder had high cheekbones and a straight nose, his dark hair was too long hitting past the shoulder of his shirt and his silver eyes had watched Mason approach.

He finished rolling his cigarette before he spoke, "Howdy, Mason. I was wondering when you'd decide to come over and welcome me." Then he put the cigarette into his mouth and lit it with a match scratched against the bottom of his silver tipped boots.

"This isn't a welcome. We don't need your kind of

trouble here. Sweetwater isn't in need of you and I don't want any ruckus going on." Mason's hand rested on his revolver, reminding Wilder he had a gun, too. "You just in town for the day?"

"No."

"Got plans of staying?" asked Mason, thinking it was like pulling teeth to get this man to let any information go.

"Yep," he answered, again not giving much away.

"I know you aren't registered at the hotel so are you camping outside of town?" Mason asked, now becoming impatient with the one syllable answers.

Wilder, tiring of the game, answered, "I'm renting a room over at Miss Lily's house. For some reason, the lady likes me." He grinned, showing off a bright white set of teeth the sun practically glinted off.

"Miss Lily likes all sorts of down and outers. I suppose you're going to take advantage of her," replied Mason looking over the Main Street and noting a young kid across on the boardwalk entering the newspaper's office. Must be the one Victoria told him about, another rescue of Matthew's. The boy didn't look like too much trouble but he'd have to keep his eye on him, too. Mason wasn't comfortable having all these new men coming into town but Sweetwater was expanding and new faces were just part of that.

Mason turned back to Wilder saying, "Just don't make me lose any sleep watching you."

Wilder flashed that same devilish grin before saying, "Oh, yeah, I heard you got married. I wouldn't want to be anywhere but sleeping if I had some one that fine in my bed."

"Watch yourself, Wilder. I don't take kindly to

anyone talking about my wife with less than respect." And Mason unconsciously took the stance of a gun shooter, spreading his legs and balancing on the balls of his feet, his right hand still on the holstered weapon.

"No, Mason, I clearly did not mean any disrespect. Just that a man's place should be beside his bride, that's all. I guess I'm a little envious is all. We, men like you and me, don't get the chance of that kind of happiness very often. I'm really glad you found a woman that suits you."

Mason relaxed but gave Wilder a glare that would have made a lesser man blanch, and repeated, "We don't need your kind of trouble here." Then he sauntered back to the jailhouse while Wilder turned and walked to the saloon.

CHAPTER 3

Matthew St. Michaels sat in the office of Jessie Macgregor, Esq., Attorney at Law, and read the legal documents that would govern the partnership the three men present were forming. Matthew's idea was to bring a distribution center as far west as Sweetwater to service the quickly expanding territories. Jeremy Macgregor was financial partner and would design and build the structure needed while Jessie Macgregor would be financial partner and managing officer.

"It looks fine to me, all the things we discussed are covered. I'm anxious to get the order placed for inventory since anything coming from overseas will take more than three months depending on the weather. Many of the items I order are out of the Far East, silk and perfumes, especially. We can lease some interim space in the ports until the building is done if we need to," explained Matthew as he signed the papers to confirm the verbal deal the men had made earlier.

"I've ordered the posts for the frame-work since that is milled per order. It will arrive by rail in a couple of weeks. I'll send the framing crew over when it gets here to start on it. The schoolhouse should be done rather quickly except for the interior, which will only need lath and plaster then trim carpenters. I think this will work out very well as long as we get the school's roof on by mid-July," Jeremy said going over the work schedule planned.

Jessie, the only blond in the family with blue eyes reminiscent of his older brother, Jamie's, said, "That leaves me with getting the catalog ready for print, maybe getting some negatives from the new photographer moving to town or from an agency in the East. Faith is good at drawing and we can use some of her work, too, although some things show better in a photograph."

"We'll work on it and use some of both. I have copy we can use that the papers used back East so that may help cut down on the work," Matthew said and stood, shaking hands with the brothers. "Here's to new opportunities for Sweetwater and our two families."

Mary Beth, Faith, Hope and Charity sat in the parlor of Mary Beth's home and giggled non-stop. The men had escaped to the cool of the porch to get away from their women's chatter and the tears of reunion that would grip the group every few minutes. Will passed on the news from the Harrison ranch and Jeremy passed on the news from the town council and about the new buildings going up at a rather rapid rate.

"I understand there's going to be a new business in town, too," added Jessie. "I received a wire about a photographer settling in Sweetwater hoping to be able to sell some photographs to the newspaper of any news worthy projects or even the local Indians. I guess the eastern newspapers can't get enough of the 'wild west' even if the Indian's are pretty much quiet here about."

"Yep, if he wants Indian news that's more likely to be in the Dakota Territory or maybe Idaho," added Will.

"I didn't send a wire back since it sounded like he's on his way already. It'll be nice to have another business open up, probably right on Main Street," explained Jessie.

"Maybe he'll need a place built and Jeremy can design that one, too," Will added with a grin.

Jeremy said honestly, "I don't know if I dare take on another building until I get these two finished and Matthew's distribution building started. I'm in charge from start to finish on the bank and school although that wasn't my original plan with the school. But if I can do it for the bank, I may as well do it for the school. It will be fun to see the whole thing come together, a building with a schoolroom that can be separated into two when needed and the living quarters for the teacher with a nice backyard attached to the backside."

Jessie, Jeremy's younger brother added, "To use the basement room for city council meetings and town socials when winter comes will be a bonus. I think we're all happy with the final draft and as you can see from here, the foundations and basement are being dug." All three men looked over at the cleared lot next to the white church with the steeple and nodded their agreement.

Mary Beth called the men in to eat, the dining room filled with the three large men and four petit women. Mary Beth said grace and the food was passed around until the plates were filled and the men ate heartily as usual. The meal of pork roast with rosemary and thyme was one Callie Harrison had devised for her ranch hands and had taught Mary Beth to cook.

After dinner and the clearing up, the group gave a long goodbye to Charity. Will drove the buggy toward the ranches to the north and the other three women soon said their goodbyes so that Jeremy, Faith and Hope could walk back to the newspaper building.

Hope told her hosts goodnight and went to her room while Faith and Jeremy went up the back stairs to the apartment. Jeremy didn't take long to help Faith remove her dress and then he kissed her shoulders and continued as each body part was unwrapped for his pleasure.

"I am such a lucky man, Darling. Sometimes I have to come find you just to make sure you're real and that you belong to me." Jeremy felt he was on shaky ground here but thought that his wife of so short a time knew his need to claim her as his own. To know they were to be together for all time.

"And I feel just as lucky, love. Remember I came to town to live out on the ranch with Charity and never thought I would ever have more. You gave me that chance and I will be forever grateful you didn't run from me after you had heard the worse." Leaning in, she accepted a long leisurely kiss.

"Nothing in your past was your fault. I don't want you to be grateful to me for loving you. I am so glad we met and you let me love you." He kissed her mouth with the passion that always built quickly between them.

"Then let's get into bed like decent people before we end up on the floor again. I don't want to shock Hope, after all," she teased her husband.

"I think you don't want to have her envious of you. I'm a damn good lover and I don't care who knows it," he teased in return and then kissed his way over her breasts to remain licking and sucking one rigid nipple.

"I'm the one that has to face her, you fool. Married or not, one does not flaunt what one has in front of others who do not have it." She enjoyed Jeremy's attention to the other breast, stretching and giving him ample availability of her entire body.

"I'll be quiet about it then and do my best to keep you from calling out my name in your passionate throes." He again teased his wife as she turned a becoming shade of pink to go with her red gold hair.

"You either behave yourself or we forego lovemaking until Hope moves into the school house." She asked innocently, "Sometime in August, wasn't it?"

"I'm not able to hold off for that long, Darling. I had a difficult enough time waiting for the priest to say we were married. I wanted to skip the party after the ceremony, let Jessie and Mary Beth have it all," he said sliding Faith under him as he stroked her into acceptance.

"I'm back to feeling so lucky I can't wait for you to join with me," Faith said quietly. So, Jeremy did as his wife wished, as he always did as she wished, and made love to her.

CHAPTER 4

Matthew was proud of Thad when the boy announced he would be starting work the next morning on the schoolhouse.

"I'll pay you back for the work clothes I put on your account as soon as I get my first wages. I don't think I'm being paid much but I'm glad Jeremy, ah, Mr. Macgregor, took me on. I plan on working hard so he doesn't dismiss me."

"How wonderful, Thad. I'll leave something out for your breakfast in case I'm busy with the babies but I can pack-up a meal for the midday meal along with something to drink. You need to keep drinking when you work out in the heat like that," Abby told him in her most motherly voice.

"You don't have to repay me for the clothes but I'm glad you found something so soon. It isn't easy finding work when you're young and there are grown men out there looking, although those job sites are putting a lot of men to work. Once the school year begins, though, I expect you to attend classes during the day. Maybe we can find you something part-time after school and week-ends," Matthew said making sure Thad knew education was important to him.

"I don't need to go to school. I can read and write, cipher some. I don't need more than that," said Thad trying to get Matthew to agree.

"We all need all the education we can get. The world's changing and we need to keep up with things. I was back East and you should see the gadgets and machinery they have doing all sorts of jobs men used to be paid to do. Mostly steam powered but they have others. It's amazing what man can find to invent to save a little work," Matthew enthused.

"I, for one, wouldn't be able to make half the clothing I do without my Howe sewing machine and the way lace is made by machine now has cut the price by more than fifty percent. We are living in an age where anything goes. Perhaps you can invent things, Thad. That's a job that is always around." Then Abby turned to wipe Grace's mouth as she squished mashed carrots out.

Thad thought seriously before saying, "I did kind of like the press or whatever it was in the newspaper office today. It looked like it had a lot of parts and I was trying to figure out where do you get all those parts to make that one machine? I mean, do you get a smithy or something to make up what you need?"

"Actually, there are a lot of machines now that make those parts for other machines. Someone had the inspiration to fill a need for others, like barbed wire. It seems so simple now but a few years ago, we had a heck of a time keeping cattle where they belonged. They were constantly being startled into a stampede over the littlest things and then scattering far and wide, ruining crops along the way," Matthew explained.

"Now, I'd like to see a machine that washed the dishes and pots. That's an idea that would really win you a prize, Thad. Every woman in the U. S. would purchase one from you." Abby stood to start clearing the table.

Matthew grabbed Grace. "Will you help Abby clear, Thad?" And carried the baby into the parlor where the open windows brought in a little cooler air.

"Yes, sir," Thad answered and proceeded to clear

while Abby began the washing up.

Later that night at the sheriff's home, Mason nuzzled his wife's hair. "I love the way you smell." When she giggled and tried to step away, he prevented her by merely placing a hand on her breast and inhaling deeply again.

"You are such a man," she said as if that explained it all but stayed where she was enjoying his total pleasure at having her close to him, noticing his reaction to her as he pressed into her.

"Hmmm, I do like the way you smell." And he continued to rub his face over her neck and then down the front to the tips of her breasts just barely covered by the nightgown Abby had given her for her wedding night a few weeks before.

His mouth sought the rosy peaks and he suckled as a babe would at some point in their lives. But right now, Mason took the advantage, picked up his wife and carried her to their bed. He lay down beside her still wearing his buttoned trousers and proceeded to find more interesting spots on her body to enjoy.

Soon his clothes were on the floor and the two were reminiscing with parts they were learning by heart. Victoria gloried in Mason's love and passion that had taken fire so quickly between them. Almost too quickly considering he thought she had been involved with a gang of thieves and killers when he first saw her. His rescuing her twice from abductors finally made him realize that to protect her, she had to be under his watch and that meant in his bed. They had both found the thought more than welcome.

The two reached their culmination together, already learning the moves that excited, brought each other to a peak and then gentled their partner. Victoria, her nightgown now on the bedroom floor, snuggled into the curve of her husband and fell asleep.

The thought going through Mason's mind just before he fell asleep was not very generous - 'up yours, Wilder. I've got a fine woman to wife and you're going to have to pay for yours the rest of your days'.

Thad got up just as the sun was rising. He went quietly into the kitchen to get the breakfast biscuits Abby had left out for him and filled the jar with fresh water to take to work. He could hear the babies and Abby moving around in their room so took the sack with his noon day meal and went down the stairs to start the first real day of work he had ever had.

When Thad got to the school site, it was already bustling with men and tools. He went up to the man who looked to be in charge.

As soon as the man glanced up and saw him, he said with a German accent, "You must be my new barrow man. Just grab a wheelbarrow over dare and get in line. Do you got gloves?"

"No, sir." Thad felt he'd shown himself as a novice right from the start.

"Better pick some up by tomorrow," the large foreman told him.

As Thad nodded, he got the single wheeled barrow and followed one of the other men going to pick up a load at the bottom of the new excavation. There was amity between the men on the site, many having worked together since the start of the basement. The men at the bottom were called the gravediggers while the men carting off the dirt were being called dumpers. Thad liked he had been included in the men's camaraderie and was careful to keep up with the others, doing his fair share of the dumping.

Just before midday break's whistle, Matthew showed up with a worn pair of leather gloves like the ranch hands used and handed them to Thad.

"Abby thought you might need these since it seemed likely you'd be doing some of the rougher jobs. Seems she was right," he said smiling and watching the men now all going to sit and pull out their meal pails, drinking from bottles and jars brought from home.

Thad accepted the gloves. "Thanks, they might stop some of the blisters but I already have a few. My hands will toughen up as I keep working. It will just take time," he said wisely.

Matthew looked at the young boy. "I'll see you at supper, then." And left Thad to eat with the seasoned workers knowing it would be good for the lad to be treated the same as all the others.

Hope was sitting with Faith and Mary Beth in Mary Beth's house. Hope was looking at her friends and asked again, "You're telling me that Miss Lily, a woman who runs a brothel here in Sweetwater, has offered to help me? I don't understand how she even knows about me."

"I think I might have mentioned your arrival," Faith confessed but not telling how many people she let know another single young lady was coming to town. "I mean we were all excited and then, I think, she saw you going into or out of the newspaper."

"I don't feel I should get involved with her. You don't understand how easily a teacher's reputation can be compromised and for little to no reason. Even being seen with a man who isn't a direct relative can be grounds for dismissal," Hope said seriously.

"Well, it isn't quite like that here. I mean, Miss Lily has done the hair styling for most of the women in town as well as sang at their weddings," explained Mary Beth.

"Really, she sings at weddings?" asked Hope skeptical of how innocuous the woman sounded.

"She plays the organ for church services every Sunday, too. I think if we went with you, no one could say anything rude about us visiting Miss Lily during the day," agreed Faith.

"She told me she was once on stage. You know, the theatre in New York and San Francisco, where she sang, danced and acted in plays. That's where she picked up her skills," Mary Beth explained to Hope.

At her friend's knowing smiles, she said, "No really, I mean about working with styling hair and dresses and things like that. The other I think she learned on her own." They all laughed at Mary Beth's blushes.

"If you're sure it won't be seen as something bad, I'll visit her and see what she thinks she can do to help," said Hope grasping at the sliver of a chance the discoloration of her face may be gone or, at least, diminished.

The three young women finished their tea, then Mary Beth put her hat on and they walked around the corner to Miss Lily's, climbing the front steps and knocking lightly on the door.

An attractive older lady with white hair done in a very intricate style bid them to enter. In a pleasantly refined voice as she swung the door wider for her guests, she said, "Come in, dears. We don't have any clients this early in the day, I assure you. Please have a seat. Can I get you some tea and cookies?"

Mary Beth, who knew Miss Lily best or at least the

longest, spoke for them all. "No, thank you. We just finished a whole pot trying to build-up the courage to walk over here." She smiled at the kind older woman to soften the words.

"Well, I understand that. This house or, at least, its reputation can be quiet daunting but really very little excitement happens under this roof. Merely comfort and cookies for single men in need, no more than that really. Only perhaps, I have said too much." Miss Lily turned to Hope. "You're Hope St. Michaels, I presume. I really shouldn't talk too much business around an unmarried young lady. Please forgive me."

"We came because we thought, well, someone said you thought you could make Hope's birthmark less noticeable. We, I mean Faith and I, don't notice it but Hope seems to think men find it repulsive," explained Mary Beth.

"I can see that you would think that, Hope, and at first it may be startling to many, especially if they approach you from the left side and then see the darker pigmentation on the other. I have worked with similar and although we can't do anything about ridding your face of the mark itself, my experience of making young actors look old and old actors look young has taught me much about fooling the human eye," Miss Lily told the young women.

"So, you think you can cover it up? I've tried but it smears or sweats off and looks worse than when it started," Hope said despondently.

"I use a mixture of theatre make-up and casein paint." At the expression on Hope's face Miss Lily added, "It's completely safe. I've used it myself for weeks at a time. Casein is merely a milk-based paint and

187

we can use it to cover the mark. Let me have a closer look, if I may."

Hope turned the right side of her face toward Miss Lily as she said, "Oh, Hope, this is good. Your skin is as smooth as silk, the discoloration is simply that, just under the skin. The make-up I am suggesting can be applied daily by you and if you wish to wear a lower cut dress you can cover that portion, too."

Hope peered at her two friends and they were both clasping their hands under their chins and smiling for her good fortune in having Miss Lily mixing up a concoction to cover her birthmark. They were happy for her but she was unsure what she felt.

"Can you all come back tomorrow afternoon? I should be able to have what I need and then I'll want to match the color to your skin tone which is flawless, my dear. I rather think of it as porcelain, quite pretty and has a slight pink undertone. I think I can match it very nicely," Miss Lily said letting go of Hope's chin.

As they were standing to leave, Mary Beth and Faith said their goodbyes to Miss Lily. Hope's gaze was drawn to a man watching her through a partially open kitchen door. His eyes were startling in their intensity, a flash of silver cutting the distance between the two of them. Hope glanced away then back but he was gone, only the closed door greeted her.

Turning back toward the others, she said her goodbye and the three young women returned to Mary Beth's house, talking all the way there about what had recently happened. Well, two of them were anyway.

Hope was lost in thought trying to concentrate on whether she really saw a man with silver eyes staring right at her from Miss Lily's kitchen or was it some kind of fantasy or vision. Miss Lily had said there weren't any customers in the house. Trying to shake the memory from her mind, Hope began to talk of finding the books and items needed for the school. Faith said she would speak with some of the sales representatives who stopped in at the newspaper to see if they knew the best places to get readers and other books at a decent price.

Faith and Hope walked back home together and then fixed dinner. Jeremy came home from the bank site and took off his coat, placing it over a chair. He kissed Faith on the lips and then smiled at Hope.

"Smells wonderful, ladies. I'm a lucky man." He looked at his wife with a silent message.

They all sat down to enjoy their supper together but no one mentioned the trip to Miss Lily's. Hope was quiet, still lost in thought trying to remember ever seeing the man from the kitchen doorway before. Some far-off memory teasing at her subconscious.

Thad climbed the stairs to the apartment over the dress shop slowly, feeling muscles he never knew he had. His hands were so sore he couldn't make a fist. No wonder men who had jobs didn't street fight. They were too sore and tired, to do so. As he reached the top, he saw Matthew holding Abby close to him, his face against her neck. Thad tried to scuff the step but remembered he left his shoes at the back door because they were so dirty. He found himself upon them before he could make a noise.

Matthew stood up straighter but didn't push Abby away or jump back from her. He was unembarrassed being caught in a tender moment.

"Well, what do you feel about your first day of construction work? Going to go back tomorrow?" Matthew asked with a grin.

"Sure, there's three more days in the week left. I can make it. The other men told me my hands will toughen up with more work and everything else is fine. I'll get used to it," Thad assured them.

Abby moved out of Matthew's embrace and went to the stove to stir the stew and dish up supper. "Come and get some food and then I can give you salve for your blisters and scrapes."

Thad sat down heavily and began to eat but didn't eat with much enthusiasm being too tired to enjoy the tasty beef stew and fresh bread. He drank three cups of coffee and a glass of water and then asked to be excused.

Abby and Matthew glanced at one another and smiled in commiseration with his pain. She rose from her seat, bringing Thad the salve and offered to help him. At his blush, she offered Matthew's help but Thad declined both.

That night as Matthew hugged his wife to him, he said, "Well, do you see us as parents of a teenaged boy?"

"It came a little sooner than I thought but I think we can help him find his way and that's all any parent can hope for, isn't it?" answered Abby nestling her behind into her husband as they laid in the bed together.

"I guess. It just seems too easy. This kid was real trouble in Three Rivers. His name being St. Michaels was the only thing that had the sheriff calling me instead of arresting him. I hope the move out of a bad area into Sweetwater will make the difference for him."

"He had some good basics. He was at St. Michaels and the nuns' influence during a very important part of his life. Let's hope their teachings and us placing some faith in Thad's basic goodness he'll be able to find his way. Grow into the man he can be proud of," replied

Abby sleepily.

"When will we be able to, mmm, resume our activities? I really find I need you lately. You know, closely." He stroked Abby's back from waist to thigh.

"Rebecca said not yet, but perhaps I can help if you'd just move over this way and I can get very, very close to you," she offered.

Matthew gave a contented sigh. "Not exactly what I was hoping for but damn near to it."

CHAPTER 5

The three young women, Faith, Hope, and Mary
Beth walked with more confidence toward Miss Lily's
this afternoon. They were sure the one-time actress had
the covering cream to help Hope feel better about going
out in public, moving among strangers who wouldn't
stop and stare or whisper. And maybe some man would
talk with her long enough to find out what a wonderful
person she was and how much love she had to give. All
these thoughts were going through the three women's
minds as they climbed the steps to the front door.

Miss Lily opened the door as she had yesterday and
welcomed the young women. There was a plate of
cookies on the side table and a pretty woman in a
summer dress with a double flounce around the bottom.
Her light-brown hair was pinned up on top with several
large rolled curls hanging down in the back. She gave a
shy smile but didn't meet the young women's gazes as
she brought in the pot of tea.

"This is, Lacy. She steeps the best tea I have ever
had," Miss Lily said.

The three young women nodded their heads in
acknowledgement but didn't quite know what to say to a
woman who lived in Miss Lily's house. Some questions
were completely off the table and others seemed too
personal so, they smiled and agreed the tea was indeed
the best they had ever had too, and they weren't lying.

Miss Lily picked up a small jar saying, "This is what
I came up with but I can alter the shade a little. Now the
mixture won't last long so try to keep it as cool as

possible. It will probably be good for about a week or so. When it begins to have an odor then I'll mix up another batch. It only takes a few minutes."

"I appreciate this very much but I'm not sure I feel right about using it. I mean it's like lying to people, isn't it?" Hope asked worriedly.

"Well, we women do that all the time. I mean, we wear corsets to lift up certain parts and hitch in others, we add hair pieces to enhance our own, we pinch our cheeks to bring a becoming blush and then we behave the way society dictates simply so we won't be ostracized. It's all a type of lie, I suppose," Miss Lily explained her philosophy of life.

"When you put it like that, I guess it's not much different. I'll have to think about using it daily especially around the children," Hope replied.

"Let's try it, my dear. I'm going to use this little piece of damp sponge and simply pat this on like so." Miss Lily started at the top edge of the discolored skin under the eye and worked downwards. "I dip it lightly in this water if it gets too dry and then into the jar and then pat, pat, pat until the mark is hidden. There. Look in the mirror and tell me what you think."

Hope opened her eyes, which she had closed at the beginning of the process. Standing, she faced the mirror she knew was on the parlor wall. She stared at the woman in the mirror and for the first time was able to view her whole face. She looked like her friends. She looked young and pretty and her smile showed her lips for once as a separate part of her instead of disappearing into the purple haze that was her skin.

"Oh, I look so different. I look so normal," she said lifting her hand to her face but hesitating to touch it.

"It will be dry in a moment and won't smear off. It may sweat off in hot weather but then merely pat it back with a damp sponge and it should look good as new," assured Miss Lily admiring her handiwork in the mirror's reflection.

Faith said breathlessly, "Oh, Hope, it's better than I ever expected. You look as I knew you always could."

Mary Beth simply sat there smiling and holding her hand to her trembling lips.

"Thank you, Miss Lily. Whatever I decide, I appreciate you showing me what I would have looked like if I had been born normal. My parents wouldn't have thrown away a daughter who looked like the woman in the mirror. I know they wouldn't have. It makes me grateful for the friends and the nuns who cared for me even though I was disfigured." Tears were rolling down her cheeks, both of the now perfect looking cheeks.

Miss Lily placed a clean hankie into Hope's hands and saw that everyone, including herself, was in tears. Tears of happiness for Hope's new face and tears of sorrow for a girl who thought her value was tied to her marred skin.

Soon after another cup of tea and a cookie, the friends were conversing with Miss Lily, Lacy and Stella, the other lady at Miss Lily's. As they were rising to leave, Hope felt someone watching her and looked toward the kitchen door thinking herself a fool for even considering such a man actually existed. She found those same glittering silver eyes watching through the small opening of the door, staring straight at her. Ignoring the other women in the room. Hope turned away self-consciously then remembered her reflection, lifted her chin and glared right back at the man in the mirror's reflection.

He grinned, a white flash across his face then tipping his hat, let the door close between them.

Hope hurriedly picked up her brocade reticule now holding the precious jar of cream and repeated her thanks to the ladies of the house. Soon all three younger women were walking back to Mary Beth's house right around the corner on Main Street.

Faith returned to the newspaper office and Jeremy. Mary Beth waited for Jessie then the three had dinner together. Hope tried to give each of the newlyweds some private time, dividing her time between them both in the evenings evenly, one with Mary Beth and husband, Jessie, and the next with Faith and Jeremy.

Neither would allow Hope to merely sit in her room, even when she claimed the need for a quiet read. Hope was walking home from Mary Beth's when she felt that other presence again.

She saw a red glow near the side of an unoccupied building and turned quickly, ordering firmly, "Stop following me."

A shadow became a man as the stranger took a step into the moonlight. The glint of his eyes confirmed who the man was while he asked, "Do you always know when you're being followed?"

"That's a stupid question. How would I know when I'm followed if I never see anyone? But I do know that you're following me and now I want to know why," she demanded unafraid of confronting this man in the dark.

"I'm not following you as much as watching you," he said casually in his deep, rich baritone.

"That is not a comfort to me. The question was why," Hope demanded again facing her demon in the dark.

"Can't a man find a lady fascinating?" came the flip reply.

"No, not me, so why do I keep finding you where I'm at?"

"It's a small town."

"All right, now I'm becoming angry. I am going to talk with the sheriff tomorrow and we'll see if he thinks you are as innocent as you want me to believe." She turned to step around him.

"If you answer me one question, I'll tell you why you interest me so much," the handsome stalker replied.

Hope was a little intrigued and not half as afraid of this man as she should have been. "All right, what is the question?"

"Do you know Jose' Vargas?" he asked straight out.

"No."

"No one by that name in Appleton where you just finished teaching?"

Unsurprised he knew where she was from, she answered again, "No, did he have children at the school? They must have had a different last name then. And that is two questions."

"Well he's a real bad man and he has the…he is very interested in you and I am interested in him. There's a reward out for him, dead or alive, and I plan on earning that reward," he stated calmly.

"But I don't even know him and almost no one knows where I went. It was after school was out for the summer that I decided to come to Sweetwater. Just the family I boarded with knows where I am."

"I might have let it be known you were here. I wanted Vargas to be able to find you so I could find him," he said trying to make her understand her position. That she was in danger due to his drive to see Vargas behind bars.

"You're using me like bait, like a piece of cheese in a mouse trap," she accused almost hissing in her anger at this new disruption in her life.

"Well, Babe, I wouldn't put it just that way. I'm here protecting you. You should show a little gratitude," he said and she could hear the smile in his voice, his rich velvety voice.

"I would not need protecting if you had not set me up to get found. And don't call me, babe. It's, it's, it's disrespectful," she finished lamely.

"Sorry, Miss St. Michaels, and I am sorry now that I ill-used you. I should have devised another way to lure Vargas to me, stayed in Appleton till he showed up from his hide-out," he admitted honestly.

"Now I don't know if I want you watching me or simply leave to find this Vargas in some other way," Hope said aloud, wondering what the best way to handle this new information would be.

"I can't stop the wheel now that it's rolling, Ba, Miss. I've got to stay on you or hang you out to dry, so to speak. I'd rather watch over you till I can rustle up Vargas," Wilder explained.

"I guess I can't stop you but I won't sleep very well from now on. I sleep in a downstairs room and the others are a distance away." Before she could think of the wisdom in telling this dark stranger such personal information, he spoke again.

"I can teach you how to shoot a gun. I take it you don't know how and haven't got one." Wilder offered the only self-protection he knew.

"I don't know about that. I don't think I could shoot anyone," Hope admitted doubtfully.

"You will surprise yourself at what you can do when you're protecting your life or that of others. What if you get attacked in the schoolroom, the children unprotected? Would you be able to shoot someone then?" Wilder asked reasonably.

She whispered, "When? When can you teach me?"

"Meet me tomorrow afternoon behind the livery stable. I'll bring a pistol for you." Then tipped his hat before sauntering toward the livery.

Just after noon the next day, Hope found herself walking toward the livery. She nervously wiped her hands down the simple blue print skirt with a wide flounce around the bottom, dusting the path with each step. As she arrived on the far side of the stable, she could easily see Miss Lily's and the well-worn path between the two buildings.

Then she saw the stranger, well not a stranger but Hope still didn't know his name, standing in the center of the barren lot.

Altering her direction, Hope walked up to the man, head high and birthmark covered with the special lotion.

She thought Wilder knew exactly where she had been the whole time but took this opportunity to look her squarely in the face and then flashed a grin that made her heart literally skip a beat. Hope took a moment familiarizing his whole face - black hat with silver tassels shading dark brows over those piercing silver eyes and high cheekbones, straight nose leading to sensuous lips, lips made for kissing. Hope realized he was studying her as closely. She was glad she had succumbed to her vanity and used the cream Miss Lily had given her.

"I don't even know your name," said Hope who had worried over that void all night.

"It's Wilder."

"Thank you for helping me, Mr. Wilder," Hope said in her best schoolmistress voice.

"It's just, Wilder." Then continued with his first lesson. "The first thing I want to show is how to make yourself difficult to abduct. You're little but there are ways. Scream your guts out even before they touch you. You want attention from others who may come to your aid. If a man grabs you, like this…."

Grabbing Hope from behind around the waist, Hope immediately tried to pull his arm away and struggled as he pulled her backwards toward the stable. "By fighting me, you're actually helping me move you along. You keep stepping back with me and taking your weight on your own legs. Now listen to me. It will be hard to do because it's against your natural leanings, but drop, let all your weight lean into my hands. A dead weight is difficult to move - even someone as light as you are. I have to drag you and that gives you time to think about when you can make a run for it. Pretending to faint is a good plan, then run when the abductor thinks he doesn't have anything to worry about."

"Like this, then?" Hope went limp, making Wilder bow down with the extra weight suddenly in his arms.

"Exactly, just drop and that throws the abductor's balance off." Wilder said as he stood Hope back on her feet.

Lowering her gaze, she watched as the dark stranger continued taking a gun from his waistband. "All right, I chose this pistol because it's not too heavy but big enough to get the job done. The longer the barrel the straighter the bullet will fire. The closer you are to your target the better your aim will be. The barrel gets hot after its shot so always hold it by the handle. Now I'll show you how to load it."

Hope watched avidly as he flipped the gun and the cylinder opened to display the holes, chambers, where each bullet fit. Six, there would be six chances of shooting someone, of killing someone. No, not merely anyone, but someone who is trying to hurt her. Hope had to think of this as protection, not as maiming or killing anyone. If they didn't come after her, she wouldn't shoot at them. Shaking herself, she tried to concentrate on the lesson.

"Now take the weapon in both hands...there's nothing wrong in using two hands. You're not going to be graded on stance so take the pistol and point the barrel toward the cans I have lined up over there." He glanced over at a board lined with cans set up away from the town and buildings.

Turning her body to face the direction he indicated, she held her arms out straight toward them turning her head to avoid the noise and smoke she knew firing would cause.

"Not like that, you'll shoot him in the foot, if at all. Aim a little higher." Wilder critiqued her aim.

Hope raised the pistol but again turned her head and the barrel lowered.

"If you shot now, you'd take the guy's manhood. Lift it higher, at least give him a break," he said teasing her.

Wilder came up right behind Hope and brought both his arms around her, covering her hands with his own darkly tanned ones. His body was almost touching hers and Hope began to tremble. Wilder pulled her tightly into him. "Don't let your emotions get the better of you or you're dead. Now brace your feet, spread them to take an even amount of weight and put your finger over the trigger."

Hope had stopped trembling once Wilder began giving her directions without indicating there was anything between them other than the lesson. He was holding her to help her learn how to protect herself, nothing more. She wasn't a woman to him. She was a student.

Taking a deep breath, she lifted the weight of the pistol and tried to sight down the barrel.

Wilder corrected her. "Lift the gun and let it be an extension of your arm. You're pointing toward something and when you fire the bullet, it will go in a direct line from that point. You don't have to take aim with a pistol, lift it, point at what you want to shoot and pull the trigger. Now pull the trigger." And Hope did, unconsciously closing her eyes as she did so.

The blast of the shot was a surprise. Hope jumped dropping her hand, clutching the gun with her finger still on the trigger. Wilder grabbed the weapon and pointed it where it couldn't do any damage.

"Not bad for a first try, Babe. Let's see if we can keep it in the county this next time."

"I shouldn't be trying this. I'm going to hurt someone by accident. This simply isn't me," Hope sighed in despair.

"Now don't quit on your first try. It takes a little time to get used to the noise and smoke and smell. You need to use all the bullets today, at least, so you won't jump like that when the shot goes off. Now try again. I'm right behind you and I'll help steady your arms."

Hope extended her arms, seeing that the barrel was pointing toward the cans and placed her finger on the trigger, then keeping her head up and closing her eyes, she pulled the trigger.

This time Hope didn't flinch as much and was actually used to the explosion coming from between her own hands. She opened her eyes to see all the cans still in place and then lowered the pistol and looked toward Wilder who was nodding his head.

"There, you see that bullet went right between the two cans on the end. Nice shooting, Babe."

Pressing her lips together, she lifted both arms again, took aim as far as selecting a can to shoot at and tried not to close her eyes. She pulled the trigger and fired. The bullet missed the cans but did hit into the fence post the board was sitting on. The sound of splintering wood followed the louder blast of the shot.

Turning to Wilder, she met his grin with her own wide smile. "I hit it. I hit the post." The fact that she hadn't been aiming at the post didn't seem to lessen her excitement. The bullet hadn't simply gone out there into the fields to land without notice.

"See you're getting there. Now you've got three more shots so don't waste them," he said encouragingly.

Hope shot three more times and with each got a little more confidence in handling the weapon although the cans remained unscathed.

At the end of the session, she went to hand the pistol back to Wilder and he told her, "No that's yours now. I want you to keep it on you or at least in your room until I get, Vargas. Here's the bullets and when you get home, load it and keep it where you can reach it quickly."

Then before Hope could turn and leave, Wilder pulled his pistol, fired in rapid succession, then flipped the weapon to his left hand and continued the shots. A tin can jumping into the air with each one.

Wilder holstered the still smoking gun and turned to Hope, a grin proudly placed on his face. "I don't expect that out of you, but at least you know it can be done."

Hope thanked Wilder once again and walked back toward the Main Street and the newspaper office.

As Wilder turned to leave, he saw Mason leaning against one of the livery's hitching posts, his long legs out in front of him.

Walking over to him reloading his gun, Wilder said, "I knew the shots would bring you out from wherever you were. I tried to let you know I was going to have a little shooting lesson but couldn't find you."

"I would have appreciated the heads up. You know in a sleepy little town like this, we don't hear shots ring out very often. Maybe New Year's Eve and such," replied Mason. Finally, curiosity got the better of him and he said, "I would think she's not your usual type."

Wilder, his eyes narrowed, a slight flicker of an eyelash the only hint that more was at stake here than a discussion of a stranger, asked, "What kind of a crack was that? Miss St. Michaels is a beautiful, refined, well-spoken lady any man would find attractive."

Mason stood, a few inches taller than Wilder's six foot, and said deadpan, "That's what I meant. Not your usual type." He turned to leave adding, "Just to let you know, Matthew is only one of her protectors so you may as well move on down the road. You'll not be an acceptable friend for her."

"I'm not trying to be anything to her. Just teaching

her how to defend herself out here in the west." Growing tired of the conversation, Wilder continued on his way to the saloon.

Hope was in her room before she inhaled a relaxing breath. Carrying the large weapon, even unloaded, was nerve racking and she left it on the small table beside her bed, the bullets next to it. She went upstairs to get a cup of tea and sat at the kitchen table. There was a covered steaming pan on the stove that smelled delicious but it also made the room overly hot. Taking her cup of tea, Hope, returned downstairs to offer her help to Faith in the pressroom. Faith gave her some advertisements to proofread and that's how Jessie found them when he came in.

"I met our new neighbor. The photography equipment arrived yesterday and the photographer today," he said with an unusual grin on his face.

"Oh, is he married?" asked Faith. "How old?"

"Does he have school aged children? Does he seem nice?" asked Hope.

Jessie looked at them both and then said, "Her name is, Colette Delmar, and she isn't married. No sign of children, I'm afraid, Hope. She's not much older than me, maybe Jeremy's age and seems very nice."

Faith repeated back what Jessie had said and then, "A female? The photographer is a female? Now why did we simply take for granted it was a he? Aren't we chauvinists."

"Usually men have their own businesses while women merely work for them, especially if he is married. No offence, Jessie, but Faith could run this newspaper as well as you," Hope said knowing Jessie wouldn't take offence.

"I agree. I wouldn't even be up and running, yet, if I hadn't had Faith to guide me, no pun intended. I was lucky she was willing to move here from Callie's ranch and work for me. Lucky for Jeremy, too, I suspect, but they would have found each other someway. Jeremy would have just hung around Callie's until Faith put him out of his misery," he told them as he found the ink he needed on the shelf.

Faith put down the papers she was reading and said, removing the ink stained apron she always wore in the print room, "I'm going to just run next door and offer her a dinner tonight so she won't need to worry about that."

"Wait," said Hope, following Faith from behind the counter. "I want to come meet her, too." Both women hurried out the door, almost squeezing through it together in their haste.

Jessie called out, "And that's why men own businesses. We don't get off-track at every little thing. We stay on course." But he was speaking to an empty room.

The women turned back to him but he couldn't make out the words they mouthed or maybe he could but didn't want to admit they knew those words. He continued back to his office where he finally had some legal matters to work on.

Faith and Hope entered the front door to the store and looked at the many crates and boxes yet to be unpacked. There was noise from the rear of the building so the two called out.

A beautiful woman with black hair and brown eyes emerged from the dark hallway. She was wearing a simple, yet elegant, skirt and shirtwaist and clearly had been busy in the back.

"I don't want to interrupt what you're doing but just thought I would drop in to welcome you to Sweetwater. This is, Hope St. Michaels, and I'm, Faith Macgregor."

"Oh yes, your husband, he stopped in earlier *ne'st ce pas?*" asked Colette with a slight accent.

"No, that was my brother-in-law, Jessie. My husband is, Jeremy Macgregor, the architect here in Sweetwater," Faith explained the tricky situation.

"And so, you are the sister?" asked Colette as she turned to Hope trying to get the relationship correct.

"Well, not really but for all general purposes, I guess I am, yes," answered Faith.

While Hope added, "We were raised as sisters."

"I will see when I know you better, yes?" the full-figured brunette asked with a slight smile.

Faith and Hope both breathed out a thankful, "Yes."

While Faith added, "If you would like, I'm happy to have you come to dinner with us tonight so you don't have to worry about getting food out or cooking."

"I don't cook too often, but yes, a meal with new friends will be more than welcome. The door right next to this, *ne'st ce pas?*" And Colette pointed to the newspaper side of her building and both of the other women nodded.

"Come over whenever you're ready. We aren't very formal here." Then Hope and Faith returned to the newspaper to finish the proofing. Both content now they had met and liked their new neighbor.

Dinner was very festive, with Jeremy taking out a bottle of wine once he learned their guest was French and offering it to everyone. Hope declined but everyone else drank a glass. The coq au vin was a little over done, the meat hardly staying on the bone but tasted delicious and

Colette proclaimed it to be one of the best she had ever eaten.

"Callie, another sister, taught me how to make it while I was out to her place cooking for the ranch hands," Faith told her new neighbor.

"These ranch hands get meals like this? I may have to become good with roping cows just to be fed so well each night." Colette chuckled, wiping her mouth with her napkin.

"They are very well fed but that's what makes them stay at the Harrison ranch. Callie is making it difficult on the other ranchers since she gets the best of the lot each year plus having the experienced crew Seth, her husband, had already. He has some of the best cow ponies around, too," added Jeremy.

"I only have canned peaches for dessert, I'm afraid," said Faith as she passed out the dishes of cool peaches drenched in their own sweet syrup.

"But these are delicious. Home canned peaches are the very best. Did you do them yourself?" asked Colette evidently impressed.

Faith laughed saying, "No, another sister did. Jessie's wife, Mary Beth, but we are planning on canning a lot of things together this summer and fall as things ripen. Another of Callie's gifts."

"How many sisters are there? Your parents must have been very busy," teased Colette.

"We were raised by nuns in St. Michaels Foundling Home in New York. Some of us started to gravitate toward Sweetwater and now we can see one another anytime we want," Faith explained.

"That sounds pleasant. All my family are back in Nice. I don't think I will ever see them again and now we write less and less. Our lives are simply too different and the younger ones don't even remember me. It is a shame when families lose one another." She finished the wine in her glass.

"It has worked out very well so far," said Jeremy. "I got a wife and sister-in-law all because of Callie trying to gather her family around her." He smiled at his wife and raised his half empty wine glass as a toast before finishing it.

Colette took that as her hint to leave, so stood. "I must be going. Faith and Hope, the dinner was lovely. Thank you for thinking of inviting me. I did not make any plans for food and did not even pack any. It was too expensive to bring by train since they charge by weight and size. I packed all my equipment and supplies but nothing too much for my living quarters." She lifted her hands shrugging. "It will all come in time."

Hope walked Colette to the boardwalk and then waved when Colette got into her own door. Taking a moment to look into the street, she searched the shadows for Wilder. She never saw him but she was pretty sure he was there - watching.

The next day began with exciting news of a much-awaited event. Jessie came in and announced, "Daniel came over early this morning to get Mary Beth. Rebecca is having her baby and that is going to be the headline. Can you come up with a drawing or something of a baby?"

"What about a photograph? Do you think Rebecca would consent to having her baby's picture taken? Perhaps with Daniel and her? I mean the whole town goes to his church and she has helped so many women in town even though she's only been here a little over a year," offered Faith.

"Oh, the first photograph in the paper. So many new things happening," Hope said clapping her hands silently together.

"Well, at least let's wait until the baby is born before we make all these plans. I want Rebecca's blessing on this before we get all worked up about this article. She isn't one for a lot of notoriety in her life and Daniel is pretty low key, too," Faith warned.

Jessie and Hope both calmed down and put their heads together for the story behind the photograph that would be printed later. They, also, had to put in information about Sweetwater's First Annual Fourth of July Extravaganza.

"The name was thought-up by Mrs. Thompson who has begun her campaign to give the young people in town a way to meet each other - specifically her oldest son. She is intent on keeping him in Sweetwater and thinks that a wife will do the trick," Jessie explained to Hope as he pulled a blank sheet of paper towards him while standing at the counter.

"I'm going to go down and see if I can be of any help, keep Daniel from pacing holes in the carpet or something. I'll be back if Mary Beth kicks me out," Faith called back to the two working on the story.

Victoria, Sheriff Mason's wife, opened the door to Faith's tentative knock at the parsonage. "I came over to see if there was anything I could do for Mary Beth," Faith explained to the woman she had met a few times while visiting Abby's dress shop.

"I had the same idea so come on in. I've not had to do much. Boiled water and let it cool down and I'm trying to keep Reverend Walters from worrying himself to death. He's sure they're hiding something from him but Rebecca doesn't want him in there with her, says he will be too much of a distraction," Victoria whispered to Faith, trying not to upset the reverend with the facts.

"I'll let Mary Beth know I'm here if she needs anything I can do," Faith said. She walked back to the bedroom she knew belonged to Rebecca and Daniel as a married couple but found that room empty. The room she and Charity had talked in was closed up but Faith could hear Mary Beth talking encouragingly, must be to Rebecca because Daniel was in the kitchen.

Faith tapped lightly but Mary Beth opened it immediately, turning back into the room telling Rebecca who it was. Mary Beth stood back and ushered Faith in pointing toward the washstand.

"Wash your hands and go to the head of the bed and hold Rebecca's hand when she has a contraction."

Faith washed her hands and dried them on a clean towel laying there and quickly went to Rebecca's side taking her hand. "I'm not sure what you need but I can certainly hold your hand. Just let me know what…."

Rebecca half sat up as a wave of pain took over her body and sweat beads formed on her forehead.

Seeing the bowl of water with ice chips floating in it as Rebecca let go of her hand, Faith squeezed out the cloth next to it and wiped the beads of sweat. After rinsing it again, placed the cool fabric on Rebecca's forehead.

Between contractions, which Faith soon found were coming quicker and lasting longer, Rebecca talked about what her body was doing. Mostly trying to impart as much information to Mary Beth as she could as she went through the process she had always been at the other end of the bed for.

Then Rebecca did something strange, she got on her hands and knees on the bed and rocked slightly as she explained to Mary Beth, "I've found this helps with the back pain like I've been having. I think it has something to do with taking the baby's weight off the spine and hangs it in the womb. Its not touching any bones other than if the head is in the birth canal but my baby isn't there yet." The last few words were rushed as another contraction brought on the panting as Rebecca tried to keep breathing through the pain.

Faith saw the fan, deciding helping Rebecca stay as comfortable as possible was the best help. She began fanning Rebecca as that lady again went through a surge of pain.

Rebecca asked Faith, "I allowed you in because I thought you could handle seeing a birth without it causing you to give up lovemaking. I didn't make a mistake, did I?"

"No, I knew what occurs. Mary Beth has been educating us as to what to expect. I'm not a wilting flower any longer. I left that behind me, as you know. Life brings pain and I am here to help you through it as you will probably be with me to do the same." She met Rebecca's gaze as the other woman nodded and braced for another swell of pain.

Mary Beth sent Faith out to give a brief account of what was going on with Rebecca so Daniel wouldn't come barging in with pent-up frustration at not knowing. As she entered the kitchen, Daniel jumped from the table, a full cup of coffee in front of him. He appeared rumpled, evidently having pushed his fingers through his hair more than once.

He stared expectantly toward Faith and she immediately said, "It won't be right away though she's doing well, has a lot of strength and is in good spirits. She and Mary Beth are working well together and I am there to help keep her cool with a fan and cold water."

Daniel looked a little more relaxed, saying, "I have more ice. Got it from the butcher this morning."

"I'll take some in a glass and then Rebecca can suck on it or drink cool water," Faith offered. Daniel retrieved the covered bowl and handed it to Faith.

"I don't know how she can go through so much pain for so long. She didn't let me know until this morning when I woke up. I don't think I would be able to do it," he confessed.

"It's His plan and we must bear the pain as its given to us. We are to give children to our husbands to strengthen the family and it is not our place to question how that comes about," Faith said reasonably, repeating something she heard the nuns say when she was much younger.

"Throwing back one of my sermons at me? I agree, it's His plan but part of the plan must be to drive the husband to distraction while waiting for his child, knowing his wife is in pain," Daniel replied.

"Try to relax, Daniel. You don't want Rebecca worrying about you, too, do you?" Faith asked him.

"No, I'll pull myself together, perhaps clean up a little. I don't want to meet my child looking as if I spent the night out on the town." He tried to pull the wrinkles out of his shirt and coat finally giving up.

"I'll tell Rebecca you're doing well and she has nothing to worry about." Then Faith went back to the room with a cup of sugared tea and the ice.

Rebecca was still on her hands and knees, wearing only a lightweight nightgown. Faith offered the ice and tea to Rebecca who drank the tea after having Faith put ice into it. Rebecca didn't sip it but drank it down practically in one swallow. Then prepared herself for another contraction rocking but making no noise other than the sounds of her panting breaths.

Faith tried to distract her from the pain and relayed some of what she and Daniel spoke about. That he was cleaning up from the hectic morning. He was worried but more relaxed now he knew Rebecca was doing as expected and no problems were present.

Rebecca said, "Thank you. If he saw me in this much discomfort, he would never make love to me again. Some men are simply too protective, too ready to take the blame for the pain, and I want more children even though I haven't given birth to this one, yet."

The ladies all laughed at Rebecca's issuance of that statement, knowing that each faced the possibility of having an over protective husband. The truth was there in front of them every day.

The hours passed slowly but finally Rebecca was sitting up, pillows pushed behind her back at the head of the bed. She was straining with the contraction and Mary Beth was encouraging her pushes, letting her know when the baby's crown showed and when the baby's head was through. When the entire baby slid out, there was no need to say anything, except that it was a boy. Rebecca and Daniel had a son.

All three women had tears rolling down their cheeks while seeing to the needs of the baby and the mother. Faith handed the baby to Rebecca after he had been cleaned off leaving Mary Beth dealing with the rest of

Rebecca's care.

Rebecca was completely ignoring Mary Beth's work and was unwrapping her son to make sure all looked as it should, counting fingers and toes as she had seen mothers do at almost every birth. She now knew why. It was to verify that the mother had done her job correctly. That she had grown an infant and it was perfect. She smiled at her son and then said, "You can let Daniel in now."

Faith looked at Mary Beth as she nodded so Faith jumped up and went to tell Daniel he was welcome in the birthing room.

Daniel looked up as Faith opened the kitchen door. Her bright smile had him on his feet and taking off to the room he had been banned from all day. Victoria had been sitting at the table too, a piece of small clothing in her hands as she embroidered. Were those really a row of yellow ducks?

Victoria said, "I made a stew. Would you like some? There's plenty. I guess I was worried so the more I worried the more I cooked and baked. I finally got some work from Abby when I gave her the update and brought it here to finish. They're actually for Rebecca's baby." She held up the little dress and bib.

"They are lovely and he will look adorable in them. And the stew smells delicious but I couldn't eat a thing. I was so involved with it all I still have trembles, like excited or after hearing a gun shot. I'm going to head home as soon as I know Rebecca and Mary Beth no longer need me. I want the family to be together for a while and I'll come back tomorrow if they need help. Mary Beth will tell Jessie, I suppose." Faith went outside to finally use the privy.

Victoria was leaving when Faith returned to the house. She had a couple bundles of linen and Faith offered to help her carry them to the laundry across from Miss Lily's. The two young women went down the front porch and across to First Street and down about half a block to the Chinese laundry. Miss Lily was out on her porch as they passed and she enquired about Rebecca.

"She has a beautiful baby boy. The baby was fairly big with healthy lungs. Mother and father made it through fine." The three women laughed at the truth of the last statement.

"I'm so glad. For some reason I've been on edge today and was worried that it had to do with Rebecca but evidently not. Now maybe I can settle," Miss Lily informed her young friends still standing in the street.

"I'm tired knowing what she was going through. I'm going to go home and be with my husband," admitted Faith.

"That is where I'm headed, too," said Victoria as she walked toward the livery and her apartment with Mason behind the hotel.

Victoria felt eyes upon her and an uneasy feeling crept across her shoulders but she couldn't find anyone around who seemed to be paying her any attention. She was going to mention it to Mason in case there was someone in town from Louise's old gang still trying to get revenge on her or Mason for ending their criminal career last fall.

Feeling like someone was watching her, Faith scanned the area but saw only a Mexican cowboy enter the livery. No one seemed to be paying attention to her so she continued home to the newspaper and Jeremy. It had been a long day.

Jessie had the tub almost ready, simply had to add the hot water that was still on the stove. As soon as he saw Mary Beth heading toward home from the parsonage, he had his welcome home complete.

"You look happy and worn out so I take it the birth went well," he said to his wife as she entered and set her bag down with limp hands.

"Well, you know, Rebecca. She handled everything as it came. Not a whimper out of her and she even made time to compliment my bedside manner. She sent me home and I'll stop over tomorrow for a few hours if she needs me. Faith was a lot of help, too. She stayed almost the entire time and was there when the baby was born." She accepted the cup of tea he placed in her hand.

"I have to know, the newspaper man in me is anxious for the story. Umm, not the whole story just the when, where and who sort of stuff." He laughed at Mary Beth's expression.

"He arrived at five-forty-five, at home at the parsonage of Sweetwater Methodist Church and his name is, Jacob Daniel Walters. He weighs six-pounds four-ounces and is beautiful," she finished as she stood.

"No, no, no. I have another surprise for you - a warm bath. Not hot and I can add more cold water if that sounds like what you want." He led his wife into the back room where he had set the tub. "And I'll wash your back if you want me to or your front or anything you need washed." He kept stepping closer as he spoke and now was close enough to kiss her, sliding his tongue into her waiting mouth.

"Has it been that long? I didn't mean to ignore my wifely duties," she teased her new husband.

"I know you were preoccupied, jumping every time

you thought Daniel was coming over to get you. Now the baby is here and you can relax and enjoy life again - and me of course." He pulled off her apron and then unbuttoned her shirtwaist and skirt, letting them drop to the floor. Her camisole followed and as Rebecca recommended, she wasn't wearing a corset during work duties. Something Jessie personally enjoyed and approved.

Helping Mary Beth into the tub, she moaned as she sank into the water, grateful muscles relaxing after hours of bending over a bed to support Rebecca. Jessie rubbed the scented soap into a cloth and washed Mary Beth's back, then gave the same attention to her front. Possibly a little more, then continued down both legs, enjoying the excursion as much as Mary Beth did.

Once he felt he had cleaned every inch, Jessie went to the foot of the tub. He picked up each small womanly foot and massaged it as he knew Mary Beth liked, then kissed each one as he placed it back into the water. He held out a towel and Mary Beth let him dry her in a ritual they both had decided on early in their marriage.

There wasn't a lot of talking, simply touching and feeling and knowing already what the other enjoyed. Mary Beth lay down on the clean sheet naked, the evening too hot for blankets while Jessie did the same. He reached over to touch his wife as she lay in the darkened room simply enjoying her presence.

"Aren't you going to make love to me, Jessie?"

"I thought maybe you were too tired. You've had a long day."

"For months you chased me, dogged my tracks even, intent on getting me to marry you. Now you seem afraid of doing something to displease me, like you're

217

walking on eggs all the time. Did I do this to you? Did I make you so hesitant?" Mary Beth turned to him for answers.

"I know this marriage wasn't what you wanted and that I kind of badgered you into it. I guess I'm afraid that one day you'll tell me to leave and then what will I do?" he whispered his fear.

"What I said before we were married was just that - before. I never meant for you to feel you came after my commitment to Callie and Rebecca and the church. I made that decision. You are the most important thing in my life. If you can't believe that, then at least believe the vow I took in that church across the street." She pulled him closer to her. "I love you. I've always loved you and once I decided to marry you then my priorities changed. You may have to share it with our children but us, our family, is what matters most."

"I don't know why I feel you're going to disappear and leave me. Maybe because I can't believe I'm lucky enough to have found the one meant for me. I mean, what are the chances of that, really?" He leaned over and kissed her mouth.

"Make love to me now and I'll show you how much you mean to me. Give me a baby," she whispered.

That request stopped Jessie's movements toward his wife, as he asked, "Are you sure you want to do that so soon? I thought maybe you were doing something to prevent it or…"

"What have you been thinking? It's God's plan as to whether or not we have children and when. I would never think to try to alter His wishes. And I would want your children even if I didn't think it a sin to do otherwise. Where did we start to misunderstand one another, Jessie?

I feel so badly that you've thought I didn't love you or wasn't committed to our marriage," Mary Beth sounded sad.

"It's probably just me. I'm not confident about you as I am with everything else in my life. You're my one weakness," he confessed.

"No, I'm your strength and never doubt it. I love you, Jessie. Now, I'm ordering you to make love to me." She pulled him to her so that he could do as they both desired.

Hope was setting print for the next edition while Faith took bread and a pie to Rebecca's house to nourish the new mother and father. But mostly it was to check on Mary Beth since Jessie hadn't shown up at work, yet, and to spend time with the new baby.

Looking up and through the front window, Hope thought she saw a man slip between the buildings and another right behind him. Not the usual actions of the towns' people and not slim enough to be Wilder. Besides, you never saw Wilder unless he wanted you to.

The men kept staring toward either the newspaper or the newly occupied shop next door. Hope knew Colette was there alone as she had been the last few days. The photographer was setting up the front in what Colette referred to as a studio and one of the back rooms as a lab with chemicals and trays and all sorts of interesting things.

Hope wanted to warn Colette of the men and their strange behavior so she walked over to the store next door and casually entered. Colette looked up from arranging some wicker chairs with a smile of welcome.

"I don't mean to alarm you and it may be nothing but there are at least two men watching our buildings. I wanted you to know." The more she spoke the more she worried that she wasn't merely seeing things. "I have a pistol back at the newspaper and I plan on having that close to me. If you wish, you can come back with me."

"I have a derringer, too. It is good at close range and I will blow their heads off if they are up to no good with me," she said, craning her neck to see where the men were still hiding.

"I'm going out the back door so they will think you aren't alone. Faith will be back and possibly Jeremy with her in a few minutes for the midday meal. Be careful, maybe lock your doors?" Hope went back by way of the rear entrances.

Once inside the newspaper building, Hope tried to load the weapon Wilder had given her but was shaking so badly the bullets kept dropping to the floor. She tried to remember Wilder's warning about not allowing her emotions to get in the way of her need to protect herself. She was calling herself all sorts of foolish for not having the gun loaded and ready as Wilder had advised her.

Finally, the cylinder was full as she had been instructed and Hope locked her private room's door. She waited crouched down by the bed, the pistol pointing at the door, praying and waiting for Faith and Jeremy to arrive home and calm her silly fears.

Next door, the brazen men had finally gotten up enough nerve to walk into Colette's place of business and peered around.

Colette smiled and asked in a heavy French accent, "Iz there something I can do for you, gentlemen? A photograph for your loved one to put in a locket perhaps or possibly a tin type of you with your guns, *oui*?"

Both men wore huge sombreros with braids hanging

off the wide brims, blousy grease-stained shirts and dusty trousers that seemed too tight around their waists. Their boots were some kind of snake skin with silver spurs. On their right hips were holstered guns, the straps holding them on dangling while they sported leather belts of bullets crossed over their chests. A lot of gun power for this small town, Colette knew.

Placing her hand into the pocket of her apron, she held the cool metal derringer in her palm, her finger already on the trigger. She would shoot right through the dress if she felt the men were aggressive towards her. She was worried when they didn't seem to want her at all.

The bigger one, the one that smelled the worse, asked roughly, "Where's the other one? The little school teacher?"

"I do not know diz school teacher. I am new in town," Colette stated partly truthfully.

"She was just here, we saw her," the other man snarled.

"I am de only one here, I can assure you," said Colette trying to buy Hope time to hide or get to someone who could help.

"No, the little bitch is here," growled the larger man who shoved Colette out of the way so he could go down the hall.

Colette knew there were only two shots in her gun and the chance of her hitting both men before one of them shot her was slim. She prayed for Hope to be to safety and repeated, "I am here alone. Maybe you made a mistake."

With that, the second man hit her across the mouth knocking her to the floor.

The larger man yelled, pointing, "There, that's where she went. Out that door. Maybe she went back to her room. It's right next door."

Both men squeezed out the rear door and into the backdoor of the newspaper building which Hope hadn't taken the time to lock, expecting Faith and Jeremy to return. Not that locking it would have stopped these men more than a second.

Stomping down the hall, they hesitated outside the only closed door. They looked at each other and smiled wicked, evil grins. The smaller man picked up his booted foot smashing it against the doorjamb, splintering the frame and door as it crashed open.

Hope fired the gun, startled by the sound it made here in her cozy little room. She saw the startled faces of the men in the hall and then the anger as they realized she had tried to shoot them. They both roared and headed into the doorway at the same time, catching each other in the too small opening before Hope shot again.

This time the bullet was more head high than ceiling high and that stopped them in their tracks. Neither pulled a pistol to return fire but jumped behind the hallway wall, instead.

It wasn't more than a few seconds but seemed like forever to Hope before she heard Wilder snarl something in Spanish at the two men. Mason yelled for them to put down their weapons or be shot.

Then Hope heard a scuffle and something hit into the wall with a crash. Wilder peered in at her. He seemed like he wanted to come to her but had one of the men in cuffs in front of him. Mason must have had the other and then the hall was empty and silent.

Colette ran into the hall from the backdoor calling

out for Hope and found her when she saw the broken door. "Oh, I am so sorry, Mignon. I wanted to stop them but I worried if I missed and they got to you, there would be no one to get the sheriff. I chose the sheriff."

Hope looked at Colette and realized her mouth was bleeding. "Oh, they hurt you, Colette. Come and let me help. I have medicines upstairs. Come with me."

Hope stood up from her hiding place next to the bed and realized she still had her finger on the trigger and gently laid the gun down beside the bed.

"Oh, no, Mignon. We will take this big gun with us up the stairs. I do not trust anyone anymore but you and me." Colette picked up the pistol taking it with them.

Jeremy came up the steps two and three at a time, rushing into his home to find Colette on a kitchen chair being administered to by Hope. Hope had applied a salve to the split in Colette's lip then gave her a cold cloth to place over it to help with the pain and swelling.

Jeremy asked both women, "Are you hurt? Do you need me to call the doctor or get Mary Beth?" He looked at Hope for an answer.

"No, Colette's stubbornness in not giving them any answers earned her a cut mouth and gave me a chance to get my pistol loaded," she said gratefully.

"I didn't even know you had a pistol. Thank God, for that at least," Jeremy said studying both women to see if there was anything, he could do to help them.

"I've had it for a while but it wasn't loaded," Hope fabricated a little.

"I need to go home, I think, now. I am so glad you are all right. They were very set on getting you, my little friend, but I do not know why," Colette told Hope worriedly.

"Thank you for getting Mason. I wasn't sure he was in his office. I was so thankful when I heard him and Wilder enter the downstairs' building," Hope said gratefully.

"Ah, it was 'Wilder' this Mason was yelling as he ran across the street. I could not understand what he was shouting but it was for the other man that came so quickly with his gun drawn. I like these men, Mason and Wilder. They are quick and smart. Now I must go home." Colette rose from the chair then went down the stairs to her own backdoor.

Jeremy looked at Hope with more questions but decided to leave it to Faith. She at least could handle Hope if things turned to tears and he wasn't very good with crying women. Hell, was any man? He grimaced and told Hope to stay upstairs until he retrieved Faith. He had made his wife stay at Mary Beth's when they heard the commotion in town but by now, she would be worrying, too.

Faith came home with Jeremy and immediately hugged Hope to her. "Did Jeremy get it right? There were actually men here after you? Why?"

"I don't know but if it hadn't been for Colette, I wouldn't be here now. She called in Mason." For some reason she didn't want to disclose Wilder's part in all that had happened.

"And you have a gun and you shot at the men?" asked Faith unable not to sound astonished.

"I, I have a gun and I fired, twice," confessed Hope.

"How wonderful. You must teach me to shoot, too," enthused Faith getting her friend's mind off the men who attacked her.

Overhearing the conversation, Jeremy said, "I'll

teach you to shoot if you must know how. I guess it probably isn't a bad idea since Sweetwater is getting larger and more and more strangers are mixing in all the time. I hate to think my building sites are bringing in disreputable people."

"Let's have supper and you will stay up here with us from now on, Hope," said Faith sitting her friend in one of the kitchen chairs.

"I'll help with the meal but I won't sleep up here. I won't be that much of an imposition so don't force me, please," Hope insisted.

"We'll see," was all Faith said.

After supper, Hope took the still loaded pistol and went down the steps toward the rear door and her room when a male voice called out her name.

"Hope, it's Wilder." Hope changed direction.

Jeremy had been listening for Hope to get into the locked building with her key and yelled out, "Hope, who's down there with you?"

Hope called up to Jeremy, "It's Wilder. He helped Mason this afternoon, capturing the men who had me cornered."

"I know, Wilder. Don't stay out there too long and, Wilder, I expect you to make sure she gets in safely," warned Jeremy.

"I'll make sure she's safe," he called back.

Hope faced the man who had taken up so much of her thoughts lately. "Thank you for today and for the gun. As you heard, I was able to shoot it at someone if I felt threatened enough. I just wasn't a very good aim."

"Yeah, but I heard two shots. The third would have downed one of them," Wilder teased.

"I was getting used to the noise and they wouldn't

stop so you may be right. I had given them time to back off but for some reason they kept coming. If I had known they had hit Colette, I might have fired all of the bullets at them. I should go and see how she is."

"Don't worry, Victoria has been checking in on her. Mason is staying close to the jail until the Federal Marshall can send men to pick those two up."

"So, it's over then? You've got Vargas?"

"No, I'm afraid not. The two we have were sent by Vargas but there's no proof of that other than I know these men are part of his gang. They have all been hiding out somewhere. So far, we don't know where and I don't think these gang members will turn on Vargas. He's known to have a very violent temper and holds a grudge," Wilder said watching Hope's reaction to this information.

"So, it's not over? He could send more men after me? What about my friends? They hurt Colette this time. What if Faith and Jeremy try to protect me?" Tears formed in Hope's eyes.

"Oh, Babe, don't cry. I'll stay closer to you now I know you're going to be a target." He pulled Hope against his chest, for comfort, his arms wrapped around her.

Hope felt calmer leaning against Wilder, his warmth, his strong body, his heartbeat under her ear as she felt something tugging on her skirt.

Wilder must have felt it too, and said, "Sit." The tugging stopped.

Looking down, Hope saw a small wired-haired dog, tan and black, his tongue hanging out as he kept moving his feet lifting first the left than the right but not jumping up on her again. Bending down, Hope scratched the dog behind his ears and won a friend for life. Wilder squatted down and scratched the dog's underbelly and in a moment the dog was on its back with his belly exposed for more of the same.

"He's darling," said Hope losing herself in the moment. "What's his name?"

"I call him, Bullet, but you can call him whatever you want. He's yours now. I want you to keep him with you, in your room. He'll warn you if there are any strangers nearby. Just introduce Jeremy and Jessie to him in the morning and then he won't bark at them. Otherwise, he'll warn you when they come near, too. Just tell him they're a friend."

"Oh, I can't take your dog, Wilder."

"He's not my dog. Look." When Hope looked down, the dog was sitting next to her feet.

"I'll take him back when this is over if you don't want him but it will break his heart," teased Wilder.

Hope shook her head in resignation and when she turned to go into the building, the dog was right on her heels, not giving a backward glance at Wilder. Once in the door, Hope locked it before going to her room. The damaged door was still swinging open and Hope pushed the chair in front of it to hold it closed.

After putting on her nightgown, she looked for Bullet to find him already curled up on the rug next to her bed. She told him goodnight, said her prayers and thought of Wilder until she fell asleep.

In the morning she must have slept in because she heard Bullet growling, facing the door and sniffing under it. The growl turned into yapping when she heard Jeremy walk into his office.

"Hope, do you have a dog now?" asked Jeremy

through the broken door.

"Wilder thought he would be protection. If I introduce you to him, he'll stop barking but I must get dressed first," explained Hope.

"That's a good idea. I think I could hear him upstairs, too, if he barked at night," replied Jeremy still on the hallway side of the door.

"Let me get dressed and I'll explain it better." Hurrying around, Hope, got ready as quickly as she could and took Bullet outside. While she used the privy, Bullet used a nearby post.

As they entered the back hall, Bullet's neck hair bristled even more than normal and a growl started deep in his throat as he spied Jeremy.

"Bullet, he's a friend."

Bullet looked up at Hope and his growling stopped, his fur regaining its normal unruliness.

Jeremy smiled, saying, "Well, that works as long as he remembers me tomorrow. You can introduce him to Jessie, he just came in. Does he have to be introduced to Faith, too?"

"I don't know but he seems smart so he may know I love Faith and accept her as he accepted me." Hope walked toward the pressroom, Bullet right beside her.

Bullet walked up to Faith's skirts, sniffed and his tail went wild. Jessie had to be introduced as a friend and then Bullet sniffed his way around the room passing the ink and paper quickly to return to Hope's side.

CHAPTER 6

Mason was in plain sight, as usual, sitting on the boardwalk in front of the jail. Victoria brought him a cold drink and later a meal he ate in the office, the door propped open so he could see across the street.

Going next door with Bullet right on her heels, Hope wanted to make sure Colette was all right. As soon as the two women saw each other they went into one another's arms for a hug.

"I'm so glad you're looking better today. I was afraid there would be more bruising and I didn't want you in pain simply for helping me," Hope told her new friend after searching for any further damage.

"I wish I could have done more but I could not. Anything I have that got bruised can be mended, I assure you." The two women stepped back from one another as Colette spread her hands wide encompassing the front portion of the building. "How do you like my studio? It is ready for customers so now I wait."

"I know Jessie would like to have you do some work for him at the paper and I'm going to spread the word you are open for business. I think many families would like photographs and I know Jeremy wants some photographs of the new buildings, something to show the investors back East that things are progressing. And Jessie would be interested in those for the Chronicle, too."

"I think I could work out a price Jessie could afford. I know he is starting out and it takes time for a newspaper to make any money. I need to get my name out there, too, so perhaps he will give me advertising space as well as my name under the photograph, *ne'st pas*?"

"I am sure Jessie will consider that a fair trade but I'll let the two of you work out the final arrangements. I'll tell him when I get back."

Colette stopped her new friend from leaving saying, "And Hope, Victoria is keeping me informed of Andy, the young stable boy. He was tied up and stuffed in a grain bin but is all right now after some water and food. That is how these men were able to stay in town unnoticed, Victoria said. She tells me what is happening with those men and their boss so do not be concerned about watching over me. And Mason, too, is doing a beautiful job of it."

Hope looked across the street noting the large sheriff. "Yes, I feel much better knowing he is in charge."

The two women said their goodbyes and Hope went to speak with Jessie, Bullet silently following close behind.

The next day was quiet. The two Mexicans had been picked up and taken away by train. Hope decided she could return to her usual activities even if Vargas himself wasn't under arrest yet.

Earlier, she had wanted to meet the students she would be teaching in the fall and had already made acquaintance with the nearest family, that of the butcher next door to where she lived. She met the three children there who came downstairs and they all went outside and sat on the tree trunks placed in a circle for that purpose. Mrs. Burgess, the children's mother, came out and offered Hope a delicious smelling dish of food Hope was unfamiliar with.

"Oh, thank you, Mrs. Burgess, it looks wonderful but I just ate so I'll have some a little later, if that's all right?" she said trying to speak slowly to the woman who she knew spoke almost no English.

The younger daughter, Anna said, "Mamma wants you to take it home. You can bring the dish back and then she'll probably fill it for you again."

"She wants to pay you for helping us. She wants us to do well in school and doesn't want to take charity," explained the older sister, Helga.

"Oh, tell her that I'm paid by the town. She doesn't need to pay me extra. I enjoy teaching and I don't have any other students yet so you three get the benefit of my time." Her gaze and smile encompassed all of the family.

Hans said, "I'd rather be fishing."

"If I left right now would you be able to go fishing, Hans?" asked Hope.

"No, I'd have to wait for my Pa because I don't swim so well," he confessed.

"Then let's use the time to the best advantage. Do you have any questions on the story problems I gave you the other day? Are you finished with them, yet?" Hope asked trying to get the children interested in their classes.

Hans said, "It was good the questions concerned a meat shop. I could do the problems real easy that way and I didn't have to ask my Pa for help, either."

"That's good, Hans. I meant for you to do the problems yourself but if they were so easy, I will try to make them more difficult so you will need to stretch your ability. I could write some with construction items like lumber and bricks," offered Hope.

"That would be good, I think. I like the buildings and all the excitement around town. It's looking different already and I like that, the newness," he explained to Hope. Speaking easily with her because he had to converse with the adults in his parent's lives.

"All right, lets read the problems and then you can give me the answers and how you came to that answer." Hope began her impromptu outside class.

After the class with the Burgess children, Hope continued to Abby's shop knocking on the rear door and stepping in when she heard Abby call out. Victoria and Abby both came into the sales portion of the shop to discuss the recent events.

Abby immediately asked worriedly, "How are you doing after yesterday? Matthew told me about the men and the attack on you and Colette. I can't believe that Sweetwater and its residents keep getting this kind of people drawn to it. I'm so sorry you both had to go through such a harrowing experience." Abby appeared worriedly concerned. "Matthew tells me he'll look into this Vargas gang when he's out on his sales trip."

"I was unaware so many people were looking out for me. I knew Mason and Wilder were but everyone has been so kind. I seem to be putting people in danger without meaning to or even knowing why," Hope said sadly unhappy that she seemed to have brought a bad class of people with her.

Victoria commiserated, saying, "Please, don't feel badly. It's not your fault. You can't hold yourself responsible for what someone else does, someone you don't even know. I brought problems and danger to Mason and Sweetwater without realizing it, too. The people here let me know they would protect me, even risked their own lives to stop the people who were trying to abduct and kill me. It made me realize I was meant to live in a town like this. You'll come to realize that, too."

Nodding, Hope, wanting to put yesterday behind her, explained, "I actually came to bring this book. It's written by Jules Verne, also, and Thad enjoyed *20,000 Leagues Under the Sea* so much I found another one, *From the Earth to the Moon*. Tell him I am still waiting for *Five Days in a Balloon*. There is another new one out now, too, but it is a little pricey."

"I heard that," said Matthew as he came down the stairs. "I'll look for it when I'm in the bigger cities. Sometimes deals can be made. I really enjoyed the other book, too, so I'm as bad as a child, I'm afraid, about getting another exciting story."

Then to Abby, he said, "Both girls are asleep for the moment. It's difficult to get them to rest in this heat. Too hot to rock them. I'm afraid I spoiled them since I love to hold them until they fall asleep. I still seem to miss so much of their lives," he admitted without shame.

Abby smiled benevolently at Matthew. "You're always there when we need you the most. That's what matters and what they will remember growing up."

Hope watched the contented couple and felt nostalgic, "I'm looking forward to the school year to begin so I can get back to working with all ages of children again. I have so many ideas and plans. I'll meet most of the students on the Fourth, I'm sure. Let Thad know I expect him to participate in the spelling bee since I'm using some words from his favorite book and *Moby Dick* so he can practice at night like he's been doing."

"I'll see that he makes time," Matthew said as Hope began to leave the shop. "He's very involved in reading that book from Shelly, *Dr Frankenstein* or something? He won't let me near it right now but I'm reading it next."

Smiling, Hope said her goodbyes then returned home for a light meal and cold tea. It was going to be another scorching day.

Hope was already in bed when Bullet began whining and stepping quickly back and forth in front of the newly repaired door. "Didn't you go when I told you to, you silly thing? I better not get any mosquito bites waiting for you," she scolded teasingly.

Picking up the loaded six-shooter, she carried it with her in her hand because her robe didn't have a pocket let alone one big enough to hold it. Opening the door to let out the now very excited Bullet, she watched as the dog went directly to a pile of what appeared to be rags under the stairs to the upper apartment. Whining, Bullet scratched at the mound of clothes.

Leaning toward the pile, she saw the glint of his eyes as the moonlight slipped through the clouds. "Wilder, oh, Wilder what happened? How can I help you? Tell me what I can do," she said trying to get Wilder to answer her.

He moved raising his hand listlessly toward her as she stayed bent over him. He was trying to point and then Hope saw his horse with a whip and rifle still hanging on the saddle. Going over to it, she softly spoke as she took the reins dangling to the ground. Placing her gun inside the saddle bag, she flipped the cover over it.

Returning with the animal, she bent nearer. "Should I get, Jeremy? Do you want to get onto the horse?"

Wilder reached for her shoulder, struggling to get on his knees then to a standing position. Hope helped him get on his horse by pushing his back-side up.

"Where do you want to go?" she asked not knowing

how to help and then realized she had blood on her robe and arms. "Oh Wilder, you're bleeding, you need more help than I can give you."

"Miss Lily." Was all Hope could make out.

She led the horse down the alley, through the open lot to cross the street and through the livery yard coming to a stop outside Miss Lily's kitchen door. Miss Lily's was the only house with any light showing so maybe going there was the right thing to do.

Trying the door, Hope found it unlocked so continued to help Wilder off the horse and into the kitchen. He made it as far as a chair as she called out for Miss Lily.

Miss Lily, dressed as she always was with her hair done in the intricate pile of curls and waves on top of her head, came bustling in. As soon as she saw Wilder, his skin pale and his eyes unfocused, Miss Lily opened the kitchen door and yelled, "Stella and Lacy, finish up. I need your men down here to help me."

Pumping water into a pan, Miss Lily reached for clean towels, asking as she worked, "Do you know where all the blood is coming from? Is he shot or maybe stabbed?"

"I don't know. I found him behind the newspaper," Hope answered helplessly.

Just then the door burst open and Stella, wearing a lovely dressing gown and Lacy, in one as nice only a different pastel color, rushed into the kitchen. Stella gave a little shriek when she saw the blood saturating Hope's robe.

"I'm not hurt but Wilder is," explained Hope moving so the women and then the men trailing them could see Wilder slumped in the chair. The men, their hair all tussled, one wearing an open shirt and hastily pulled on trousers while the other was wearing only his coveralls, followed the women.

Miss Lily said, "I need you two to carry Wilder up the stairs but be careful, he's hurt. Put him into the front bedroom and I'll follow." Then she turned saying, "Lacy, can you run over to get Mary Beth for me. She's the closest we have to medical help right now. Then wake up Andy and send him to get the doc."

Stella ran upstairs first and lit the lamp before turning down the bed. The men, groaning with their burden, half-carried half-dragged Wilder who had finally succumbed to the pain and passed out. They thumped Wilder down on the bed and Hope tucked clean towels under the side that showed fresh blood pumping out. She wasn't sure how to proceed but decided that finding the wound would be the next step.

Failing to remove the vest, Hope finally decided to pull the shirt out of his trousers and that is when she saw the gash in his side. She was too inexperienced to know what had caused the wound but knew she had to stop the bleeding. Placing another clean towel over the laceration where blood kept seeping with each heartbeat, she pressed it as tightly as she could, trying to stem the flow. Keep his life from draining out in these rhythmic spurts.

Miss Lily came in with scissors and cold water in a pitcher which she took over to the washstand pouring some into the basin to wet the cloth again. Returning to the bed, the older woman gazed down at Wilder, a worried frown on her face.

"I'm going to cut off this shirt and then get a look under that towel to see how bad it is. Sometime these things bleed and aren't very serious," explained Miss

Lily as she cut the shirt to expose Wilder's broad tanned chest, a smattering of dark hair between his breasts and tapering downwards disappearing into his trousers. Miss Lily continued making Wilder comfortable. Removing his boots and shaking out a small knife with a pointed blade from one and then rolled off his socks leaving his feet bare.

Miss Lily unbuckled his gun belt and his black trousers exposing more of his body to Hope's eyes. The gun belt was pulled out from under his body and then Miss Lily reverently placed it on top of the dresser across the room.

Mary Beth came in carrying her bag, going to the washstand and washed her hands as Rebecca had taught her. She gazed at Wilder lying on the bed saying, "I don't have any experience with gunshot wounds, Miss Lily. I'm going to need some help here." Then kneeled next to the bed to examine the injury closer, moving the lamp to get better light.

Miss Lily did the same and they finally came to the conclusion that a bullet tore through the soft part of his body just above his right hip and exited.

Mary Beth expelled a held breath. "I'll clean up the gash and then suture both holes. He seems to have started to clot before the moving restarted the bleeding. I think it's already beginning to clot again."

The two women raised Wilder enough to remove his leather vest and cut up shirt. Miss Lily brought Mary Beth her bag and Hope turned away unable to look at Wilder's injury again or Mary Beth putting a needle in and out of his already damaged body.

"That's all I can do. I hope the doctor isn't angry but I didn't want to wait any longer. At the amount of dried blood, I'd say this man had been shot hours ago," Mary Beth explained.

"His name is, Wilder. He's the one who helped save me when those men attacked," Hope explained to her St. Michaels' sister.

Mary Beth took another look at her patient and said, "I see. And that's why you brought him here. I wondered how you got involved in a shooting. Now I understand." She sent Hope an unreadable expression but said nothing more.

The midwife stood, saying, "Keep him still and keep watching for a fever. If he starts thrashing about or feels hot to your hand, come get me again. Hopefully, before any of that happens, the doctor will be here and he can take over."

"Thank you for coming, Mary Beth. I know this isn't really what you do," Hope told her friend.

"You'd be surprised at how often I end up doing things that have nothing to do with birthing. I've learned a lot watching Rebecca but I've gotten a lot of hands-on experience, also, in these past few months." The two women hugged because it seemed like the thing to do. "I'll come back if I'm needed."

Miss Lily said, "I'll take the first watch while you go change and get some rest, Hope. I'll get one of the boys here to see you home."

Hope looked at the kind older lady and pleaded, "I really would rather stay. He came to me for a reason."

"All right. I'll bring you something to change into until we can get your clothes," Miss Lily said leaving Hope standing beside the bed.

Returning within a couple of minutes, she handed Hope a folded pile of material. When Hope let it unfold, she found what appeared to be a duplicate gown to the one Lacy had worn that evening in a different color.

"I'll come back for your things in a little while. I want to get them soaking in saltwater while there's still a chance to save them," Miss Lily said with the practicality of someone who has been in charge often.

When the older woman left the room, Hope untied her robe and let it fall to the wood floor then pulled her nightgown over her head, turning to get the negligee set off the bed. Raising her arms, she let the silky fabric slide over her head and down her slim body.

A voice from the bed said, in a hoarse whisper, "There are angels in heaven."

Jumping in surprise, she grabbed up the matching peignoir clasping it to her breasts, trying to cover as much of herself as she could. "You're awake," she stammered - fear, embarrassment, and something else vying for emotional control.

"Am I? I thought I was seeing my just rewards for being such a good guy my whole life," said the still raspy voice. "Do you think I could get some water? I've been dying for a drink of water for so long."

Hope slipped her arms into the garment she held and went to the pitcher. Pouring a glass, she brought it to the bedside, helping Wilder raise himself slightly to drink.

"Now this isn't going to pour out of me in a dozen or so holes, is it?"

"No, only two. Mary Beth sewed them up so you won't leak much," Hope teased, glad he wasn't in so much pain he couldn't find silly things to say.

"You didn't need to dress on my account, Babe. I don't seem to be able to do much besides look. Are you denying a dying man his last chance to see a beautiful woman?"

Hope was then aware she was without her make-up having washed it off last night before bed. She tried to hold the robe tighter around her neck, obscuring the purple stain that continued under the collar.

Wilder's eyes had gone closed and Hope didn't know if he fell asleep of was trying to blot out the sight of her. She tied the wrapper closed and stood, looking about the room for anything that could make Wilder more comfortable. Finally, pulling a chair closer to the bed, she sat, checking Wilder's forehead for a fever every half hour or less. Miss Lily returned for the bloody clothes and left after feeling Wilder's forehead, too.

The doorway was filled by a large figure. Startled, Hope raised her gaze to see Mason's interested look as he took in her negligee and bed mussed hair. "He been awake, yet? Say anything about how this happened?" he asked.

"No, well he woke up and talked nonsense but nothing about who shot him or even where he was before coming here."

"Well, it looks like he wasn't shot anywhere near Sweetwater since there was a lot of dried blood on his saddle and horse. Looks like he rode quite a ways to get to you. You got any idea why?" he challenged.

"No, I, I have no idea." At Mason's unbelieving expression, she continued, "I don't know, truly. Bullet was whining, which is unusual but I thought he needed to go out, you know, so I took him to the back. He went right to Wilder lying on the ground. His horse was nearby and Wilder asked to be brought to Miss Lily. I got him up on his horse and then we came here. Wilder was still conscious and he could walk with me helping."

Hope thought she had covered everything that had occurred.

"Hmmm. Bullet the little mongrel that tried chewing my boot off to get into the house with me?"

"Wilder gave him to me for protection after the two men attacked me. Bullet doesn't like strangers, especially men, so he warns me when someone new comes near. If I introduce them to him then he knows that they're friends," Hope explained.

"So, you had no plans to see Wilder tonight?" He made a point to look at her peignoir set again.

"As I said, he showed up wounded. This," she lifted the end of the diaphanous negligee, "is something Miss Lily gave me to wear because my things were soaked with blood."

"Well, Wilder's missing out then, isn't he? I'll be back later and I'll send Vicki to get you some other clothes when people are awake over there. Keep them from calling me when they find you're missing. I'll ask Miss Lily to let the little mutt in to keep him from attacking anyone else. That kind of dog outside a place like this could be bad for business." He tipped his hat then left.

A few minutes later a blur of fur came running into the room, first checking on Hope than sniffing the bed and checking on Wilder. He circled a couple of times and lay down with a final "whiff" and went to sleep. Hope was sorry she hadn't thought about the little dog. Bullet had been probably frantic knowing Wilder was injured and that both she and Wilder had disappeared into the house. She smiled fondly at the sleeping pet and made a mental note to give him an extra good breakfast.

Hope must have fallen asleep when murmurs from

the bed awakened her. She jumped up going over to Wilder finding him feverish, trying to speak. Hope thought he was talking in his dream, or more like, nightmare. She could hear him say, "never" and "no" then his eyes opened, glittering with the fever. He stared at Hope and said very clearly, "mine" and "cherish," then some words that seemed garbled to her ears.

She tried to get him to drink some water, urging him to calm down and that he was safe and that she was safe with him. Bullet began to whine and hopped from one front foot to another, unable to help either person he was meant to protect. Using soothing words to both Wilder and the dog, she put a wet cloth on Wilder's forehead to help cool him.

Then she took another wet towel and began wiping it over his chest, the hair becoming damp curls and his nipples reacting to the cool brush against them. She dampened his entire chest area but stayed away from the bandaged wound. Raising his arm, she bathed that area knowing it responded to cold water and helped the body cool off faster.

The other was in the groin area but Hope wasn't going to resort to that unless his fever got worse. If that happened, then any embarrassment on either of their parts would be sacrificed. She even placed cool towels on his feet hoping treating those exposed areas would be enough.

The doctor finally came as day was breaking. He looked tired but didn't introduce himself or say much. He looked quizzically at the wet cloths draped over Wilder's feet and chest but other than that peeled back the bandage and grunted.

"Looks like that woman did a good job with this. I

should have stayed home and got to bed." Then he stood and gazed at Hope who had stood up while the doctor checked Wilder. "The cold cloths were a good idea. His fever is down and I think he's through the worse of it. Keep him from moving around and when he feels like it, light meals. He can be up in a day or two but nothing strenuous." He looked at her negligee and smiled.

Hope withered a little inside but thought it didn't matter what people thought of her. She decided last night Wilder was more important than her reputation, or her job, or anything else that made up her life. She was going to live as if her life was her own.

"Of course, doctor. I'll keep him down if I have to lay on him to do it," said Hope and wasn't a bit sorry she had said it.

The doctor picked up his bag, answering, "That's the kind of attitude we need in this town. It made the west what it is." He left speaking a few words to Miss Lily in the hallway as he went.

Victoria came in a half-hour later carrying a cloth bag, which she emptied to reveal clothes she had gotten from Hope's room. "I told Jeremy and Faith what happened and where you were. Faith was upset at first that she hadn't realized you were even gone but I explained that Jessie knew and Mason, too, so she calmed back down. I think she's worried she won't hear if anything bad happens downstairs."

"Well, if I had been abducted or something like that, Bullet would have sent up a warning and everyone within a half a mile would be wakened. Because it was Wilder, he didn't sound an alarm," Hope explained.

"Is he doing better? Mason said he was still unconscious," said Victoria as she looked over to the bed

243

and the near naked man.

"He became feverish but the doctor was here and thinks the worse is over. I've been keeping him cool and he doesn't seem to be in a lot of pain."

"I've got to get back. I'm working with Abby today since Matthew needs to go out of town. Is there anything I can do for you, first?" Victoria asked as she turned to leave.

"No, these clothes help. I keep getting some strange looks wearing the gown Miss Lily loaned me," Hope said, laughing at the memory of the stares she had received from the men she saw then remembered one was Victoria's husband. "Tell Mason I am not sleeping with Wilder. I think he may have gotten the wrong impression."

Victoria laughed. "I'll make sure he understands the situation. I think since we got married his mind goes there a lot more often. Don't take any offence. He's not judging you."

"It's simply that as a teacher, I need to be careful what people think about me." Then she reminded herself she had just decided she didn't care what people thought, but that evidently wasn't true. It was a hard habit to break after a lifetime of nuns and her student's judgmental parents. Hope added, "Thank you for bringing over the clothes and tell Mason I'll let him know when Wilder wakes up."

Hope walked Victoria to the door, pushed it closed and locked it. She returned to the clothes on the chair. Removing the lovely negligee set, she bent to pick up her under garments when she quickly glanced toward the bed. Again, Wilder was watching her, an unreadable grin on his face as she held the camisole up to cover what was attracting Wilder's attention the most.

"Please, a dying man's last wish?"

"You're not dying, Wilder, so stop trying to play the sympathy card. Now close your eyes so that I can get dressed," she ordered.

"What if I won't? What are you going to do?" he asked merely to continue the conversation with her as she stood there delectably trying to hide behind a small piece of fabric.

Hope stared directly into his silver eyes and let the camisole fall to the floor. She glanced down as if contemplating whether or not to pick it up and then nonchalantly bent down and lifted it up slowly, letting her breasts swing slightly with the motion.

Glancing at Wilder, she warned, "Both Mary Beth and the doctor said you shouldn't move or the bleeding may start up again and then it will take forever to heal."

Standing, she raised her arms to let the camisole slip down them and cover most of the important parts - barely. Since it was summer, Hope had foregone wearing a corset therefore that left simply the dress and stockings, which she sat down to put on. Raising one then the next leg into the air, she rolled the light weight material to just above the knee before tying them off with the ribbons. Standing, she bent over the chair to retrieve the dress, letting her fanny show slightly. She stood and like a ballerina, raised her arms and let that garment shimmy down her body.

As she buttoned the tiny buttons going down the front of the bodice, she heard Wilder mutter, "Babe, you're killing me."

Hope, without a bit of sympathy said, "You could have closed your eyes, Wilder."

"No, I couldn't. I tried. I couldn't resist you and you knew I wouldn't be able to. Where'd you learn to move like that, Babe? Or is it your natural female instincts to know how to turn a man into a hot coal?" he ended on a whisper.

Alarmed, she moved quickly to the bed placing her hand on Wilder's still cool brow. "You beast, you scared me."

"I didn't mean to. I was just letting you know how you affect me. I'm here trying not to move and all I really want to do his hold you and kiss you. Can you kiss me, Hope? It would do so much to make me feel better," he asked seriously but with that grin trying to escape.

Hope relented because if she were honest, she wanted to kiss, Wilder, too. Wanted to make sure he was going to be all right, that he was safe. Leaning over, she kissed him lightly on the lips.

"No, I said a kiss," he growled. Wilder, having more strength than Hope thought he had, pulled her down onto the edge of the bed. He covered her mouth with his, sucking and tugging lightly on her lower lip as he pulled away and then swooping in for another kiss. Finally, his tongue entered her mouth to bask in the warmth for a moment. Hope pulled away and Wilder let her.

Standing, pretending her world hadn't been shaken by his kisses, she brushed the wrinkles out of her skirt saying, "I told Mason I'd let him know when you were awake and able to talk."

"Mason can go and, well, it doesn't matter. I'm stuck in this bed for the day so he may as well come and hound me. You aren't leaving, are you? Maybe have another kissing session later today? I think it made me feel a whole lot better," he said truthfully.

"Wilder, what am I to do with you?"

Wilder said nothing because he either understood it to be rhetorical or what he wanted to say would get his face slapped, wounded or not.

"Could you take a little broth or something? I could send Miss Lily up with some." She offered as she headed away from the bed carrying the borrowed nightgown. "I need to tell Mason you're awake."

"Before you leave, could you help me drink some water?" At her disbelieving expression, he said, "I am thirsty and I guess it must be over a day since I've eaten. I'll behave myself."

"Sure." After helping hold the glass to his lips, Wilder drained it.

"Thanks, Babe," he said lying back on the pillow seemingly exhausted.

"Don't call me…. Never mind, I guess I'm getting used to it." Then Hope, followed by Bullet, left the room to find Miss Lily.

Miss Lily heard Hope descend and knew it meant Wilder was awake and doing better since she knew the young woman wouldn't have left his bedside if it were otherwise. "So, does he want some broth or beer or both?" asked Miss Lily.

"Both probably and he probably needs a bed pan but I think it best if I draw the line somewhere," confessed Hope remembering that striptease she had performed simply to torture Wilder. She rather enjoyed the power she felt over him and his body. Maybe not the most altruistic thing she had ever done but she found it educational to see the lust cross Wilder's face.

The married women were right. The woman has the power in a relationship and she can be benevolent or malevolent to her mate. It was something Hope would need to think about.

Miss Lily turned toward the stove after Hope's answer so didn't see Hope contemplating the morning's events.

"I need to tell Mason he's awake," said Hope.

Miss Lily opened the back door and called across the yard, "Andy, Andy get Mason, will you, Hon?"

Hope saw Andy wave back and start to run toward the jail.

"I should go home and explain to Faith and Jeremy what's been going on. I know they know the basics but I'll feel better telling them myself," Hope confided to Miss Lily.

"You need to go home and get some rest. We'll take good care of Wilder, don't you worry."

And then Hope remembered seeing Wilder in this very kitchen, twice, and felt a sting of jealousy the women in this house were taking care of Wilder even before she had met him. A weight came over her that she hoped didn't show to Miss Lily. After all, it wasn't the older woman's fault Wilder sought out this house and her girls for 'comfort'. It simply made Hope wonder if she wasn't as important to Wilder as he made her feel.

He never promised anything or offered anything besides a few kisses. What did Hope expect from a bounty hunter? He went where his job took him. He wasn't setting up house. Mentally shaking herself, she realized she had been planning on more, much more. And a man like Wilder wasn't made to give more.

Faith showed up a little while later with Hope's hat and gloves. "I thought if we walked home from Mary Beth's direction the towns' people will assume, we had been visiting together. No one need know more than that. Jessie knows how important a teacher's reputation is so no one's been told you aren't in the office or upstairs."

"Thank you, it sounds like you've thought of everything. I think we should go as soon as we can. I'm very tired and should try to be seen in the office a little so people won't believe any gossip that may get out. I know Victoria or Miss Lily and the ladies here will keep a secret," Hope said, relieved now that a plan was being formed to cover her absence this morning.

Stella and Lacy were in the parlor knitting when Hope and Faith came through. Hope had combed her hair into a simple bun and tucked it under her hat, making it appear she and Faith had simply been visiting. Taking a last look into the mirror on the wall, she regretted not having the cream to cover her birthmark. Then remembered she hadn't been wearing any the whole time since last night and no one remarked on it.

She said her goodbyes and gratitude before descending the front steps with Faith, smiling and chatting as they always did, the little mutt following.

CHAPTER 7

Mason appeared in the doorway of Wilder's room. "You still among the living?"

Wilder didn't bother opening his eyes. He felt too weak to pick up his gun to protect himself if he had to anyways. "Yes, if pain means I'm alive."

"It's a sign, I guess. Want to tell me what happened?"

Wilder sighed but felt Mason had a right to know. "The good news is that it didn't happen in your jurisdiction. I knew of a place Vargas has been known to frequent. A woman who works there felt she owed me a favor so let me know when he showed up for his, ah, entertainment. I went and staked it out. Then in the middle of the night a guy that appeared to be Vargas came out and got on a horse that had been tied up since before I arrived. I followed to try to make sure it was Vargas. If I could find his hideout, I could get the whole gang and that would be a few more hundred in bounty."

"Well, was it worth it? Did you find out anything about where he was headed? Or just catch a bullet?" Mason asked without sympathy.

"I was keeping well back. I would swear Vargas didn't know I was there but someone else sure as hell did. I was shot from the back. The bullet went through me but I stayed on Diablo. He's trained to take off if I'm hit like that and I must have been out for a few minutes. When I woke up, I just kept thinking I had to get to Hope. Make sure no one was coming for her thinking I was out of the picture. She found me, well, Bullet did and the rest

250

you know." And Wilder's story was told.

"So, you don't know who shot you but you knew where?" Mason asked to be sure.

"Just this side of Preston," supplied Wilder.

"Doesn't give me anything more than what we knew before. You got shot for nothing sounds like to me," Mason said as he turned to leave.

"Not nothing. I got to spend some time alone with Hope." He coughed holding his hand over his wound trying not to do that again.

"There is that, then. Get better, Wilder. I may need your help." Then he was gone.

Jessie looked up with a smile when Faith and Hope came through the front door, Bullet coming in with the skirts. "How goes the vigil? Any story for the paper?"

"I don't know much about the how," said Hope. "But Mason may be able to give you some information later today. He's was going to talk with Wilder and get more facts."

"You look tired, Hope. Why don't' you go and rest. There's nothing to do here anyways. Are you hungry? You can go upstairs, have a meal and rest in the second bedroom. It should be quiet," offered Faith peering closely at her friend.

Just then Mrs. Thompson, the wife of the owner of the dry goods store came in all aflutter and made a bee line to Faith and Hope. "I saw you come back from your, er, walk. But it's funny, I never saw you leave with Faith or that beast you call, Billet."

"Bullet and I went out earlier through the alley. It actually seems a little shorter that way," fabricated Hope.

"I needed to speak with Abby so I went there while Hope went directly to Mary Beth's. We were visiting for a few hours. I guess time got away from us," Faith lied without a flicker of an eyelash.

Mrs. Thompson had an 'aha expression' in her eyes and said, "I thought Mary Beth was taking care of Rebecca and the baby." She watched the two young women closely for any sign of fright.

Jessie jumped in saying casually, "No, she was home this morning with me. Rebecca told her she didn't need any help and I guess people have dropped off so much food, Rebecca thinks she or Daniel won't need to cook for weeks."

Faced with all three telling the same story, Mrs. Thompson backed down. "Well, I came in to see if the article about the Fourth of July celebration is done and if I could get a copy to review."

Faith replied, "Surly, it's right here." She pulled out a sheet of paper with typing on it and handed it to the older woman.

Mrs. Thompson didn't even glance at the sheet but turned toward Jessie as she left the office. "I'll let you know what I think of the article."

The three friends glanced at each other in amazement that Mrs. Thompson was so transparent in her need to gossip about everything.

Jessie, as he began his own work again, said, "She can let me know what she thinks of my article but I'm not changing anything in it."

Hope felt Mrs. Thompson's visit was the last thing she could handle and went upstairs to rest, Bullet following on her heels.

Later that day, Jessie relayed to Hope that Wilder was doing well and seemed to be in full recovery. The truth was brought home when Hope saw Wilder leaning against the wall in the walkway between the jail and the hotel's restaurant. A favorite place for him because he could watch the newspaper and the full length of the street. Mason wasn't in sight.

Then a bustle of dark-green caught Hope's eyes as she saw Colette, without a hat or gloves, cross the street to speak with Wilder. They spoke for several minutes and then Wilder tipped his hat and followed Colette back to the building next door, her studio and home.

Hope tried not to think of what the lovely dark-haired woman and Wilder were doing, what they could possibly have in common to talk about. Unless they weren't talking. Unless Colette saw Wilder and wanted him and Wilder saw a beautiful woman and wanted her. Hope shook her head. She mustn't think like that. She had no ties on Wilder nor he on her. She had to remember that - but it was so difficult.

"I'm going to go to my room for a while. This heat is making me fatigued I think." Hope said excusing her low spirits as tiredness.

Next door Colette was in her glory. She had found an unusual face to photograph and was placing the chair so the light coming in from the window crossed it at the correct angle. Wilder stood gazing around at the camera and stands and the wicker chairs with a palm tree in the corner. He had agreed to this because somehow being in this room made him feel closer to Hope next door.

"Come here, Mr. Wilder. Take a seat just so, no? Do you wish to hold your gun in your lap? You know, show it off?" the French woman asked him.

Wilder's head came up fast but then realized the women meant exactly what she said, and he replied, "Ah, no, I'll keep my gun right where it's at. In the holster."

"*Oui*, that is good, too. Now when I say, do not move until I tell you, no?" Colette moved the camera tripod a little closer then turned and twisted it on its stand and finally said, "I will make the shutter open so no more moving, not even a blink." She lowered the black cloth over her head and a flash went off but Wilder remained as he sat, no movement, not even a blink. He was good at that.

"You must be part Indian*, ne'st pas?*"

"So they say."

"That is so exciting, it gives your face, your cheek-bones a very attractive aspect, you know? A dramatic look, a warrior look." And there was another click and flash.

Wilder thought the remarks a little romantic for what a half-breed was usually called but didn't say anything.

"But those eyes, those glorious eyes, these are not Indian, no?" she asked moving the camera base to another spot.

"No, those I got from my Welch grandfather," Wilder admitted.

"Just one more, turning just a little more toward me, *oui,* that is it." And Colette began the process all over again much to Wilder's amusement.

"Now you may go visit Hope. She is usually not busy in the afternoon. I could go and get her to come here if that is more better. You can, umm, meet in my private quarters in the back *ne'st pas?*" asked Colette trying to help her friend and this man have some private time together.

"No, I mean, you're mistaken as to my and Miss Hope's relationship. I'm just helping Mason, the sheriff, keep an eye on things here," he said trying to deflect Colette's interest in Hope and himself.

"*Oui*, but who is to know if you are here with me or there with Hope? She would like to see you, I know."

Alert now, Wilder asked, "Did she say that? To you, I mean, that she needs to see me?"

"*Non*, but she does, I know. She is sad and a little lonely and it is you she wants to see, not the others."

"I can go and see her, if you think she wants me to?" Wilder asked hopefully.

"*Oui*, she is right next door. Her *petit un chien*, her little dog is always where she is so, find him and you will find her, I am sure," added Colette as she walked Wilder out through the back of the building and right into Hope's backyard.

Colette left Wilder standing next to the building Hope's room was in and disappeared back into her own apartment. He smiled as he realized he might have been set up but then shook his head and decided to see if the rear door to the newspaper was unlocked and it was.

From the rear hall, Wilder could see the room Hope had been in during the attack was closed. As he got closer, he could see Bullet's little paws peaking from under the door, trying to dig his way out. Wilder tried the knob and it opened so he slid into the darkened room and could see Hope lying on top of the bed, dressed except for her shoes.

A tightness in his groin hit Wilder like a punch and his wound ached with the tightening of his abdominal muscles. He hadn't realized what gut reaction he had to this woman and he gave up the fight right then. He was never going to want or love anyone else the way he did Hope. He accepted that fact and went toward the bed, trying not to startle her. Seeing the gun on the table next to the bed he felt a little safer being there.

Whispering, he said, "Hope? Babe? Wake up, I need to talk to you." He lied. He wanted to do a lot more than talk but he knew, even with her teasing, Hope wasn't a girl he could make love to and then leave. She deserved more than that.

Hope turned sleepily then sat up realizing that this time Wilder wasn't part of a pleasant dream. "Is something wrong? What are you doing in here?" She peered around for some sort of danger.

"I haven't been able to talk with you since you left me at Miss Lily's. I wanted to come and thank you for getting me help and staying with me, taking care of me." And because he couldn't resist added, "And for giving me that little strip-show. It really raised my morale."

"I am sorry I did that. I must have been overly tired and let my sense of the ridiculous get the better of me." She smiled at the memory of the expressions that had crossed Wilder's face as she did what she had done.

"I'm more than ready for another any time you say," he assured her.

Then Hope remembered what had made her want to be alone in her room. "Perhaps you can talk Colette into one. I'm out of the competition."

Wilder smiled and sat on the bed, pulling Hope unto his lap, saying, "You have no competition, my green-eyed little cat. I was having my photograph taken and it was Colette who suggested I visit with you by way of her back door." He rubbed his day's growth of beard against Hope's neck and cheek. "I liked the suggestion."

"I find that hard to believe. You reek of her perfume," said Hope denying herself the luxury of wrapping her arms around his neck and accepting his lovemaking.

Wilder sniffed at the sleeve of his shirt saying, "I can't possibly. She never came closer than two feet of me but I'm glad you're suspicious. Tells me that in some way you feel possessive of me." He kissed her neck just under her ear because he couldn't stop himself.

"I do not. There are way too many women to fight off if I felt possessive of you," she said petulantly.

"I know a jealous woman when I hear one, Babe. But don't worry. It makes me feel kind of, I don't know, proud, I guess, that a beautiful woman like you could find me attractive." He continued the mapping of her neck and shoulders as he unbuttoned the top few buttons of her shirtwaist.

Hope was enjoying his attentions and wasn't paying much thought to anything else when she blurted out her worse fear, "But you visit Miss Lily's, probably daily."

"I think of the place as a second home. I've known Miss Lily for years from when she lived near my family and Lacy and Stella are just part of that family now. I've never bedded those ladies. What do you take me for?" he asked, feeling hurt at her lack of faith in him.

"I'm sorry but I saw you there every time I visited," she admitted.

"First, I was following you and second, I was staying in that upstairs room. By myself," he said to prevent Hope from adding another sin against him. "Then Mason moved me into a front room at the hotel so I could watch over this building during the night. He took the day shift."

"I'm sorry, Wilder. I shouldn't act like I have any part of telling you what to do or how to live."

"Like I said, I'm proud of knowing you care something for me. Not that I deserve it." Wilder lifted his head saying, "You're going to hear things about me, about my family and I want you to know they're not true." He hesitated, licking his lips in nervousness.

Hope gazed worriedly at Wilder, knowing that not much threw him off-guard but waited for him to continue.

"You'll hear that my grandmother was raped by a Comanche and that my father is a bastard. It's not true, none of it. I knew my grandparents and my grandmother was Comanche. She and my grandfather were married under tribal law because no one else would hold with a white man marrying an Indian squaw. But I know they loved each other. I saw it every day of my life until she died of a fever and he died of a broken heart. Never believe it was otherwise," he finished emphatically.

"I won't. It's a lovely family story and you should let others know."

"I don't care what others think but I wanted you to know my family isn't from bad roots," he confided.

"I'm glad to know more about you. I think a man who comes from so much love must have love in him, too," she said as she nuzzled herself under his chin.

"I want to tell you one more thing." His voice got very deep and he said quietly as if admitting to a sin, "My first name is, Coyote."

"Coyote." She let the sound roll around on her tongue then said, "I like it. It suits you. Your parents did a good job." She continued to kiss his rasping chin and then his jaw line, moving toward his lips.

"I hate to do this but if I don't leave right now all my good intentions of just stopping by to thank you will go up in flames. You heat my blood so easily I need to stay away or we'll both end up miserable," he told her too honestly.

"Why would we be miserable?" asked Hope, confused by his comment.

"Because I am what I am and you are what you are. We aren't ever going to be able to openly live together. I don't want you shunned or worse because of me," he told her bluntly.

"I have no say in this?" asked Hope hurt that he thought so little of her character.

"You have no idea what the rest of the world is really like. Let's leave it as it is. That way no one will get hurt." He put Hope onto the bed and stood, cracking open the door to see if it was clear to leave. Wilder told Bullet to stay and slid through the door opening closing it behind him.

Hope lay back down but wasn't sleepy any more, merely sad. Sad for Wilder and sad for herself. She wasn't unaware that the people in the west were still separated by origins even if the new states and territories seemed like a melting pot of all nationalities. The split between Indian and homesteader went deeper, like the pain and anger still present in some Southerners and Northerners. It wasn't going away soon but as more and more families integrated, the harsh differences and anger would dissipate. Become less with each generation.

Being raised by the nuns and knowing their benevolent views of children of mixed heritage, Hope had a different idea of what made up a family. She had looked forward to the time she would have one of her own when she was still too young to realize why she had never been adopted like the other girls. No one needed to explain it to her but eventually she stopped accepting the invitations to join the others in parading in front of potential couples looking to adopt. She knew her appearance would make couples turn away and even leave without a child after realizing the chance of adopting a non-perfect child was a proven possibility.

Of course, Hope wasn't the only child rejected merely on appearance. Those children of mixed heritage also stayed in their rooms while the potential couples visited with the more adoptable orphans seeking homes. They all seemed to have given up any expectation of having a family or parents who wanted them. They formed a sort of family within the orphanage and she felt closer to them than any of the others except for Faith and Charity, the other parts of the trilogy.

Could she see herself as a wife to Wilder, though? That was a different story. He seemed unsettled and possibly unaccepting of his own worth. He was seeing himself through the eyes of others who only meant him harm. Was she strong enough to help him see himself differently? Was she strong enough to fight for him? Was she worthy of finding a life and family with him?

CHAPTER 8

The whole town was abuzz with the excitement of the Fourth of July, the newspaper having put out articles the last three weeks plus the Special Edition Jessie was running off the press at this moment. Although the entire town was decorated, the actual celebration was being held in the front yards of the church and the new school building.

There had been an old-fashioned barn raising for the roof of the school the day before. Many of the men from the outlaying farms and ranches, along with their families, came into Sweetwater to help raise the rafters for the roof. Many of them camped outside of town near the river adding a festive mood to the whole event. The mayor was well pleased with how the new school was bringing the townspeople and those living within the county together already.

Hope and Faith baked a couple of pies and had fried chicken staying warm in Mary Beth's oven. Abby and the babies were going to be at Mary Beth's house for the day, as well as, Charity, who came in from the ranch. That meant a lot of people to watch the children so Abby and Matthew could have some fun without worrying about the babies getting too much sun or not enough sleep.

Callie was bringing Warren and staying with Rebecca, who was planning on making a visit to the celebrations but probably not with baby Jacob. Seth had sent money and men to the roof raising the night before and the rest of his hands were driving in that day. The

Macgregor's were staying at home rather than bring the new babies and their mothers into town. Jessie and Jeremy made plans to take their wives for an extended visit to their brothers' ranch the next day.

The town had been trimmed in bunting of red, white and blue while signs were posted as to special activities and things of interest happening throughout the day. There was to be a marksmen contest also known as a turkey shoot and then women would be urged to throw a fry pan as far as they could. The winner being the one to toss it the farthest without hitting any of the spectators. There was to be a three-legged race and the boys' only wheelbarrow race, mostly for the young people and a pie contest.

Abby was holding a prettiest hat contest as she had at Easter. It was being judged by Colette since, as a newcomer, she didn't know Abby's creations from any others. The Mayor had disqualified his wife from entering to keep peace in the home, he said. Abby was furnishing the winner with a new willow, which was the starter for building a new hat.

Hope had set up a spelling bee, which gave her a chance to meet some of her new students. She had a book of stories set aside as the prize for the winner. Later in the day there was to be singing led by Miss Lily and then dancing after the potluck supper.

The spelling bee had just finished with the winner being, Helga, who had beat out several older children. Mrs. Burgess was all smiles wearing the blue ribbon her daughter had won.

Thomas Thompson, the oldest son of the Mayor and dry goods store owner, strolled over to Hope. He had his straw boater in his hand as he said, "Miss St. Michaels, I think it was a great idea to add so many things for the young people to do, to make them more a part of the event. I think it makes them aware of why we celebrate this day."

"Thank you, Mr. Thompson, but please call me, Hope. There are several St. Michaels in town." She smiled at this friendly man with sandy-brown hair and brown eyes. He had a wide forehead and strong jaw, with a nice smile and appeared to be open and welcoming. Hope knew he was newly back to town after a trip to the southern states. He asked if he could get her a cool lemonade and Hope agreed, sitting at one of the tables with benches the men had set up last night for the communal supper later that day.

Thomas returned with the drinks. "Please call me Thom, my Dad is Thomas or Mr. Thompson, so I don't answer to those names without someone nudging me." He sat next to her asking, "So you've been here a little over a month now?"

"Yes, my previous position was over for the summer and parents in Appleton weren't sure they wanted to keep a female teacher. Many parents felt a male teacher would be able to make their children smarter out of fear and physical threats." She shook her head showing her feelings of such motivation. "But it was their decision. Then Callie Harrison wrote and offered me this position. It will have less children, at least to start, but I look forward to teaching a wide age group again."

"How many do you think there will be?"

"I think seven in the lower grades and five or six in the upper grades. I have been working with the Burgess children and they have been a joy and eager to learn. Well, except Hans, but he is competitive and will work hard once he's put against the other older children. He's very good at arithmetic already. I think working in the butcher shop honed those skills," she explained because she felt Thom was seriously interested.

"It sounds like you really know some of your students well already. It's nice to see someone take such an interest in their work," he said approvingly.

"It's not work to me. I enjoy teaching children new things. How to learn is as important as what to learn. I'll do a lot of reading in class as well as writing assignments so the children can see how what they read is useful in their lives now. I like to do plays, also, since it brings the books to life." She smiled knowing how some of the older boys will re-act to those.

Thom smiled and leaned in toward Hope. "Makes me wish I could attend school again. My teacher was old mean Mr. Green. I think I still have the welts of the willow branch on my backside." He laughed out loud at his audacity of speaking of his backside to a complete stranger. "You make me forget myself, Hope. I better watch it or you could go right to my head." He looked at Hope as if seeing her again for the first time.

Mrs. Thompson hustled over from where she had been talking with friends and said sharply, "Thomas, I need to speak with you. Now."

"Yes, Mother, how can I help you?" He stood and followed his mother a few feet away where Mrs. Thompson imparted some very important information, pointing her finger at Thom's chest and making hissing noises in her emphatic speech.

Thom, red faced and obviously angry, turned away from his mother and started to return to Hope when Mrs. Thompson could be plainly heard to say, "And that disfiguring mark could be hereditary, you know. I don't want some grandchild of mine looking like a pinto pony." As her son ignored her, she screeched, "Listen to me, Thomas, there will be more to choose from."

Thom turned and said loudly, evidently past his breaking point, "Mother, stop showing your ignorance and shut-up." Then he looked at Hope, a pleading for understanding in his eyes. Hope shook her head slightly, telling him not to come closer. He stalked away toward the store leaving his mother standing there, her mouth opening and closing like a beached fish.

Hope stood and brushed her skirt down, smiling to her neighbors at the adjoining table before excusing herself and walking down the alley toward her home.

Faith went to follow but Mary Beth whispered, "Let her have her dignity. If we interfere now, she may break down and cry and then she'll never stay in Sweetwater. Many of the children heard and are appearing worried at the disturbance."

Just then Miss Lily announced they were starting the sing-a-long and a man with a concertina and another with a fiddle began a popular song that drew a group over to the stage where Miss Lily was leading the singers.

Things seemed to calm immediately and people not singing went back to what they were doing before they were so rudely interrupted. Mrs. Thompson eventually realized people were staring at her with contempt and she hurried after her son.

Hope was still walking, head up and eyes tearless but a slight tremble was threatening her mouth. If she could hold off the tears until she was in her room, she would be all right - just a few more steps. Finally, she made it through the back door. Bullet not understanding what was wrong but somehow knowing Hope wasn't to be bothered with his usual exuberance followed quietly.

Removing her hat, she set it on the five-drawer chest. She finally let the tears fall as she laid down on the bed facing the wall. Then she heard Wilder as he sank down on the bed spoon fashion, pulling her into the curve of his body.

"Babe, she's not worth the tears. She's a stupid woman with stupid thoughts," he said, the anger plain in his voice.

"I know but they are her thoughts and if she thinks that way then there are others," she said through the tears.

"Well, if there are, they weren't there today. Not one person agreed with her and many made it plain she should leave," said Wilder, trying to make Hope realize how many friends she had here already.

"I shouldn't have tried to cover up my disfigurement. I should have been honest with everyone," she said, her voice getting steadier.

"I can't believe that, Hope. You are more than a mark. I mean, I see it but I see you, too. It doesn't define who you are. You're not the woman with a birthmark - you're the woman that happens to have a birthmark. It's a big difference to me. I don't see it when I look at you. I never have." He kissed her neck and rolled her over to face him.

"You will not convince me you do not see half my face is purple," she snapped angrily.

"It's more of a lavender but, no, I don't see it. I know it's there but also I see your lovely sun streaked hair, your hazel eyes and long lashes, the tip of your nose that twitches when you giggle." As he listed Hope's attributes, he kissed that part. When he was finished with her facial features, he began on the more physical attributes starting with her breasts, which he kissed through the thin material of her muslin dress.

"All my life I was the girl people stared at, whispered about behind their hands or called names outright. I am well aware of my disfigurement and that it causes most people to turn their faces away from me. It's always been who I am," Hope confessed.

"Sweetheart, my problem has always been written on my face, too. Half-breed. I got beat up so many times I just started hitting first if I got even a sideways glance. By the time I was thirteen, I was carrying a six-shooter and that kind of put an end to the beatings. Any man would have to think himself pretty good with a gun to come up against me. I made sure of that so I know what being shunned because of what you look like means. I'm sorry you had to go through your life feeling like that but I'm here now to tell you how wrong they were. And you have dozens of friends that agree with me," he said urgently, pressing kisses upon her face again.

"I almost believe it when we are like this. You make me feel like the most desirable woman in the world, Wilder." She sighed.

"You are the most desirable woman in the world and if you let me, I'll try to show you just how much." Wilder took Hope's lips and kissed her as if she were the most precious thing in the world. The best part of that was, to him, she was. He covered her mouth, sucking and stroking and finally inserting his tongue and urging her to return the favor, which she did to his satisfaction.

Wilder palmed the eager nipples through the muslin and then unbuttoned the front of the dress to give him better access. He reached in to cup one side and rolled the rigid nipple between his thumb and forefinger. Hope pushed herself into Wilder's body, arching to get closer to him and the pleasure he was giving her.

He left Hope's lips and opened the dress so his mouth could then lave the nipple that had been ignored, urging it into the same hard pebble the first one was. As he suckled the breast nearest to him his hand moved downward stroking Hope's hip. He slipped his hand under her skirt and up to the soft flesh leading directly to the mound covered by soft fluffs of hair.

Returning to Hope's mouth, Wilder inserted his tongue as he inserted his finger into the soft, silky warmth, letting the wet welcome of her body almost un-do his intentions of merely pleasuring her. Hope pushed into Wilder's hand, slowly moaning as her body stretched to reach a pinnacle, she was yet unaware of existing.

Still moving his hand, Hope's breathing increased and her body surged against his. He began urging her to her climax. "Let it come, Babe. Let it come." And then a few strokes later as Hope was unable to even voice her questions a stiffening then shudder rolled through her body, interior muscles clamping around Wilder's finger.

He stayed holding Hope tightly, his body having rocked against Hope's during the last most intriguing moments but he hadn't embarrassed himself completely, at least. Hope's climax had affected Wilder much more than he had expected and his breathing was almost as stressed as hers. Almost. He kissed her, letting her examine her reactions to what they had just done together.

"That was, that was…I don't know but what did you

do? Am I still a virgin?" she asked with naiveté.

"Yes, I am sorry to say, you are still a virgin. Just a better educated virgin," he said hugging her to him, enjoying the sheer amazement in her eyes. "In the future when you think of this day, this is what I want you to remember." He kissed her, praying that Hope would remember only this time, this place and remember him as he was today.

After a few minutes, he said, "I better get out of sight. Your friends might begin to worry and start looking for you. They won't be pleased to find me here. Stay as long as you want but be back to the celebration by the time the dance music starts or I'll carry you back if need be."

Then opening the door, Bullet, who had been banned from the room when Wilder got there, ran in trying to see what he had missed out on.

Back at the celebration, people were milling around after the children's games and the cake-walk began. Wilder appeared next to Mason as he stood on the outside of the group looking in.

Mason glanced at Wilder, still dripping wet, and asked, "What happened to you?"

"I made the acquaintance of a horse trough," Wilder told him bluntly.

"Yeah, I used to do that, too, only it wasn't the hot weather that usually was the cause. It sounds almost refreshing after the heat of today, though," Mason confessed.

Wilder didn't say anything but wondered about a guy like Mason having to take a cold bath when his body was in need. And nobody ever had more need than Wilder did today. Hell, he was getting an arousal just thinking about Hope and her first climax. He would have to stop thinking or he was going to be sopping wet all afternoon.

The meal was being brought to the table. The long boards hastily nailed together last night and the matching benches were beginning to fill. There already were jars of pickles, preserves and breads wrapped in gingham cloths lining the long table. Then there were pies, cakes and the sugar cookies Miss Lily was famous for baking.

The women began carrying pots and pans and dishes, spacing the foods along the boards, making sure there was some of each kind of food for each group of people. Callie's table was very sought after, everyone knowing her reputation for tasty dishes. People sat down with their own place service and spoons were produced to dish up the hearty stews and sweetened baked beans, Boston style.

No area of the U. S. was left out and several countries were represented as well. Mrs. Burgess had brought a big kettle of fat sausages and potatoes and what she called *sour braten*. Colette had a pot of chicken cooked in wine with lemon and capers. The aromas of all the different foods tantalizing the hungry gathering.

Reverend Walters called for quiet and led the group in grace, ending with God Bless America and a chorus of Amen. Then the food began to disappear.

Hope had rejoined her friends and was happily sitting at one end of the tables, passing dishes up and down the line of people. Soon all the plates were filled and the group settled into eating. Hope got up with her plate and took it to Wilder who was sitting on a tree stump brought in for the celebration.

She held the plate out to him and he grinned up at

her saying, "This is yours, Babe." He was glad she felt self-confident enough to face him after what they had done together that afternoon.

"I'm not very hungry any more. You need your strength," she said as he took the plate and she sat on the stump next to him.

He took a bite then took another forkful and lifted it toward Hope's lips. She smiled and opened her mouth for the bite, watching as Wilder's mouth opened mimicking what he wanted her to do. She licked her lips, tasting the sweetness lingering on them and taking it back into her mouth.

Wilder felt himself go stiff all over again and tried not to watch Hope so closely as he fed her from the food on the plate.

They spent the half-hour alone and laughed and talked about everything and nothing but definitely not about what they had done together that afternoon. Faith and Charity came over to see what or who was keeping their friend so entertained. Wilder stood and tipped his hat as Hope made the introductions.

Wilder felt like a young boy on his first date being vetted by the maiden aunts. It made him smile since he and Hope were a lot further along than a first date. Then he realized how much he smiled since becoming close to Hope. He hadn't realized it had become such a rare occurrence. He looked with pride-filled eyes at Hope and the others seem to fade away, leaving only the two of them as their gazes met across the small space between them.

Thad came up to them and admired Wilder's gun but Wilder didn't encourage his interest.

Hope said, "I haven't seen you much lately. Are you

getting anything done besides your work with the building crew?"

"I'm learning a lot of new skills on the job, Miss Hope. I mean, I've learned how to make and use a twist drill." Pointing to the framed building behind them, he explained, "There needs to be a dozen holes drilled into each of those beams for the wood pegs to hold the mortise and tenon joinery. And then on some of them we use a hand crank drill but I really want to try the ratchet wrench. I haven't been given a job that needs it, yet, but there is still a lot of work to do." Thad couldn't prevent his excitement from showing.

"That sounds like a lot of good information. You can help me make up some story problems for the younger students and perhaps a quiz as to what tool is needed for what job, even if you've never used the tool yourself," said Hope trying to get Thad as excited about going to school as he is about going to work.

"And the new, ah, urinal came in for the bank. It's for, ah, it's for…." Then looked to Wilder for help and Wilder simply shrugged leaving Thad on his own.

"It's for men. I understand, Thad." She gave a reprimanding look at Wilder who merely grinned back at her.

Suddenly a gunshot went off nearby and Wilder put himself in front of Hope and the others. His weapon pulled and pointed outward, his gaze taking in anyone who seemed threatening. Then another and another gunshot went off as some of the men fired into the air, celebrating the Fourth in a traditional western way. Wilder holstered his pistol and smiled at the ladies, politely ignoring the fact he had been poised to protect only Hope.

The musicians tuned their instruments and then they were playing a lively song, urging the people to grab a partner and dance. The next was a type of square dance, the fiddler calling out the moves as the couples formed stars and bowed to their corner.

Hope stood tapping her foot and Wilder said, "The next is going to be our dance, Hope. I'll insist you honor our bargain." He grinned proprietarily. A smile he had been using with her since she came back from her room that afternoon. He wasn't sure it had been such a good idea to pleasure Hope but he wouldn't do it differently if he had it to do over. Simply seeing Hope happy, enjoying her friends and standing near to him had him wishing things could be different.

Hope enjoyed her dance with Wilder and then Thom approached her, taking off his hat, asking, "May I have the pleasure of this dance?"

Hope, knowing what it took for Thom to approach her in front of all his neighbors, smiled and said graciously, "Certainly, sir." She dipped a pert curtsy then accepted his proffered hand. She followed him unto the dance floor, joining the other couples as they got ready for the music to begin.

Thom held Hope very properly and tried to make small talk, making sure a smile remained on his face at all times. Hope tried to ease his stiffness by answering and asking nonconfrontational questions.

Finally, Thom said, "Miss St. Michaels, I want…need to apologize for my mother's crassness."

Hope interrupted by saying, "Please feel free to use my Christian name as you did before. And I understand why your mother is so upset."

"I don't, not really. I know she wants me to stay in

273

Sweetwater now but I don't feel comfortable here. My mother got a bee in her bonnet that it was because there weren't any young women of marriageable age but the truth is, I don't want to stay because she's here."

Hope looked up at the man. Still trying to keep a smile on his face while confessing personal problems in his family. She waited for him to finish.

"I would be delighted to court you under any other circumstances but I don't know if I'll be staying. I wouldn't want to begin knowing there may not be a proper conclusion." By now Thom was red-faced and had difficulty meeting Hope's gaze.

"I don't mind, Thom, since I find myself committed elsewhere. I won't take your noncommitment as a sign you find me or my disfigurement repugnant," she told him, a real smile on her face.

"Your commitment, ah, could that be with a rather frightening looking ruffian who's been staring daggers at me since I brought you out unto this dance floor?" he asked, a little more relaxed talking with her now he made clear his hesitation over becoming involved.

"Very intense silver eyes?" she asked still smiling up into his face.

"Yes, and his hand on his gun. Is there something I should know?" His smile started to slip.

"He's simply unsure of me. He thinks I'm too good for him but he doesn't want anyone else around me either," she admitted softly so Thom had to lean in to hear her. He noticed that evoked the dark man to tense and Thom felt the hair on the back of his neck stand on end.

The music faded to a conclusion and Thom bowed slightly stepping away from Hope without appearing as if he had received a reprieve from a death sentence. As they walked back to the edge of the dance area, Thom headed directly toward Wilder standing in a gunfighters' stance, a challenge in his eyes.

Once in front of Wilder, Thom thanked Hope for the dance and faded into the crowd as the musicians started up the next set. Hope saw Thom next to Colette a minute later walking onto the dance floor.

She turned to Wilder and said calmly, "Wilder, you must not scare every man I come in contact with. Thom simply wanted to apologize."

"He was doing more than apologizing. That could have been done in a minute right here." Jealousy and suspicion were evident in his tone.

"He was letting the town know there isn't any animosity between us. He was doing it for his benefit as well as mine. Putting any future meeting between us on a polite footing although he did explain why he couldn't pursue me," Hope said adding the last to see if she could get a rise out of Wilder.

"I knew he was up to no good. Something about the way he kept looking back at me. Did he say anything he shouldn't have? Was he rude?" Wilder asked, peering in the direction where Thom and Colette were dancing. Letting Hope know that Wilder had never lost track of Thom all the time they had been discussing him.

Placing her hand on Wilder's arm, she said, "Wilder, stop this immediately. I have no interest in him and deep down you know that. You're acting out of, I guess, frustration because we can't be together right now." Her eyes pleaded with him not to make a scene, another scene surrounding her.

"You're probably right, Babe. I've had little to

occupy my mind besides this afternoon and its driving me a little crazy." He gave Hope a look that warmed her all the way to her toes.

CHAPTER 9

The crowd began to thin out and every once in a while, a burst of rifle shots would ring out from the camping site as men, a little worse for wear on the free beer, tried one last time to celebrate the birth of a nation.

Hope had been laying on her bed still dressed, half expecting Wilder to show up although the goodnight kiss they shared seemed to indicate he was going to his room in the hotel. Finally, unable to sleep, she got up and went to the back alley, letting Bullet run around investigating the new smells of night.

Turning, she began walking back to the celebration site, the glow of the campfires used to keep the mosquitoes away still showing in the darkness. As Hope got closer, she noticed the church windows had candles or lamps still burning in them.

Hope knew why she had walked in this direction. She hadn't had the consolation of confession for months and felt the need to commune with God in his house, alone, where she might hear His answer. So much was happening inside her, she needed some solace, some way to know what she should do.

Her time with Wilder, the feelings he evoked within her had opened up new possibilities. As a teacher, she couldn't be married. As a married woman, she would be expected to stay at home and keep house for her husband. But she wasn't that kind of woman and Wilder wasn't that kind of man. He spent his time bringing criminals to justice. He didn't even have a home. Something she learned as they ate supper this evening. A man without a home certainly didn't need a wife to care for it.

Yet, she knew she was in love with the man. Knew she couldn't turn him away if he showed up in her bed again. Knew she didn't want to turn him away. The reason for her turmoil and lack of peace was easily found – the answers wouldn't be.

Looking down at the little dog, bounding after a moth, she said, "This isn't a place for you, boy. Stay out here and play with the bugs. I won't be long." She slipped through the double doors of the church making sure to close them after her.

Walking directly to the front pulpit, she genuflected making the sign as the nuns taught all the children of St. Michaels. She knelt and began her prayer, looking for forgiveness and guidance and peace from the Source she knew could provide it.

A man's hoarse, accented voice startled Hope into jumping up and facing the sound.

"I knew you would come to the church. It is the holiest place in this town even if it is not for us Catholics."

Hope wasn't sure who or why this man was here this time of night but she followed her instincts saying, "God's house is open to all. Everyone is welcome to pray in their own way."

"I am glad you remembered why you are here, St. Michaels. I am in need and you shall relieve me of my pain." The man kneeled down in front of an astonished Hope, bending his head as if in prayer.

"I, I am not St. Michaels. I mean, I am but not like that. It is my name, Hope St. Michaels. I'm not special in any way." She tried to reason with the man who seemed to be under some mistaken idea she could help him spiritually. His grasp on her dress seemed unbreakable.

"No, you are my blessing, my relief from this constant pain and the buzzing voices. Put an end to the bright, splintering lights and colors that plague me until I lose all reason. I need to sleep. It has been days, I know, but I can't remember how many now." After the long dialog, he became quiet panting for breath.

Hope was looking toward the backdoor leading to the graveyard and farther on the parsonage wondering if she could make it there before the man caught her. He was a little over-weight but otherwise seemed fit enough. He didn't seem violent, simply confused and Hope made plans for an escape as she stood rooted to her spot.

"That witch, that Selena…after I paid her hundreds of pesos, she tells me she cannot help. That only you can help me. She told me, find the woman with the two faces, half the face one color, half the face another. Then I see you and you are a saint and you seem so good and you give me hope." The man looked up, an expression of gratitude on his face.

Hope tried to explain, her innate honesty guiding her, "I cannot do miracles or anything like that. I am not a saint. Let me take you to the doctor. He may be able to help if you are in pain." She tried to help him stand and leave with her.

"No, you shall not turn me away. I deserve your help, your miracle to save my sanity." Hope felt his nails dig into the skin on her arm.

"All right, I will pray with you. I will pray for you."

Hope fell back on her days at St. Michaels and began the rosary in Latin and when she had gone through that, seeing the man was calmer, she tried to again get him to leave or to let her leave.

Becoming more distraught, he held her in place as he said in anguish, "The pain is still there and the voices, the buzzing like bees in a wall. I cannot stand it. Help me or you will be sorry. I need you to take this evil from me. Release me from this hell!" The man's eyes were blood-shot glazed with pain or madness, possibly both.

Hope began the Beatitudes because she knew them by heart and had always found them comforting. "Blessed are the poor in spirit…"

Suddenly, the man roared and grabbed his head, rocking forward. Hope's instinct was to give aid, get the man to lay down so she could find help but that only seemed to make his pain worse.

"I will not lay down while you deceive and lie. You are not a healer. You are a pagan." He pulled out the six-shooter that had been resting in the holster up until now.

"Sister, Sister Hope, please help me. It's been four years since my last confession and I need to unburden myself." A youthful voice said from the darkness surrounding the lamp on the pulpit.

Hope recognized Thad's voice but was fearful of what this man would do to the boy interfering with his blessing. "Come back tomorrow, my son. I am helping another with a more desperate need than yours."

"But I am in need, dear Sister Hope. Please see to my soul, as well." Thad came into the circle of light.

The man raised his head and snarled, "Do something useful, give this boy comfort."

Thad went on talking, "I have sinned in many ways. I have stolen and I have drunk liquor and I have smoked opium knowing that I was defiling my body. I coveted my neighbor's wife and dishonored his daughter."

Hope prayed Thad was manufacturing a list this bad to make it sound as if he needed her help more than the man did.

She said her expected part, "And are you truly remorseful for all these sins? Only one who is truly repentant shall bask in the glory of God's light."

"I th-think so," said Thad hesitantly.

"You may need to go and pray on these sins if you cannot say sincerely you are remorseful and want to be forgiven. Welcomed back into the good graces of the Church." Hope again tried to get Thad to leave while the man was still calm.

The man roared and grabbed Thad, placing the gun on Thad's shoulder and yelling, "These are but sins of a puppy! I have done worse and I need the sacrament to stop this pain. I need God's forgiveness, your forgiveness. I will shoot this boy unless I hear my forgiveness!"

"Of course, of course but you can't mean to defile God's house in such a manner. Let the boy go so he may start his prayers and I will hear your confession and give you the sacraments," Hope said, trying to make an unreasonable man hear reason.

There was a noise at the front door and then a blur as Bullet dashed under the pews grabbing the man's leg with sharp teeth and didn't let go. The man shoved Thad to the ground and grabbed Hope, placing her in front of him as he tried to kick the dog off, swinging Hope back and forth with the effort. Finally, raising the gun, he hit the little dog on the head and Bullet dropped with a soft thump.

Hope yelled at Thad to run into the darkness and he appeared to follow her instructions that time.

"Vargas, give her up. You're surrounded and there's nowhere for you to go," Wilder called out from the shadows.

Searching the gloom, Hope looked toward where she thought the voice was coming from but couldn't be sure. She tried to send him a message of love in case this didn't end well but she wasn't sure he would understand something he had so little knowledge of as an adult.

Vargas held Hope in front of him swiveling this way and that, trying to see into the blackness to his nemeses. Wilder had been trailing him for weeks, probably months and may be the reason for this pain in his brain.

"Get out Wilder or I will kill her. I know you took her from me so I would suffer. You took her and tried to hide her but I found her. It took me a while but I found her. She is the only one to heal me, my very own saint. Leave or I swear I will kill her."

Wilder stepped out of the dark and into the light, his gaze never leaving Vargas. Glaring, daring Vargas to make one move that appeared threatening towards Hope, he stood there.

"I'm going to put my gun down, Vargas. See I'm going to place it on the floor right here. Hope doesn't have to be a part of this. This is between you and me and now you have a gun and mine's there on the floor." Wilder had placed the pistol in his right hand down.

When Vargas's gaze followed the gun to the floor, Wilder yelled, "Drop, Babe."

Hope let her legs collapse under her, throwing Vargas off center, his arm letting her fall rather than getting pulled over with her weight.

Then shots rang-out over her head, a flashing light from Wilder's left side lightened the whole room. Hope remained flat on the floor, praying Wilder wasn't hurt trying to save her once again.

Then Wilder was there pushing Vargas's dead legs away from her as he gathered Hope into his arms. He was there holding her to his chest, murmuring soothing words, trying to keep her now trembling body from shaking with spent emotion. Trembling caused by funneling her fear which had nowhere to go, to escape now the danger had been eliminated.

There were a number of other people huddling around and all talking at the same time. Wilder helped Hope to her feet and walked her outside. Faith rushed toward her cooing, tears of joy and relief flowing down her friend's face.

Victoria stood to the side, dressed in her nightclothes as were most of the people there. Hope could tell Jeremy had pulled on his pants hastily and was carrying a hand gun. Jessie was heading across the street toward them with a shotgun. Holding a rifle in one hand, Matthew had hold of Thad's shoulder with the other - looking more like a father than he ever had before.

Wilder basically pushed Hope into Faith's arms. "Take her home. Give her a stiff drink. The shakes will probably be started by then." He turned to return to the church where Mason was waiting for him.

Faith and Jeremy turned Hope toward the alley. Faith finally stopped crying and began quietly praying, giving thanks for the safe return of her friend. The three of them went to the upstairs apartment and Jeremy did as Wilder suggested pouring three glasses with a couple fingers of good Kentucky bourbon. He took them into the parlor area where Hope was sitting, staring and trembling while Faith tried to find a way to comfort her.

"Do you want to talk about it? Should I send Jeremy for Mary Beth?" she asked worriedly not knowing what evil had happened in the church that night.

"I'm all r-r-right. I love you all and I'm sorry I caused this all to h-h-happen," said Hope through chattering teeth. Jeremy tipped his glass to her mouth, forcing her to take a gulp of the fiery liquid.

Coughing, Hope wiped her mouth on the back of her hand, her eyes beginning to water from the strong drink and no longer fear or even relief.

"Thanks, that probably helped," she said smiling at Faith who was trying to sip from her own glass.

Jeremy finished his and poured another, placing the cork into the bottle firmly. Evidently deciding everyone had had enough, he came back into the parlor.

Hope felt she had to tell them what happened. "He was a man who went mad, I think. He didn't want to hurt me but I think there was real pain, in his head, that made him go a little insane. He made me sad and I really wanted to help him. Until he hurt Thad and, oh, I forgot all about Bullet. Is he dead, do you know? He was only trying to protect me. He didn't deserve being hit like that."

The tears Jeremy had been waiting for came rushing outward. All the held back emotions and fear and relief streaming down Hope's face.

Then Faith began crying in empathy with her friend and Jeremy felt his throat tighten. He had to gulp a couple of times to keep the tears from his eyes. He walked back to the kitchen table, uncorked the bourbon and poured another two fingers.

The next morning Bullet was brought back to Hope. He licked her face and wiggled as his tail slapped the padded bottom of a crate. His ear had a poorly fitted bandage over it and two short pieces of wood on each side held a back leg in place. Hope petted the brave little dog and told him to stay which he seemed to understand but whined whenever Hope left his sight.

Thad looked through the large window and entered the pressroom. "I just wanted to make sure you were all right, Miss Hope."

"I think after last night, you can call me, Hope. After all, we are brother and sister and you saved my life."

"I didn't do that much. I just felt I had to do something to keep him busy until Wilder got there."

"How did you know I needed help?"

"I was down at the camp, you know, with boys my age that came in for the Fourth. I was headed home when I heard, Bullet. He was all tangled up in a rope or something so I untied him and he tore down Main Street. I realized there was a lamp on in the church so I went in to turn it out. I thought it had been left on by mistake. That's when I heard him saying all those strange things and I had to think of something to get close to him."

"That was brave of you, Thad. You should have gone for Mason or Matthew instead of putting yourself in danger, though," Hope told him thinking of his safety.

"I thought about Matthew, of all the times he's gone in dangerous places to save our sisters or other women who needed his help. I guess I didn't want to chance this lunatic doing more than talk. I think he was getting more and more…insane as he kept talking."

"I think you're right but I don't want others hurt trying to save me," explained Hope.

"I was praying Bullet was doing what he was doing. He brought Wilder who brought Mason while Andy got

285

Matthew. Every house on Main Street was lit by the time it was over. I was never in any real danger. That Vargas - he seemed intent on you," Thad said looking at Hope in a bewildered manner.

"Well, it was comforting to know you were there. I was frightened of Vargas even if I felt a little sorry for him. Whatever demons were eating at him, he believed I could help him and that meant he did not believe in God. That was the beginning of his end," she said softly.

"Well, I think he was just plain crazy and I'm glad Wilder put a bullet in his head," Thad admitted.

Hope had known Wilder had killed Vargas. She hadn't realized how. "I'll pray for the man's soul, Thad. We need to remember those less fortunate. And I'll pray for you, too. You are turning into a fine young man and that means you need to find your way back to Him, too."

"That's why everyone loves you, Hope. You always see the good." He glanced out the window saying, "I've got to get back to work. I'm glad you're feeling all right." He turned to leave but stopped when she spoke.

"Thad, one more question, what you told me, your confession. Was all that true?" she asked worriedly.

"Just the first part and then I couldn't think of enough sins and couldn't remember the commandments except that one about coveting," he said with a shy grin.

"I'm glad I don't need to pray quiet so hard for your soul, then, but I will add you to my list." She smiled as he turned and ran toward the school.

As the Macgregor's packed to go to the ranch for a visit, Hope and Faith conversed. "I don't want to leave you, Hope. We had planned on all of us going to the ranch and I know both Emily and Mavis are looking forward to the visit. They've been house-bound since months before the babies were born and now with both Aileen and Elliott old enough to have visitors, it would be good to get all four Macgregor brothers together. You'd be more than welcome," Faith said, trying to convince her friend to go with them.

"I agree. Nothing is more important than family and babies grow so fast you and Mary Beth are missing out on knowing them. And Jeremy hasn't been back in Sweetwater for all that long. You all must make the trip and stay as long as you want. Jessie can ride in and print the paper and then ride back. I can help him," Hope said reasonably.

"Hope, you've been through so much, I don't want you to be here alone," Faith said still trying to convince Hope to attend the family function with her.

"Look, Vargas is dead and that was the only threat to me. Now I'm as safe as any other resident of Sweetwater, maybe safer since Mason sits on the boardwalk within an easy call. And Colette says she's going to be checking on me several times a day plus we plan on having meals together. I can stay with Victoria and Mason if I feel nervous about anything here. Isn't that safe enough for you?" Hope explained the plans she had in place for the next week.

Faith gazed toward her husband as he said, "She's right about being safe, love. I mean, she has Mason and Matthew within a few yards and she can stay with Victoria if she needs to."

"I'm not happy about this but I can't knock you on the head and drag you with me. I'm warning you though, if anything, any little thing happens, I expect you to run screaming for help. Do not keep trying to handle things on your own. You're making me a nervous mess." Faith smiled at her sister to take the sting out of her words.

Hope waved her friends and their husbands off in the buggy sent from the Macgregor ranch. She went into the storefront locking the door behind her. There was a closed sign posted in the window and Jessie had said there was no reason for Hope to do anything. She decided to do some reading for pleasure, work on her class plans and rest. Feeling as if she would never get enough sleep, she was still worried about Wilder and what she wanted from her life. Not good pre-sleep thoughts.

Going into her room, she calmed Bullet since she had been out of his sight for so long. "Do you expect me to carry you around all day? Oh, what a spoiled boy." She crouched next to the box and petted the loving mongrel. "Here give me kisses. What a good boy you are. Oh, now your belly needs scratching? There does that feel good?"

"I know I'd think it did if you scratched my belly," said a familiar voice from the open doorway to the hall.

Hope jumped up and ran to Wilder, putting her arms around his neck and crying into his chest.

Holding her loosely he chuckled into her hair, "Hey, Babe. What brought this on?"

"I thought you were gone forever and I never really got to thank you or let you know things," said Hope wiping her eyes with a hankie from her pocket. She was always so close to tears she had begun to carry one on her person at all times.

"I had to take Vargas' body back to the fort. That's the prison he had broken out of and where all this started. Now it's over and I received the bounty for something I would have done anyway, once I got to know you. I saw red every time I thought about Vargas getting to you. I've ripped myself apart knowing I might have given him the information to find you," he said still not holding Hope as she wanted him to.

"Please don't keep thinking of the past, Wilder. I don't care about what 'might have been and if only'. I want to see what today brings, what we can do now." She pulled his head down so she could kiss him on the mouth.

The moment their lips touched Wilder gave up on any sort of refusal of his feelings for this woman. She was right - today and now was what was important. The past couldn't be changed but the future could be made today.

Wrapping one arm around Hope, he bent and put his other under her legs as he carried her to the narrow bed, they had so enjoyed just a day earlier.

"Where is everyone? I didn't see any signs of the Macgregor men," he said, staring at Hope as she drew circles on his shirt.

"They went to the ranch for a family get together. You know the kind of thing. Meet and play with the new babies and talk over the things that happened as a family long ago. I didn't want to go and have people worrying about me instead of enjoying one another as they should be."

"Is there something to be worried about?" he asked searching her face for any trace of a lie.

"Not any more, I swear. I have decided that I love teaching. I love seeing children get older and wiser but I love you more than even that. I don't care if I can never teach again but I will fight for us, for you."

Wilder, feeling overwhelmed, covered her lips and kissed her with more passion than he ever knew he had.

After a few minutes, he tried to catch his breath and keep his needs under control, as he put Hope from him. "I know being on this bed, having you welcome me like this is going to cause me a hell of a lot of pain but I can't convince myself to leave you. I know what I want but I'm not sure it's what's best for you."

"I told you. You are more essential than a job to me. I was in the church to find what was important and even with all that happened, I knew finding you was the most crucial thing to ever happen to me. I will go wherever you need me to be. I can work at a lot of different jobs if you need me to. I can help support us. I can use a typing machine. I can now set type and run a press. I can teach piano and I'm pretty good at embroidery and fine-stitchery. We can make it as a couple. I won't ask you for more."

Wilder held Hope closer humbled by her love and admitted, "You won't need to do anything you don't want to do. I have the horse ranch my father left me and I make very good money as a bounty hunter." He held up a hand as Hope began to protest, finished by saying, "But it isn't a job for a married man."

"Oh, Wilder, I never meant for you to give up your livelihood. I don't like you being in danger but if it's what you want or need to do, I can get used to it."

"And I don't want you worried about me, Babe. My job was something I did because it was exciting, kept me moving and no one else wanted to do it."

Hope lifted her head in question. "You said married man. Are we really going to get married, Wilder?"

"Absolutely. I decided you were what I wanted whether or not I was the best thing for you. I'm not wonderful husband material but I'll never hurt you and I think I'll be a good father. I had a good example and I forgot that till I met you, started talking about my family."

"I never doubted your ability to take care of me. I wasn't sure you would ever leave your way of life," she admitted her fear.

Wilder laughed, "My way of life, is it? I was just living day to day, letting the criminal set the pace and dictate where I would be. I'm going to choose my own way from now on. Well, you're going to choose my way."

"We will decide together. From now on everything will be together."

"I like the sound of that but I want to feel free to make love to you, not soil you with my lust."

"I like your lust. Give me your lust." Hope began to writhe against his body, which was happy to receive the attention.

"Babe, get your hat and the prettiest dress you have. We're going to see if we can be husband and wife by this evening. If not, I'm going to tie myself to the hitching post at the livery and tell Andy to shoot me if I try to get to you," he told her teasingly.

"I'd come to you and we would make love right there in front of Andy and anyone else within sight."

"Babe, I think that's one of the reasons I love you." He slid off the bed so Hope could get ready.

CHAPTER 10

The odd couple stood on the porch of the parsonage holding hands and facing Rebecca.

"May we speak with the minister, please?" asked the good-looking man dressed in all black. Rebecca knew Hope since she had been to the church but the man was a stranger.

"Certainly, he's in his office. Please, follow me." She led the two young people to Daniel as he played with his son, who was pretty much smiling at everything his father did.

As the couple entered the office, the Reverend jumped up from the floor unembarrassed to be caught playing there. He handed the baby to Rebecca who carried him from the room.

"Hope, how are you. Please have a chair." He noted the couple sat across from him but near enough to one another to touch. "I can't tell you how sorry I am about the other evening. I feel so guilty since I had forgotten to lock the church which allowed that man to have access to you."

"Don't think anything more about it. Vargas had been following me and had to be stopped sometime. I'm glad no one got hurt. I mean, besides Vargas and Bullet but Bullet will be better in no time." Hope assured Daniel, "I don't' blame anyone, only Vargas."

"I'm glad you've decided to move on with your life. Now what can I do to help?" Daniel asked as his gaze shifted between the two in front of him.

Wilder said bluntly, "We want to be married but we

don't want others to know about it."

"Is there a problem? Another woman or…?" the Reverend asked trying to make sense of this unusual request.

Wilder became defensive and bristled. Hope placed her hand on his arm and he glanced toward her, calming immediately.

Hope explained, "Nothing like that, Reverend. It's simply that Wilder knows I wish to teach in the fall and you know the state's rules on married teachers. He would rather have me teach for a year and then if people find out it won't matter as much because they would see how good of a teacher I am."

"I don't think the town council had a strict preference, simply wanting a teacher who could educate students up to and including preparing them for college entrance, if required. Few candidates seemed to want to move this far west and most of those who applied wanted more money than you asked for," he said embarrassedly. "Perhaps I shouldn't have said so much but I have a vote on the schoolboard and you being married wouldn't dissuade me from keeping you as our teacher."

The Reverend leaned back in his chair asking, "You're sure this is what you want, Hope? I mean you've gone through quite a bit of trauma these past few weeks and I know you could be grateful for Mr. Wilder saving you more than once."

Again, Wilder bristled and Hope squeezed his arm in warning. "I assure you, Reverend, I know everything I need to about my future husband. We met under unusual circumstances but I think it was God's plan we fell in love and want to be a family," Hope explained with the maturity of a woman years older.

"You make a good argument, Hope, but what about you, young man? What are your thoughts in this matter?" he asked Wilder directly expecting a direct answer.

"When I came to Sweetwater, I was following a lead in a bounty case. I never meant to meet Hope, to fall in love with her, to feel this way about anyone. I have tried to leave her, to give her the chance to meet someone else who would be better for her. I couldn't do it. I couldn't turn my back on her and then she convinced me I shouldn't. I will do anything to keep her safe and happy," he told the older man honestly.

The Reverend peaked his fingers placing his chin on them. "I am not the one to decide who should marry whom but I feel you two have spent a lot of time thinking about what is right for you. I will officiate at your wedding anytime you wish." He smiled at both of them.

Cautiously, Hope said, "We were hoping you'd marry us right now." She looked at Daniel with pleading eyes.

Reverend Walters stood and picked up his book saying, "Shall we walk to the church then?"

Wilder felt Hope tense beside him. "We'd rather be married right here if that's all right, sir."

The Reverend looked at Hope's pale face and nodded. "Certainly, I'll call Rebecca. I know she'd love to be a part of this."

Within minutes, the Reverend wearing his collar, Rebecca holding her sleeping son on her shoulder, Colette, for the second witness, along with Hope and Wider all stood together in the parlor of the parsonage while Reverend Walters officiated at the first wedding held there.

"Dearly Beloved, we are gathered together to join

this couple…" Then he hesitated when he realized he knew Wilder only by his last name.

Hope supplied, "Coyote Wilder."

The Reverend continued, "and."

Then Hope supplied, "Hope Francis St. Michaels."

He then repeated her name, adding, "Together in Holy matrimony. Coyote, repeat after me…."

As the ceremony continued, Wilder, his gaze locked with Hope's, repeated, "Hope Francis, I give you this ring as a sign of my vow and with all that I am and all that I have. I honor you in the name of the Father, and of the Son and of the Holy Ghost." The ring he'd slipped off his finger and given to the minister to bless was placed on Hope's finger.

The Reverend had Hope say her vows and announced they were husband and wife. Hope's eyes filled with happy tears. Wilder's smile couldn't be wider and Rebecca and Colette wished them a happy marriage and many children which made Hope blush.

Colette said, "I knew when I saw his eyes that he had found his love. I am so glad you found one another in this large world. Not everyone is so lucky."

It was almost dusk as Wilder and Hope entered the backdoor of the newspaper building. "We could go to my room at the hotel. It has a bigger bed and we could have a nice meal at the restaurant and maybe some Champaign or wine, at least," offered Wilder, trying to make the day special for Hope.

"I'm not hungry, Wilder, not for food anyway. I have been dreaming of what we did on the Fourth of July and can't get it out of my mind," she said as she led him into her room, removing her hat and unbuttoning her dress.

Wilder's eyes glittered with passion and desire, both vying for dominance but love won out. "Come here, Babe, let me help you."

"All right but only if I can help you," she said reaching for his top button and starting to undo them. Wilder felt he was behind and quickly sat pulling off his boots and socks before standing in front of his bride.

Smiling, he told her, "Lift your arms. I'm going to pull this up over your head." Hope put her hands into the air and was soon standing in only her camisole facing her husband of less than an hour.

Hope continued working on his shirt buttons then removed the leather vest and shirt which she put on the chair. Confused when she reached his trousers, she took hold of the first button and started to un-do it slowly. She was afraid of hurting Wilder having been told by her friends, men could be very sensitive at these times.

Wilder held his breath and then let it out in a long hiss, his eyes slit to keep his emotions hidden, even from Hope.

Hope hesitated and leaned into Wilder, kissing his lips then saying, "Help me. I don't know how to please you."

"You please me with every move you make, Babe, never doubt that. But I'll show you what I really like, if you let me know what you really like," he told her pulling the camisole over her head and pushing his trousers down before kicking them off.

Pulling her now naked body against his own, his erection came between them nesting against her stomach. He pushed Hope back to the bed while keeping his mouth on hers, kissing her deeply and delving his tongue into the moist warmth.

Hope stretched out on the bed as she had on that momentous day. Wilder followed her retaining his mouth over hers, his tongue thrusting and retreating. His hand covering a breast, he kneaded it to an impatient peak. Replacing his hand with his mouth, Wilder sucked and licked the nipple as Hope arched up, offering the other breast for his attention, too.

Wilder continued kisses down Hope's body, his hands lightly squeezing the rigid tips still wet from his mouth as he reached the soft furry mound hiding her most precious gift. He nuzzled into the warmth and then met another peak rising for his attention, his intimate kisses and his tongue thrusting, licking the nubbin into a blossoming bud.

Hope's breathing quickened while Wilder helped move her hips. She started the slow rocking causing her to grip Wilder's hands as he palmed her nipples. Stiffening, the familiar waves of pleasure flowed through her entire body leaving her breathless.

Bringing himself up to reach Hope, he kissed her into calm serenity. Smiling at her open enjoyment of his lovemaking, he wasn't unmoved by her release and holding himself back caused Wilder to shake, a trembling Hope questioned.

"Wilder, make love to me as a husband. I enjoyed what you did but let me pleasure you. She reached down and found the strong erection between them, marveling at the soft tip and the firm velvet covered shaft.

"I don't want to hurt you. I'm not sure how to go on," he admitted, kissing her neck and tops of her breasts.

"I've been warned, it can be as little as a pinch or feel like a knife cut on your finger. I can handle anything

297

to give you the love I feel, the need to join with you in every way." She squeezed her hand gently around him.

"I love you, too, and I can't control my need for you." He held himself up as she slid under him, letting him nestle between her legs. "I love you so much," he said as he pushed into the warm womanly part of her, stopping to savor the feel of being encompassed by the silky muscles.

Hope urged him with the slow movement of her hips and soon they were in synchronized euphoria, both tensing as the ecstasy peaked and the bliss raced through their bodies, gone too soon.

"Oh, Wilder, that was fantastic. No one can explain it. I thought my married friends were being coy but whatever you did was the most wonderful thing I've ever experienced." She kissed his chest as he held his weight off her, waiting until they were no longer joined before leaving her.

"You're going to make me blush, Babe. I only did what comes naturally." He laughed into her neck then slid to her side, an arm over her stomach and his body along her full length.

"I'm so glad we found one another. It could have ended so differently and then what would I have done?" Hope said sleepily as she snuggled against her husband.

The next morning Hope woke Wilder up for an encore of the night before, urging him to join with her and ending with the same wondrous rapture. Wilder was as disbelieving as Hope when they matched each other stroke for stroke reaching the pinnacle together. Hope didn't know the rarity of their compatibility so early in their marriage but Wilder did and he thanked whatever star he was born under.

Wilder took Bullet in his box out back while Hope went upstairs to make a breakfast of toasted bread and coffee. Bullet walked across the kitchen floor wagging his tail as Wilder followed him.

"Bullet's leg looks like it's better. It must not have been broken because he was running around on it," said Wilder watching the brave little dog investigating every crevice of the room.

"Jessie told me Mary Beth put those sticks on his leg to keep it immobile until Bullet wanted to use it. She figured he'd know when it felt good enough. We may as well take off the bandage, too, since he seems to have it mostly off anyway."

"I'm going to need to check on my horse and pick up my gear but I'll be right back here," Wilder promised, kissing her quickly and forcing himself to leave.

"I want to run over to the Mercantile and get some provisions," Hope said cleaning up the kitchen.

"I'll pick up some things from the butcher. Anything special you need? Here, let me give you some money," Wilder offered as he reached into his trouser pocket.

Hope smiled and teased, "My, what an old married couple we sound like. I like that, I think."

"That's all I want now, to be an old married couple." He kissed her again as he carried Bullet down the steps.

As Wilder left the livery, carrying his saddle bag, Mason was waiting outside. He said slowly, "I thought your work was done the other night when you killed Vargas. I was told you checked out of the hotel. Planning on staying around?" He glanced pointedly at the saddlebag.

"Maybe, is that a problem?" Wilder said, his eyes squinting into the morning sun behind Mason.

"No, just asking because with the past few days and all, city council wanted me to find another man to kind of watch the town when I'm not. A deputy, of sorts. The town's getting bigger and I can't be everywhere all the time. And sometimes it takes two to get things done right. I know you're good with a gun and bull whip and smart enough to catch the bad guys." Mason put out a feeler.

"A deputy, huh?"

"It'll pay the same as my job, plus bullets."

"I'll think about it," Wilder promised.

"And Wilder, what about Hope?" asked Mason watching the other man closely. There it was the slight flicker of an eyelash that if he wasn't looking for might have missed it this time.

"What about her?"

"Just wonder how your silver ring you always wore on your little finger is now residing on Hope's left hand," Mason said with a grin.

"Just keep wondering. And keep your nose out of my business." He threw the saddlebag over his shoulder and walked across the street to the butcher shop.

"Babe, you up here?" called Wilder as he entered the upstairs kitchen and dropped the packages on the table. He looked over to where Hope stood, fanning herself with a paper fan.

"I can't seem to get cool today. It's hotter upstairs during the day but there just doesn't seem to be any breeze at all downstairs, either." she complained.

"I know what you'll like. I'm going to fill the tub with cool water. It will be just like skinny dipping and I can join you." He raised his eyebrows in question along with his sexy grin.

"I think that sounds wonderful - the cool water at least. Though I don't want you splashing water all over that floor. Faith will not be happy with me."

"There's a couple of room-temperature water buckets under the sink and I'll bring up more as soon as we pour those into the tub." Soon the tub was half-full. Hope stripped out of her clothes quickly, stepping gingerly into the tub, giving a little shriek as she lowered her rump under the water.

Wilder's mouth went dry watching his love settle her naked self into the water but brought himself up short lathering his face to shave. He sharpened the straight edge, began as he had since he was sixteen years old and then blood flowed.

"Damn," he said and dabbed at the streak of red with the wet cloth. He continued but could see Hope squeeze a sponge of cool water down her neck and over her breasts.

"Ouch!" And another spot of blood under his chin spouted.

"Babe, could you just scoot down into the tub so I can't see you. I'm going to bleed to death if I keep trying to watch you and shave," he said chuckling. "And I need to get rid of this stubble or you're going to have a bad case of whisker-burn."

Sliding down, she almost went totally under the water. Soon she felt Wilder join her, stark naked also and lifting her to him as he sat opposite her in the tub, the water still several inches from the top.

"Come here and let me wash you," Wilder coaxed.

"If I can reciprocate. I want to get to know your body as well as my own." She squeezed the sponge down Wilder's chest, watching the dark hairs spring back as

301

the water ran off them. She reached into the water, smiling when she grasped her target, taking him in both her hands, rubbing carefully.

Wilder's silver eyes went closed as he savored her touch. His body reacted in obvious pleasure, which increased Hope's attentions to his ablutions.

Unbelieving of his good fortune, Wilder leaned back to give full access to his wife. Hope took advantage of his slumbering position, straddling his hips and lowering herself onto him, beginning the new dance they had devised to bring them both to a completeness that filled a need they both had.

Later, Wilder and Hope were lying on a rug on the bathing room floor, a towel draped over their lower-halves. A quick nap had overtaken them before they could even dress, the tub still filled with water.

Wilder raised his head and then got up saying, "We must have slept longer than I thought, Babe. It's almost dusk." He looked at the watch in his inside vest pocket laying on the stool then glanced back outside. "It's only late afternoon."

Slipping his trousers on and carrying his shirt with him, he said quickly, "Get dressed, Hope." He went to the front of the apartment and stared out the window.

Looking toward the western horizon, he yelled out the window, "Mason! Mason there's twisters. Several of them off to the southwest about two to three miles out."

Mason rushed out of the jail, yelling to Andy to start warning people. He rang the bell on the side of his office, the gonging sound echoing down the street. People checked to see why the fire-bell was ringing and realized the danger. Soon the street was a bevy of activity as people rushed into their homes to gather their families and get into their basement root cellars.

Wilder ran back to Hope carrying his gun belt and pushed his feet into his boots. "I'll get you to a safe place and then make sure everyone else is warned."

As they descended the stairs, the rain started pelting down, hitting with surprising force but not as hard as the hail that came next. The Burgess family was scurrying into their cellar as Wilder and Hope headed around their building to cross the street. Then they saw Thom Thompson, half drag Colette against the strong winds to his family's home while Andy came running back after warning all the workers at the bank building site.

Wilder and Hope were continuing across the street with Bullet circling urging them to move faster. Miss Lily's was their destination. Wilder tried to be heard over the wind as he and Hope fought the force of this strange wind, heading directly into it.

"Is anyone being left behind?" Wilder yelled over the wind and hail.

Mason, holding his hat down to protect his eyes from the pelting rain and hail, shouted, "No, most have cellars in their homes, just had to warn the new comers. I'm going in to the hotel, come with me."

"No, I want to make sure Miss Lily's all right." And the now howling wind carried his voice away but Mason waved them off turning toward the hotel and his wife.

Wilder urged Hope on and soon they were close enough to see Miss Lily standing by an angled outside-door leading under her home. Wilder yelled for the older woman to climb down the few short steps while he pushed Hope through the open doorway, pulling the double doors closed behind him. There were two metal brackets meant to hold the wood board in place to keep the doors from flying off during a tornado and Wilder secured them.

As Hope turned to look at the space they were in, she was confronted by six round faces with wide anxious eyes staring back at her. She recognized the two younger ones as the girls who usually helped her at the Chinese laundry across the street. Miss Lily must have gotten the family to come over to her house for safety.

Bullet danced around at Hope's feet so she finally sat on a crate next to Miss Lily, nodding to Stella and Lacy who sat across from them, strained smiles on their faces. Wilder stayed next to the door, trying to ensure the board held and they wouldn't be sucked out if the tornado gave a direct hit to the house.

Miss Lily suddenly said, "Oh Hope, how wonderful for you. You've gotten a real good man. I'm so happy you found one another. I was praying for it since you brought him to us wounded. I could see there was more than simple gratitude between the two of you." She patted Hope's hand.

"I, how did you guess?" asked Hope a little embarrassed that people could tell she and Wilder had been making love.

"The ring, dear. That is Wilder's mother's wedding band. He always wore it but now you are." And she smiled. "I knew his mother. She was a very beautiful woman from out east. Boston, as I remember. A highly educated woman who played the harp. The only person I ever met who played the harp." Then she was lost in past remembrances.

Hope gazed over at Wilder as the doors shuddered as if someone was trying to get in, pulling and tugging to get at them. But Wilder held tight, the wind howling like a banshee. There were sounds of things hitting the house while the whole building shook and creaked as if a giant-hand were trying to tear it from the foundation.

Miss Lily hugged Hope close to her side while Stella and Lacy did the same with each other. The entire Chinese family was one mass of heads buried into each other's shoulders. All were tensely waiting for the blow.

Then nothing. No sound, no thumping, no wind.

Everyone raised their head and peered at each other as the sound of rain lightly spattering against the door became the backdrop of muted prayers and amazement, they hadn't been thrown to the four corners of the world.

"Do you think it's over, Wilder? Are we safe?" Hope asked her husband hesitantly trying not to dare the gods to return with even more vengeance.

"I'm not sure. I've heard about this, a quiet. Something about being inside the tornado but I don't know for sure. Never been through it myself." He listened, trying to hear what was happening on the other side of the doors.

Then there was a shout from outside. Mason was giving the all clear, everyone could come out and be thankful they were alive and assess the damage. Miss Lily and her group climbed out of their safe harbor and into the now clear, sunny day. The rain had passed and everything looked clean and new, except for the areas the winds had decided to bless with its presence.

Their eyes blinking from the bright light, the little troupe stood and seemed dazed at what they saw. The livery had lost most of its roof and there was a large splinter of wood pushed right through the wall where Andy usually slept. Several of the privy's were moved off their footings or gone altogether as was the chicken house behind Miss Lily's.

Hope thanked Miss Lily but explained she had to go home to see if the press had been damaged. They hugged one another one last time and each walked to their homes or what may be left of it.

Wilder took Hope by the shoulder and held her close to his chest, taking deep breaths, breathing in her scent and then putting his head into her neck saying, "I was afraid it was going to be like this. I fear for your safety constantly, your life comes before mine every time. Hope, never leave me. I won't endure without you."

With tears in her eyes, Hope whispered, "I feel the same. I worry when you leave me for only an hour. That you'll find some danger and end up getting shot again. I couldn't bear it if you left me."

"Maybe that's what love is - a lot of different fears and feelings rolled up together. But don't worry, I don't plan on going anywhere." He kissed her on the lips right out in public and no one stopped to say a word.

Wilder went to inspect the rear of the building while Hope checked over the press and other machines but the building didn't seem to have suffered any interior damage, merely a lot of debris blown up against the front under the overhanging roof. The rest of the street was blown clean except for pieces of metal roof here and there.

Wilder came in. "I think we have Abby's chicken house and a few of the chickens but no sign of the goat, I'm afraid. It could have just run off. Matthew's outside and said they lost some shingles and a couple of their upper windows are broken. I saw at least one pane gone in the front bedroom here."

"Does it look like anyone got hurt?" Hope asked,

wondering if she really wanted to know if there were lives lost.

"No, Matthew says the men at the work sites came through. Some were in the school's basement and a few stayed with the bank in one of the interior rooms. That whole building is masonry so it can withstand a lot. Train depot and tracks all seem fine, too," he informed her so that she could stop fretting.

"That's a blessing then. We need that train badly. I suppose the telegraph will be down for a while."

"Yeah, no way knowing how many poles got wiped out between here and Preston."

Hope was silent for a moment and then asked, "Do you think the ranches fared as well? Do you think Faith and Mary Beth are in danger?"

"No, the ranches probably had more warning then we did. I would have noticed the sky changing color if we hadn't been napping in that other room with the curtains closed. Everyone had time to take cover and that's all we have control over. I'm sure Jessie and Jeremy kept everyone safe. I know Mason sent men to check and I'm sure Jeremy will want to know how his building projects stood up to the test." Wilder informed her, letting her know he was getting to know her family well.

"You're right, I'm worrying for nothing. I should go and make sure Colette is doing all right. She may need help if there is damage to her building."

Later that evening, Hope made a dinner of the beefsteaks Wilder had brought from the butcher earlier that day. She served fresh sliced tomatoes, Mrs. Burgess's home baked brown pumpernickel bread and fresh berries.

"That was great, Babe, but I was thinking I should go and relieve Mason. I think he plans on staying up all night to keep a lookout for any more storms. I'll be right across the street if you need me," Wilder said placing his hat on his head.

Wilder approached Mason, saying, "Go home and get some rest. If I'm going to be your deputy, I might as well get used to the job."

Mason took off his hat brushing his hair back off his forehead. He looked closely at Wilder. "You get hit by flying glass or something?"

"No, self-inflicted. Just a little shaving accident," Wilder admitted touching the still sore nicks on his throat.

"Hell, Wilder, don't you know not to try to shave if your wife's taking a bath?" Mason wore a shit-eating grin on his face.

Wilder gave himself away when he replied. "How did you... hell, no, cuz no one bothered to warn me, now, did you?" And smiled at his own ignorance.

"It's best to find out these things yourself. Makes for a better learning experience, I've found," said Mason as he headed toward the back of the hotel.

"Asshole," Wilder called out after Mason as he pulled the chair out with one booted foot and sat down.

Wilder watched as the lights went out one by one up and down the street, the debris already out of the way of the morning commerce. Finally, he saw Hope in the upstairs window, wave and blow him a kiss like little children did. Wilder smiled at the spurt of happiness that went through him at the simple gesture and settled back to contemplate his luck and keep vigil for any danger to his town.

Mason showed up to relieve him just after sun-up, smiling and holding a cup of coffee out to Wilder.

"No thanks, Hope brought me some a while ago and said she'd be waiting for me so I need to get home and not disappoint my bride," Wilder explained, glorying in the truth of every word he spoke.

"I don't blame you," said Mason taking up the post in the now vacated chair.

"Mason, does it get any easier? You know, the feeling of needing her so much you shake with it?" Wilder asked seriously.

"I don't know. Ask me in a couple of more months," Mason replied just as seriously.

"Hell, that wasn't what I was hoping to hear. Let me know when you want me on duty. You know where I'll be." Wilder headed across the street to lay with his wife.

After satisfying lovemaking, Wilder slept while Hope watched him, marveling at her good-luck in finding and loving such a man. She heard the noise of people walking around upstairs and quickly jumped up. She redressed before they could call out for her and wake Wilder.

A flustered Hope met Jeremy and Faith as they stood in the kitchen and welcomed them home with a bright, if fidgety, smile. "I see you got the message, all right. Only a little damage to the roof and a broken window pane. Nothing to worry about."

"Jeremy wanted to make sure the building sites and all the men were undamaged so we left early this morning. We stopped by the school site as we let Jessie and Mary Beth off. A tree went down in her back yard but other than that it didn't look to be much else. I think it went right behind her house. Miss Lily's might have gotten more. We passed a swath cut right through everything. It looks like someone had gotten it ready for a road or something. All the trees laying right down in a row. Kind of an eerie feeling. It's going to take a while before that fills in again, if ever," said Faith talking a mile a minute which proved something was wrong.

Jeremy said, "I can see this place looks about normal. Honey, I'm going to the bank building to see how it came though the storm and be back in a little while. Don't wait to eat. I'll grab something later." He kissed Faith who was almost too distracted to notice. Accepting the sign of affection without really acknowledging it.

As soon as Jeremy was off the bottom step, Faith turned to Hope and asked frantically, "Where is he? That man. You've got to get him out of here before Jeremy gets back or he'll shoot him - if I don't."

Hope tried collecting her thoughts and protect Wilder at the same time. "Faith, I don't know…."

"None of that, Hope. You've had a man in here and you need to send him on his way - now!" said Faith keeping herself from looking behind the diaphanous curtains trying to find Wilder. She knew it had to be Wilder. Who else would compromise a sweet kind girl like Hope? Take advantage of her gratefulness for his saving her life. Faith whipped herself mentally for not remaining with Hope as she first intended. She knew deep down Hope was too vulnerable to be left on her own.

"Faith, wait, you need to understand. I love him, really love him and I am so lucky he feels the same," admitted Hope trying to make her friend understand.

Faith gazed at Hope as if she were a kicked kitten.

"Look, men say all kinds of things, darling. It's in their nature to get what they want. But you don't need to feel you owe him anything. He does what he does to make money and not for any other reason. We'll all help you through this but he has to go."

"If he goes, I go. I won't let my husband be sent away from me. I belong with him," Hope said adamantly, not understanding how angry Faith was at Wilder.

"Wait…your husband? You married that man?" asked Faith incredulously which was almost more insulting than anything else Faith had said.

Hope turned to stomp down the steps as Faith held out her arms, asking for forgiveness and peace. "Stay, explain this to me. I didn't realize you two even spoke before the other day," Faith said, being reasonable for the first time.

"I know you may not like what he does but being a bounty hunter was simply his way of helping keep this area safe. He has a horse ranch and we may move there if the town won't let me teach. Otherwise, for now, he has accepted the deputy job under Mason."

Faith sat down suddenly. "More than just a tornado hit this town since I left. I feel like I don't live here anymore myself."

"I'm sorry. We'll stay to my room until we can find a place of our own. If the town council changes their mind about my teaching here, we'll decide where to live then. I don't want to give up on Sweetwater but Wilder is more important than anything else."

"You're sure, Hope? It's not simply some sort of gratefulness for his saving you? For showing interest in you when you were feeling low?" Faith didn't comment upon Hope's wine-stain birthmark but it was there between them.

Hope said quietly, holding Faith's hand, "I know that he loves me. The me I never knew was there. And I love him. And yes, I would have let him take me to bed without a wedding but he refused, talking Reverend Walters into it. Convincing the reverend, he wasn't taking advantage of my gratitude or fear or for any other reason except we loved one another and wanted to be a family."

"He better be very good to you or I'll have Matthew call him out or set Callie on him." Faith smiled at her friend now she was beginning to be used to the idea of Hope's new husband.

"He was up all night on patrol. Mason and Wilder didn't want another storm catching us unawares. I left him sleeping in my room. I'm sure he's heard us by now and is worrying about me." Hope stopped and asked her friend, "By the way, how did you know?"

Faith laughed. "I noticed a pair of men's socks rolled up behind the bathing room door and there is a new straight edged razor near the shaving stand. Jeremy took his."

Hope mouthed a long, "Oh-h-h." Still chuckling, she collected the socks. She didn't need Jeremy finding out that way, too.

When Hope went into her darkened bedroom, Wilder was laying on his stomach so Hope went to see if he was really awake.

A sleepy sounding voice spoke. "So, they know? I heard some of the words through the ceiling."

"You left me to handle this all on my own while you stayed down here with your head pulled in like a turtle?" She swatted his buttocks playfully.

"A sleepy turtle. I'm reserving my energy for better things," he teased. "I thought it was better for you to tell your friends without me around to make them hold back. Better to get all the accusations out of the way and then move on." Wilder turned on his side and asked, "I was right, wasn't I? You didn't need my help?"

"No, I didn't need your help. Faith didn't realize at first we were married and I think her instinct was to protect me from the big bad bounty hunter," she said as she climbed onto the bed and lay down beside him beginning the activity, he said he had been storing energy for. They emerged together later to face their roommates upstairs.

CHAPTER 11

Colette set the tray of tea and cups on the small table in what she referred to as her studio. It appeared like a typical parlor in a fine home except for the camera equipment sitting to the side of the room.

"It is good to have all my new neighbors here, *ne'st ce pas?*" she said to the group of women gathered together for a social hour or two. "I mean, I have so much to thank you for. Your husbands have fixed my roof and the chimney. *Merci,* to all of them. *Un the'* perhaps? Or *un verre* of sherry? I prefer some of both along with these little cakes a Callie sent to me." She offered the frosted squares with a frosting rose on the top along with the sandwiches made of creamed cheese or smoked salmon, and soda crackers topped with pickled herring in cream.

"We are all glad you didn't flee after the tornado. We haven't been hit like that in years I was told," Victoria said selecting a little cake to go with her tea.

Abby looked speculatively at Hope then said in her usually Abby forthrightness, "The tornado is old news. I want all the goodies spilled on that handsome new husband of yours, Hope. I had my eye on him before Matthew came to town but he never gave me a second glance. Is he as luscious as he looks?"

The audacious comment brought a blush to Hope's cheeks. Just to show them all she was no longer a gaunt girl but a mature married woman, replied, "He's all that and more. I never knew what you married women were hiding but now I'm very impressed, very impressed indeed." She took a sip of the tea and milk as if butter wouldn't melt in her mouth.

The others hooted with mirth, teasing Hope for her good luck in getting a man who knew his way around the bedroom.

"I feel sorry if any of you haven't been as blessed," Hope said in the best matronly voice she could muster without laughing outright.

Abby said, "I think we have all been blessed in that matter and the fact that everyone married has become mothers within a year attests to that fact. I, of course, wouldn't have it any other way. I highly recommend the men of Sweetwater." She nodded toward Colette who smiled and said she would take the matter under advisement.

Then Victoria, beginning to be brave among the group even though she was as much an outsider as Colette was, asked, "Do you think they learned from the same source? I mean, did they all, maybe, visit Miss Lily?"

All six became quiet thinking about that.

Abby broke the silence. "No, Matthew is self-taught. I'm sure of it."

Mary Beth said, "I know Jessie went there a few times before university but Stella and Lacy weren't there, yet. And Miss Lily is more like a mother than a, ah, anything else."

"I know for a fact, Miss Lily doesn't see, umm, clients except for a special few old friends she has known forever. Men her own age," confirmed Abby.

"Well, someone probably deserves a thank you, but I don't think we will ever know just whom," said Faith hoping to put an end to this conversation.

Colette said in the same manner everyone else had

added to the conversation, "Well, as you know, Mr. Thompson has been paying me some attention and I hope he is as well, mmmm, not endowed…what is the word I am looking for?" And gazed curiously as the others again whooped with laughter.

Hope gave up and had to wipe the tears of mirth from her eyes.

"I think, Colette, that is exactly the right word," added Mary Beth and then they all collapsed onto each other laughing.

The tea party broke-up as the women all needed to return home for one reason or another and some simply to be with their husbands.

That night Hope lay beside her husband, both naked trying to stay cool in the newly finished teacher's apartment of the schoolhouse. She woke to find Wilder's silver eyes watching her. She stretched unselfconsciously watching as his eyes followed her undulating body.

"Haven't you slept at all, Wilder? Even after all that we just did?" she asked seductively.

"I've been marveling at my good fortune, I guess, making sure you don't disappear on me," he answered seriously.

"Why would I disappear? I love you. I'll never leave you."

Trying to explain his worry, he said into the dimness, "I spent a few years working at Fort Leavenworth as a sharp shooter. We practiced at taking long shots from the fort walls." He became quiet as Hope waited for what was really on Wilder's mind. "They had us practice. Not to shoot at the Indians as they left after an ambush but to shoot to kill any women they may have taken. So that they wouldn't have to go through being a slave to the tribe." He watched for Hope's reaction to such a confession.

"Did you ever have to shoot a woman?" Hope asked gently, "Could you have if you needed to?"

"I thought I could. I never really doubted my commitment to do so, but now…I couldn't shoot you if you got taken. I just know I couldn't. It would be more than I could bear but I know I would go after you and never stop searching till we were together again."

Hope could see the sincerity in his eyes.

His voice whispered, "I couldn't put an end to the possibility of our being together again. Knowing I would never feel your touch, hold you close, taste your lips…"

She reached over, stroked the face of this man she felt was so dear to her and admitted, "I wouldn't want you to shoot me. I wouldn't want you in that kind of pain. I want to spend as much time with you in this world as I can. I could endure anything as long as I knew you were searching for me."

Wilder let out a shuddering breath of relief as if he had actually been confronted with making that horrible choice. Knowing his feelings and Hopes were the same, he rolled over to his wife. "I love you more than I ever thought possible and that scares the hell out of me. I used to live life day by day. If I missed a meal or didn't have a bed to sleep in, it didn't matter. Now I think about you first and me - not at all. I will do anything, live anywhere just as long as you let me stay with you."

"And I will always want you with me so you needn't worry about anything else. Now how about we make better use of our time awake and I'll let you make love to me again." She smiled that seductive smile that was beginning to mean so much to Wilder.

"I'm glad we think so much alike, Babe."

A word about the author…

Author Susan Payne has always loved to read which meant she often found herself reading books she was too young to fully understand. That didn't stop her. She found a dictionary and looked up anything that she questioned.

Raising a family of five children kept her busy but also allowed her time to read. Often more than fifty books a month with her children playing at her feet. That's where her love of history met her love of words as she read the new historical romance genre.

Later, Susan found her mind filled with characters all clamoring to tell her their stories. All wanting to be heard. All wanting her to tell the world how happy they were with their chosen partners. How they had gotten through loss and survived as well as thrived.

At over eighty manuscripts, Susan is still hurrying to get the words down so that she can write the next. All stories of men and women who made their mark on life and then moved on.

Highland lairds, Medieval lords from northern Europe, Georgian and Regency then on to the western U.S. The stories keep coming and the couples keep finding their happy-ever-after.

This author has published the Sweetwater series of a fictitious town in 1873 Kansas by The Wild Rose Press beginning 2019 and Montana Lineman to be released in 2020 by Literary Wanderlust.

Website: http://www.authorsusanpayne.com.

I would love to hear from you.

www.ingramcontent.com/pod-product-compliance
Lightning Source LLC
Chambersburg PA
CBHW070045030726
47506CB00002B/346